DOCTOR WHO

VERDIGRIS
PAUL MAGRS

BBC

Published by BBC Worldwide Ltd,
Woodlands, 80 Wood Lane
London W12 OTT

First published 2000
Copyright © Paul Magrs 2000
The moral right of the author has been asserted

Original series broadcast on the BBC
Format © BBC 1963
Doctor Who and TARDIS are trademarks of the BBC

ISBN 0 563 55592 0
Imaging by Black Sheep, copyright © BBC 2000

Printed and bound in Great Britain by Mackays of Chatham
Cover printed by Belmont Press Ltd, Northampton

Acknowledgements/thanks:

Joy Foster, Louise Foster, Mark Magrs, Charles Foster, Michael Fox, Nicola Cregan, Lynne Heritage, John Bleasdale, Mark Gatiss, Pete Courtie, Brigid Robinson, Paul Arvidson, Jon Rolph, Antonia Rolph, Steve Jackson, Laura Wood, Alicia Stubbersfield, Siri Hansen, Paul Cornell, Bill Penson, Mark Walton, Sara Maitland, Meg Davis, Amanda Reynolds, Richard Klein, Lucie Scott, Reuben Lane, Kenneth MacGowan, Georgina Hammick, Maureen Duffy, Vic Sage, Marina Mackay, Jayne Morgan, Alita Thorpe, Louise D'Arcens, Rupert Hodson, Lorna Sage, Steve Cole, Jac Rayner, Rachel Brown, Justin Richards, Pat Wheeler, Kate Orman, Jonathan Blum, Dave Owen, Gary Russell, Allan Barnes, Gary Gillat, Alan McKee, Lance Parkin, Richard Jones, Brad Schmidt, Phillip Hallard, Nick Smale, Mark Phippen, Helen Fayle, Anna Whymark, Chloe Whymark, Stephen Hornby, Neil Smith, Stewart Sheargold

and Jeremy Hoad

and all other companions on the bus past and future.

Welcome to Earth, everybody.

love,
Paul
September 1999

Chapter One
A Secret, Cosmological Bonsai Thing

Tom was in a huff with her.

He lay about all morning on the settee in his dressing gown. She had given him the gown herself – burnt orange silk: an antique – and he loved it sure enough, but she believed it had given him airs.

Only a month's travelling together on the bus and they were fractious with each other already.

He was flicking despondently and rather violently through glossy magazines and hadn't said a word since first thing this morning.

Iris drove remorselessly, hunched over the wheel in the cab of her double-decker bus. She wouldn't let a sulky travelling companion get her down. Perhaps she ought to just dump him somewhere.

She flexed her leather driving gloves and used the wing mirror to adjust her floppy green felt hat.

Not looking too bad, Iris, she thought happily, pursing and smacking her lips. If she was honest with herself, her hair was looking rather wild today, lilac wisps straying from under her hat.

At this point in her extremely long life, Iris Wildthyme bore the guise of what she firmly believed to be a woman in her prime. In human terms she looked like a woman perhaps a shade over sixty, but one who had kept herself fit enough to run around with companions a fraction of her age. She had an air of raffish, haphazard, gung-ho glamour and firmly believed that dashing at breakneck speed from one end of time and space to the other kept you perpetually sexy and young.

Had Tom been in a better mood she'd have shouted down the rumbling, juddering gangway: 'Look! Driving – no hands!'

After a glance at the boy's petulant expression she decided not to bother. She put on her *Tammy Wynette's Greatest Hits* tape instead.

I'm missing good company and decent, polite conversation, she thought. I wonder where I can get it.

All around the Number 22 to Putney Common the time space continuum swirled and coruscated in brilliant shades of scarlet and blue.

It was the most fabulous sight Iris could imagine.

On first witnessing this, the jaded nineteen-year-old Tom had simply sniffed and said, 'Looks like a Milk Tray advert.'

Iris had been so cross.

Over the weeks the tone she had adopted with him had become distinctly auntyish.

'Young man,' she had said firmly at one point, 'I don't think you understand what I am offering you here. A chance to see all of time and space. Visit anyone! Go anywhere!'

Tom had sighed. He was touching up the white on his heavy-duty trainers. 'Terrific. Just make sure you get me home before Christmas.' He eyed her narrowly. 'In the year 2000.'

He had first wandered aboard her bus during early November, his time. He had mistaken it for the real Number 22 to Putney Common.

Tom had tripped aboard, somewhere between Old Compton Street and Piccadilly, after a particularly heavy night out.

Iris had been as startled to see him as he'd been to step aboard and see her. Her bus had been parked and secreted well away from any of the standard routes, she'd thought.

But there was Tom, expecting to be driven straight home to his one-room flat in Putney.

He had looked around at the interior of Iris's ship and laughed.

He laughed at the chintzy soft furnishings, the Art Nouveau lamps, the brocaded curtains and the pseudo-futurismo of her driver's cab.

Iris had flown into a fit of pique, taking them off into the vortex, leaving central London in the numinous hinge between centuries far, far, blessedly behind and here she was with yet another young travelling companion.

Hoorah!

That first trip had landed them in deepest, darkest Calgoria and into a series of hair-raising adventures with the forest-dwelling Jirat and the pathologically metropolitan Trinarr.

That whole escapade had done nothing to allay Tom's considerable ire at being – as he saw it – kidnapped.

Since then they had endured a run of what Iris called historical adventures, all of which had bored Tom, he claimed testily, except for the one that involved their meeting Cleopatra, who was fabulous.

Tom was very hard to please. He had a habit of replacing Iris's driving tapes with fairly hard-core dance music. Secretly, for all her complaints and advanced years (over nine hundred, she blithely informed him), she quite enjoyed dance music.

'Anyway,' she reminded him on a number of occasions, 'as you very well know by now, this bus is a cunningly disguised time machine. I can get you back for Christmas at any time.'

'Hm,' he muttered.

'In fact,' she went on, jumping up and pulling her silver cardigan straight, 'we could have Christmas right now, if you liked.'

'Oh yeah?'

I know what you're doing, he thought, drawing his feet up on the sofa and watching her sceptically. You're trying to make me enthusiastic. You're trying to get me to stay with you as you go gadding about through time and space.

Really, he felt sorry for her. She mustn't have many friends.

'Where do you want to go?'

Iris was unfolding an alarmingly complicated series of control panels out of the dashboard and her chubby fingers, each adorned with what looked like priceless gemstones, were jabbing excitedly at the illuminated buttons.

'Home,' he said again.

She wasn't listening. 'I know just the thing,' she said, redoubling her efforts with the myriad switches and dials. 'There's someone who you haven't met yet that you really ought. Someone terribly, terribly important to me who just adores everything about me. We'll drop in on him!'

She turned to grin at Tom, still counting on her fingers as she did the necessary calculations to come up with coordinates. 'I'll find a convenient Christmas and we'll land ourselves on his doorstep and he'll be absolutely thrilled to see us.'

'Who?' asked Tom.

He could see it wouldn't be worth the effort to insist on being taken home. He'd already learned – the hard way – how difficult it was to deter Iris from a plan once she had her dander up and her mind set.

'Who are we going to visit?'

He sighed and cast his magazines away but, secretly, he was intrigued.

He slouched down the aisle of the bus, as she made the final few adjustments to the controls and firmly grasped the dematerialisation lever with both her eager hands.

'Just you wait and see!' she laughed and the bus's engines went into noisy overdrive, every piece of furniture aboard trembling, every teacup and china ornament clattering on tables and shelves.

'Hold on tight!' she cried. 'We're coming in to land!'

* * *

Summer had come early this year. It was only May and the air shimmered with standing heat.

As the small train shunted its leisurely way through the miles of flat yellow fields towards the remote station of Thisis, Jo Grant could hardly see a scrap of cloud in the dense blue of the sky.

Well, she thought, I've brought all the wrong clothes for this trip.

She peered up at the huge, battered case on the rack above her head. It was packed with sweaters and old jeans, all the heavy-duty gear she'd assumed she would be needing for a week out in the country. But if it stayed like this she would be sweltering.

Even aboard the near-empty train Jo was stifled and overwarm in her snazzy new purple dungarees and her red plastic stack-heeled boots. Her shaggy ice-blue fur coat was up on the rack with her case.

Goodness knows why she'd brought that thing along.

Oh, she thought. I'm meant to be better at planning things than this. I'm supposed to be a kind of spy, aren't I? A shrewd sort of secret agent.

I've had all the training. Some of it, anyway. I've done the preliminaries: a bit of escapology, lock-picking, a smattering of code-cracking.

But there never seemed to be enough time for her to go back and complete the harder, more rigorous stuff. There was always something more pressing – or downright deadly – going on.

Her friend Tara, with whom she'd gone to school and who – as it happened – had a similar job (in that she was assistant to another rather eccentric freelance gentleman adventurer in secret service to the government), always said that Jo was actually better off picking up all the training she could get while she was on the job.

For all Tara's well-meant advice, Jo couldn't help feeling under-equipped for some of the menaces she'd had to confront while working for the United Nations Intelligence Taskforce.

It was all very well for Tara – whose own intelligence work for the Ministry seemed to consist of swanning about in vintage cars, doing judo and wearing a selection of not-very-convincing wigs.

Tara would never have to be dragged bodily into the future to face the Daleks, or underwater to tussle with fish people, or on to an altar to be sacrificed to the Devil.

Tara would never have to outwit a malign alien consciousness that disguised itself variously in the form of shop dummies, plastic daffodils and trimphones.

As far as Jo Grant was concerned, Tara didn't know she was born. But she was still twice the secret agent Jo was.

I can't even pack the right outfits for a week in the countryside, she thought miserably, staring out of the smutty windows as the endless, sun-parched fields at last started to give way to low-roofed stone buildings.

They were arriving in the small town of Thisis.

One thing, she realised, brightening up, Jo had the Doctor on her side.

When she was with him she always felt that it didn't matter what slavering two-headed transdimensional beastie came lumbering round the next corner.

When she was with the Doctor she felt that saving the world – or any world – was a daily and never insurmountable task that no amount of government training could teach her to cope with.

With the Doctor she would see more of the amazing, colourful universe he always promised was out there.

He made that fantastic place sound as if it was only a matter of steps away.

The train was pulling in now. She could feel it tug itself gratefully to rest at the end of the line.

There was still a thirty-mile drive to the Doctor's house. As she pulled at her too-heavy leather case and dragged her blue furry coat down on top of her head, Jo found herself looking forward to that drive – because she knew that he'd be coming to pick her up at the station.

They'd go on a spin into the depths of the countryside, thundering along in the Doctor's absurd, bright yellow roadster, Bessie.

And this time it was only a holiday they were driving to – mercifully, not another terrifying adventure.

The bus came jolting and shimmering into existence on a narrow road lined with beech trees.

Its occupants emerged in jade gloom, glancing around at the verdant woodland and breathing in deeply.

The air was heavy with the scent of wild garlic.

'It doesn't look like winter to me,' said Tom at last. 'You've made us miss Christmas.'

Iris rubbed her hands briskly and locked up the doors to the bus. 'Feels like high summer to me! But we've got exactly the right place. I can feel it in my water. Come on!'

As they trudged up the rutted road Tom said, 'Tell me more about him.'

'The Doctor?' She was wearing what could only be described as a winsome smile.

'I thought he was like you,' Tom said. 'I thought he roamed about the place like you did. Walking in eternity and all that stuff.'

'Not just now,' said Iris, rasping her heavy workboots on the dusty road. 'It's 1973 and the Doctor is quite at home here on Earth.' She peered through the dense, stirring trees. 'Somewhere near here, anyway.'

'He's retired?' Just what Tom needed. Visiting some old fogey in the middle of nowhere.

'Not retired exactly. Exiled. Licence revoked. Temporarily stranded and stymied. Aha!'

She stopped to point out a glimpse of chimneys through the canopy of trees. 'His own people punished him and cast him down out of the stars and at this point in his life he's living in disgrace on Earth. Albeit in rather comfortable and frequently exciting disgrace.'

'Cast down from the stars?' Tom asked. He was often irritated by Iris's poetic turns. 'You make him sound like Milton's Satan.'

Iris barked with laughter. 'Oh, he'd like that.' She gave him a wry smile. 'You really did get a First in English Literature, didn't you? Hm. I'm not sure I need an active deconstructionist running around with me. Milton's Satan, indeed.' Then her face darkened. 'Actually, there are others round these parts more deserving of that allusion.'

Suddenly she gave a loud gasp. 'Listen!'

Tom ducked and prepared to run for shelter. 'What is it?'

'Can't you hear the wood pigeons?'

He sighed. 'You gave me a shock there.'

'Pity I never brought a gun along,' she mused. 'We could have nabbed a couple of the blighters and taken them as an offering for dinner.'

'"Nabbed a couple of the blighters"?' Tom laughed. 'Iris, that's not how you speak.'

'I'm practising,' she said proudly. 'As you'll find, dear boy, it's how – at this point in his incredibly long life – the Doctor talks.'

'Oh, great.'

They rounded a corner and found themselves on a gravel driveway. Ahead loomed a rather gloomy edifice, all of its windows dark.

'Golly,' breathed Iris. 'It's grander than I thought. The old devil's obviously got a bob or two.'

Tom was examining the marble statues that lined the driveway. Each was encrusted with lichen; a faun with thick hairy shanks, a supine lion with a wry expression and a minotaur sitting disconsolately on a bench.

'I don't like his taste in garden furniture.'

Iris smiled. 'The Doctor is rather keen on monsters.' She turned abruptly to the house. 'Let's go and see if he's in.'

She strode on ahead, happily kicking up the pink gravel. Something, thought Tom, had certainly put a spring in her step.

He had arrived, punctual as ever, and hopped lightly out of the car with his cloak swirling out behind him.

As he helped her load her luggage in the back he asked, 'How long have you come for?' He grinned at the weight of her case.

'Just a week,' she said.

She liked the way his face creased up when he smiled. He looked weathered. Just as a man with his lifetimes of experience ought to.

In the late afternoon sunshine his hair was a brilliant white; a veritable shock. He was wearing a cherry red velvet jacket with violet trim and a blue ruffled shirt.

Unlike Jo, he didn't seem to be feeling the effects of the heat at all.

'Before we start,' he said, 'we have to make a rule for the whole week. I don't want any mention of UNIT or Lethbridge-Stewart. I don't want us talking shop all the time.'

'Oh, the poor Brigadier...'

'You know what I mean, Jo. All I want is to have dinner parties and enlightened conversation. I'm going to invite some very interesting people down to stay, and it's all going to be remarkably civilised.'

She shrugged as he revved the engine.

At Iris's suggestion they took the French windows, which she jemmied with a handy little device she produced from her handbag.

Together they crept inside what seemed to be the dining room. It was robin's egg blue and the table, which was at least twenty feet long, was a glossy red wood.

'He won't mind, will he?' asked Tom nervously, checking his trainers weren't muddy. 'I mean, us breaking in like this?'

Iris was inspecting the silverware and then the vast oil paintings along one wall.

'Oh no, he'll think it's a great laugh. Look at these!'

Tom didn't think the portraits were that inspiring. In them, a white-haired man with a quizzical expression was posing in a number of transhistorical guises.

'The Doctor through the ages,' Iris laughed.

It was true. The same man was dressed up as an Elizabethan nobleman, complete with ruff, a Victorian merchant in more sombre garb, and a Regency fop with frilled sleeves, silk britches and lacy handkerchief.

'So he's proud of his lineage,' said Tom.

'Lineage nothing,' grunted Iris. 'These are all him. That's not a family likeness. That's the very same hauteur on every face, the same beaky nose and the same thrillingly twinkling eyes – simply because these are all paintings of the very same fella! Oh, he's a conceited old thing. Paintings of himself in the dining room, indeed.'

'Are they fakes?'

'Hard to tell.'

She started to shuffle out of the room. 'I wonder if the old rake has got any pictures of me about the place.'

Her voice sounded very loud to Tom.

They passed into a room painted a brilliant yolky yellow. This was empty apart from a tapestried chair, upon which dozed the fattest cat Tom had ever seen.

The room beyond that, into which Iris confidently led the way, was a deep underwater blue and on shelves were arrayed a vast collection of blue Chinese ginger jars of different sizes.

Iris took the lid off one and a hologram popped out in front of her astonished eyes.

To Tom it looked like an orange but, on closer examination, it appeared to be an entire planet, with its own wreathed and drifting atmosphere.

'Lativus,' Iris whispered, as if worried her breath would burst the world like a soap bubble.

Tom tried one, clinking the lid off a ginger jar, and a green and gold planet bobbed up before his eyes.

Its cloud cover was whizzing round faster and faster and, as he watched, fascinated, it seemed that an electrical storm – tiny and brilliant – was raging all the time.

'Stranovitican,' Iris smiled.

Tom had never seen her so simply enchanted by anything before.

'Where did he get them all?'

'It's as if, since he can't leave the Earth any more and he can't go out to the stars, he's had these replicas made…'

She reached out to another ginger jar – a small, exquisite one adorned with dragons – eager to peek inside.

'It's like a secret, cosmological bonsai thing…'

The door at the other end of the deep-blue room crashed open then, all of a sudden, surprising them both so badly that Tom jolted into Iris and her hand flashed out and took with it the tiniest jar and they watched, horrified, as it was dashed to the ceramic tiled floor.

There was barely a second to absorb this fact before a lanky and furious figure had shot across the room and accosted both Iris and Tom.

With a deadly, full-throated shout that sounded like it had something to do with the martial arts, this figure flew into action.

In a blur of limbs, Iris was wrestled to the floor and Tom was thrown backwards, banging himself nastily on the tiles and landing amongst the sharp fragments of the broken jar.

Tom blinked and saw that it was a tall man attacking his elderly friend.

Iris was being bundled around like a sack of old potatoes.

The man was in a red jacket and cloak. He was the man from the paintings, yelling out karate noises.

Tom was about to jump up and ask exactly why he was manhandling an old lady, when it became apparent that Iris actually had the upper hand.

'How dare you!' she barked in her most thrilling contralto. 'Unhand me at once, sir!'

She had the Doctor in an easy headlock.

A very young, very pretty girl with blonde hair and stack-heeled boots had appeared at the other end of the room.

At the sight of Iris grimly fettling the man in the velvet jacket she squeaked, 'What are you doing to him?'

Iris relaxed her grip and let him go.

She straightened and brushed herself down, rearranging the collar of her blouse. 'Simply defending myself, lovey. You'd better tell him to watch his manners.'

From the gleaming chequerboard tiles of the floor, the Doctor was looking up in disbelief.

'Good grief,' he said.

Iris grinned. 'I bet you're shocked to see me.'

'Shocked!' He rubbed the back of his neck ruefully. He held out his hand to Jo. 'You'd better help me up.'

'Doctor, who is it?' Jo asked.

Iris was feeling rather smug as the Doctor clambered stiffly to his feet and shot his frilly cuffs. 'I bet if you'd known it was me, you wouldn't have gone whirling into your Venusian acrobatics!'

The Doctor rolled his eyes. 'No,' he muttered. 'I'd have probably shot you.'

'Doctor!' said Jo, aghast. 'Who is this strange woman?'

'Strange woman?' said Iris hotly.

The Doctor plunged his hands into his pockets. 'Why don't we go into the kitchen and I'll make a pot of tea and introduce everyone properly, hm?'

'Well,' said Iris. 'I'm glad you've found your manners. Tom and I are starving too, so a little lunch wouldn't come amiss, as well.'

The Doctor's mouth was tight as he led the way.

As Jo followed the ill-assorted group into the low-roofed, stone-floored expanse of the Doctor's kitchen, she was surprised at the sudden switch in her friend's mood.

He grew magnanimous and welcoming, making them tea in a vast yellow pot and flinging open the fridge and insisting that they all had sandwiches.

Iris sat herself heavily at the well-scrubbed table and gazed around. 'I should have come to visit you here before,' she said, admiringly. 'I might have known you wouldn't be living in poverty and despair.'

'Ah, no,' said the Doctor, sawing enthusiastically through a farmhouse loaf. He was laying out slices of cold roast beef and slivers of gherkins and finishing them off with dollops of horseradish sauce.

Jo realised that she was famished.

'I've got rather a good deal going with the British government,' said the Doctor expansively. 'In exchange for my helping out with various... ehm, difficulties of the more abstruse and peculiar kinds, they pay me a great deal of money.' He gave a rueful smile. 'Not that I've got an awful lot of use for that much money. But apparently they couldn't possibly pay me less for what I do. Something about their wage scales... and income tax and the Official Secrets Act. It's all quite mysterious.'

Jo had never heard the Doctor talk about money before. It seemed odd to her that someone of the Doctor's obvious powers and talents should even have to think about it.

He was looking at Iris almost fondly. 'You know, almost all of the visitors I've had here on Earth have been absolutely horrible ones. You're my first welcome extraterrestrial house guest.'

He pushed a plate of thick sandwiches at her.

'Is it too early,' asked Iris, licking her lips, 'for a gin and tonic?'

The Doctor grinned. 'Of course not, my dear.'

Then he appeared to notice Jo for the first time in ages. 'Jo, let me introduce an old friend of mine. Ms Iris Wildthyme.'

He shot his companion what she assumed was a significant glance. 'She, like me, has a TARDIS. Fully functional, in her case.' He gave a rueful chuckle tinged, thought Jo, with a curious hardness. 'Miss Josephine Grant,' he went on. 'My assistant.'

As if competing, Iris spoke through a mouthful of sandwich. 'This is Tom – my own, current, glamorous assistant. He's from the year Twenty-hundred.'

'2000!' gasped Jo. 'Then he hasn't even been born yet!' She added, for Iris's benefit, 'It's 1973, now.'

'I know,' said Iris, narrowing her eyes. She hadn't taken to Jo at all. The Doctor must be knocking about with flibbertigibbets, she thought, to make himself look clever.

She looked at Tom, who was happily munching away and slurping his tea. He was quite content now that the fighting was over and he was being fed.

The Doctor slid a gin and tonic into her waiting hand.

'Well!' she said, after a hearty sip. 'Do you mind if I smoke?

So, what's it to be this time, Doctor?'

He frowned quizzically and sat himself opposite her.

'What kind of thing are we going to get involved in this time? Man-eating insects that arrive in a swarm from deepest space and descend on Norwich? Or a power-crazed princess from Dimension Six who has a love potion to make all the men of Earth fall in love with her and elect her Empress of the Solar System? What type of mischief do you think we can set about foiling this week, hm?'

She glanced sharply at Jo. 'Fetch me an ashtray would you, lovey?'

Jo hurried to the dresser, and it was only as she passed the ashtray back that she wondered what she was doing. 'The Doctor is on holiday this week,' she said. 'He isn't going to get involved in anything at all. He's going to cook dinner, catch up with some reading, tinker with the TARDIS and have some friends round.'

Embarrassed somewhat, the Doctor smiled at her outburst.

'Really?' asked Iris. 'So, even if the Cybermen come wading up out of the Thames or the Sontarans come parachuting down over Wales...'

Tom chuckled, 'or dinosaurs wreak havoc in Scarborough...'

'You'll still sit at home holding elaborate dinner parties and entertaining old and dear friends?'

The Doctor nodded firmly. 'Absolutely. The world can do without me for a week.'

'Well, that's excellent then,' cawed Iris triumphantly. 'You can cook your marvellous dinners for us! We'll provide the company and you can play host to the two of us!'

The Doctor's face fell only slightly.

When Tom was shown to his room, near the top of the house at the end of a narrow wood-panelled corridor, he felt about ready to drop.

Iris, who was only a few doors away, told him that his sleepiness might be down to all the vortex-hopping they'd been doing recently.

She thought their adventures had become perhaps too concentrated with too few gaps between.

'I've got this terrible headache,' he said.

'Sounds to me like a touch of time-sickness. You need a little lie-down with a cold flannel over your face. You're lucky. I once had a companion called Jenny, a butch dyke traffic warden. Every time she came through the vortex she got the runs. Not very convenient.'

Tom winced. He looked down the corridor and hissed at her, 'It looks like he's going to let us stay.'

'So he should! I've been very good to the Doctor in the past. And future, as it happens. Who was it pleaded for his life with the Dalek Supreme in the Crystal Mines of Marlion?'

'You?'

'Em, no, it was Jenny, actually, but I was there.'

'The Doctor and Jo seem nice.' Tom reached for his door handle.

Iris pulled a face. 'I don't think much of Jo. A bit wet, that one.'

'I thought she was sweet.'

'Sweet!' Iris chuckled. 'Typical fella. Fancy her, do you?'

Tom coloured instantly. 'What?' His headache was getting worse. 'I'll have to have that lie down.'

She patted his shoulder and let him go.

Then she marched back to the room that the Doctor had allotted her. It had better be the best in the house. Still, if things went according to plan, she didn't reckon on sleeping in her own bed much during this visit…

Jo watched the Doctor pull his Marigolds on and start to tackle the dishes.

'Why the change of hearts?'

He was whistling happily to himself. David Bowie's 'Starman'. 'Hm?'

'Why are you suddenly playing the gracious host with them? When you first saw Iris you were horrified...'

'My dear Jo,' he beamed. 'I can't very well chuck an old woman like her out on the streets, can I? She's a very dear, old friend.'

Jo asked, 'Is she...' She glanced up at the ceiling, hushing her voice in her customary way. 'Is she one of Them?'

The Doctor was racking up steaming plates. 'I shouldn't be at all surprised.'

'Then why are you being so... charming?'

He laughed. 'It's natural charm.'

Jo was put out, she realised, because it had taken her almost two years of knowing the Doctor before he had even asked her to come to visit this house.

She had been to his flat in London, his house in Kent and she'd even been to the caravan that he kept up in the Highlands of Scotland, but this was only the second time that she'd been honoured with an invite to this, the oldest of his houses on Earth.

And there was Iris, breaking and entering and making herself right at home. It didn't make sense.

Suddenly the Doctor was looking at her, with a very serious expression.

He snapped off his pink rubber gloves.

'You heard what she said. She's got a TARDIS. Just like me. But hers is in proper working order. And while she's here, her TARDIS is somewhere nearby...'

Jo stared at him and the intensity of his gaze and her heart sank in her chest.

So, he was still looking for a means of escaping them all here on Earth.

* * *

Tom barely looked at the room before he flopped down on to the bed and curled up in the heavy burgundy duvet. His head was splitting. He couldn't even be bothered to undress before his nap.

What had Iris been on about?

He'd only said Jo was sweet. Iris asked if he fancied her. He couldn't believe she'd asked that.

Iris was so perceptive, usually. She was so sussed about things. Had she really not yet picked up on the fact that Tom was gay?

Did she really think she could have a straight male companion who'd sit up in the cab of the bus with her, driving across the desert, duetting on Dusty Springfield songs?

What on Earth did Iris think he was doing when Cleopatra showed him round her wardrobe?

It was all very odd.

And he'd be able to have it all out, sensibly, with Iris, if he could just stop feeling so achy and tired.

He slept then, as the afternoon went on the wane and the shadows of the trees outside his window started to strengthen.

As he slept, he dreamed that someone in this time was calling out to him.

More than one voice; calling out across the miles, telling him that they had been waiting, knowing that he would arrive...

'You are in his house now, Tom...

and while you are there you are in terrible danger...

He isn't what he seems to be, this Doctor...

You must come away and join us...

You must come away...

Come to join us...'

Chapter Two
The Dawn of a New Venture

Tom wasn't at all relaxed in the Doctor's house.

What am I supposed to think?

He lives in a big house, a crumbling mansion in the middle of nowhere, and his garden is full of Gothic statuary; screaming horses and bristling basilisks all of marble.

He calls us for dinner at midnight.

His manners are suave and persuasive and he wears a silk and velvet cape.

Iris tells me he was flung down to Earth by his mysterious people, who live outside of time and space.

To me, at any rate, he doesn't seem like a man to trust.

Iris, though, Iris is complacent and I'm surprised at her.

She's very peculiar in his company; lap-dog fond, panting round the kitchen after him as he sees to dinner and trying to impress him with tales of her – our – recent travels.

Can't she see she's putting his back up?

As he checks on the roasting bird in the oven, his mouth is set and grim.

He's not someone I'd want to get on the wrong side of.

Tom still had the aftershock and the lingering aftertaste of those dreams in his head and he was trying to rinse them out with the warm wine Jo kept on pouring for him.

He could still hear that voice – the loudest; teenaged, male, cockney-accented – rattling away at the back of his skull.

He could still recollect that warning, if that's what it was.

Iris had explained to him, on a number of occasions, the tricks your mind could play on you, when time travel was your game.

It was a game running contrary to many of the laws of nature and sometimes the mind revolted.

He looked at Iris and the Doctor, fussing over gravy and bread sauce.

The two of them were accustomed to this unnatural game.

Tom hardly knew who to trust any more.

Beside him, at the scarred kitchen table, Jo was trying to get him interested in her stories.

She had apparently decided he was all right to talk to and went on regaling him with yarns about her spy work.

She's talking out of line, he thought blearily. I wonder if the Doctor has cottoned on to her loose talk about the United Nations.

They were all fellow travellers in the kitchen that night.

There was a rough, wine-laced camaraderie between them, as if they all recognised and celebrated between them the fact that they shared experiences of weirder adventures than anyone else.

With Jo and her tipsy rabbiting on, it was almost like a competition.

Tom would mention meeting Cleopatra and she would have to launch into a full-scale account of her trip to Atlantis. He was learning to take everything with a pinch of salt.

'We're almost ready,' Iris said, rubbing her hands. 'Why don't you kids go and sit yourselves in the dining room?'

Tom shook his head at her wonderingly. She made herself so easily at home.

She was in a gold sequinned dress with her gold sequinned clutch bag over one shoulder. The two of them had popped back to the bus that evening to fetch a change of clothes.

He wondered why she wore a dress that showed so many of her least flattering bulges. And why was she still wearing her green felt hat?

Jo grasped Tom's hand and led him back through the sequence of colourful rooms to the dining table.

Each room was lit with green candles in sconces and the huge cat was still in its chair, glancing up at them curiously as they passed by.

Jo was making an effort. 'It's nice to have younger company,' she said. 'When the Doctor told me he was having people to stay I imagined a bunch of his old scientist cronies. All of them banging on about things I don't understand!'

She giggled suddenly and showed him to his place.

Tom was thinking: I wasn't even born in 1973.

He counted up in his head and realised that Jo was probably the right age to be his mother.

His mother.

Suddenly, with an audible ratcheting of gears in his head, a memory slid into place as he sat at the table, staring at the candelabra as Jo lit each of the candles in turn.

He was seven and his mother was explaining to him that he was destined for great things.

She had used that phrase. She believed in destiny.

That was the day she had given him the belt with the golden buckle that he had worn ever since.

It was upstairs, still on the black jeans he had changed out of. At seven he had assumed it had belonged to his father, who had died when Tom was still a baby, in circumstances he had never been entirely clear about. Indeed, that whole episode of his mother telling him that he had a marvellous destiny to fulfil had grown rather hazy in his memory.

To him, it had seemed that his mother knew rather more about him than he did himself. It had made him blush and he, up till the age of seven, an ebullient and restless child, had grown quiet and almost secretive.

As he became older this idea of his curious destiny had been only one of a number of things setting him apart from his more ordinary peers. In his mind, this destiny of his became entangled with his own, secret knowledge of his sexuality.

He and his mother had never talked about it again, but he still wore the belt, with its golden buckle and design – a hexagram with a star in the centre.

For the first time he was wondering if it had anything to do with his odd, peremptory travels on the bus with Iris. Had his mother somehow known he would end up as a traveller in time and space?

'You've got that dazed look,' Jo told him. 'You look just like someone who spends his time freewheeling – sometimes against his will – from one perilous thing into another.'

He smiled. 'Have I? Maybe I need a holiday too.'

Jo nodded at the door, at the approaching sound of the Doctor and Iris, talking loudly as they wheeled the hostess trolley through. 'I wouldn't bet on the peace lasting long.'

Tom grinned ruefully and the Doctor announced that dinner was served.

Iris heaped up her plate with more potatoes and gravy and complained loudly that they'd all get terrible indigestion for eating so late.

Jo was trying to get the Doctor interested in a recent spate of alien abductions reported to UNIT.

'Oh… it's usually nonsense,' he said. 'Simple sleep paralysis. People wake up and find they can't move. Quite natural. Don't ask me why they think they're in a space ship. I mean, really, what extraterrestrial in its right mind is going to go to all the expense of kidnapping human beings and whisking them off, just to play doctors and nurses?'

'The Nurses of Ionicaiy Six,' said Iris, with sudden lucidity. 'They would.'

'Well, granted them,' the Doctor said stiffly. 'But real abductions are far rarer than you'd think.'

'The Brigadier isn't so sure,' said Jo.

The Doctor flashed her a look.

She persevered, 'Have you talked to him recently?'

'Not for a fortnight,' he said. 'We both decided we could do with a small break from each other. Things got a little hot under the collar when we were dealing with sending our malevolent friend from Arcturus back home...'

'I'm worried about him,' Jo said, as if breaking out into what she'd really wanted to say.

Iris put in, 'Is this the same Lethbridge-Stewart I met during that business with the Celaphopods in Venice? And on Mars with the Terrible Zodin?'

'He wasn't involved with her, but the former, yes.' He looked at Jo. 'Why are you worried about him?'

'Because I haven't had a single call from him or anyone else at HQ in a fortnight, either,' she said. 'You know what he's usually like. Someone's cat dies and he's on that hotline.'

'You've been in London,' said Tom. 'You said you were staying with your pal, Tara. Wouldn't you have been miffed if your boss had been phoning you the whole time?'

'Well, yes,' she said. 'But Tara was getting calls all the time. Agents in her line of work – rather higher up in the Ministry – were getting into trouble and she was out and about all the time. It sounded rather frantic.'

'Have you tried phoning the Brigadier yourself?' asked the Doctor.

'Once or twice. They fobbed me off at the switchboard. They said he was busy. Then he was in Geneva for the weekend...'

'There you are, then,' said the Doctor, gathering plates in. 'Trifle?'

'Something isn't right,' said Jo decisively.

'My dear girl,' the Doctor began, rolling his eyes. 'Don't you think you're getting all worked up about nothing? I think we should be glad not to have him barking down the phone with his moustache bristling.'

Iris glugged the last of her wine. 'I believe Jo's right to listen to her intuition. Don't listen to him, lovey. The Doctor's got none.'

He gave her a hard stare and marched to the door. Then he looked at Jo with a sigh. 'If it will make you feel any better, I'll give him a ring now.'

'After midnight?' squawked Iris.

'I'll leave a message,' said the Doctor. 'Lethbridge-Stewart's very proud of the answer machine I built him. I'm sure there's nothing going on we should know about.'

He gave his young companion a kindly smile and she nodded. He was sure she was overreacting and it was probably down to the quantities of his excellent Chardonnay that Iris had been pressing on them all.

The Doctor went out to the dark hallway where, beside the reassuring shape of his police box, there was a small table and a black Bakelite phone.

He rang Lethbridge-Stewart's private line and frowned at all the buzzing that came back at him.

There wasn't the expected series of clicks and the standard message from the Brigadier. Instead, a rather flat, dull voice was talking in his ear.

'Hullo?' he said impatiently. 'Who is this, please?'

The bland voice intoned: '... which you might want to investigate. There is something aboard the railway carriage that your operatives will want to take a look at. It has the appearance of a somewhat outdated railway carriage, but there is no indication of how such an object could have arrived in its present location. Grid references follow...'

The Doctor snatched up a pencil and wrote down the string of digits on his doodling pad.

Once they had finished, the line went dead.

He shook the receiver.

'Hullo? Lethbridge-Stewart?'

He put the phone down and rubbed his jaw.

* * *

In the dining room Iris was slopping out their trifle with a large silver spoon and little ceremony.

'How was dear old Alistair?' she asked, with a glint in her eye.

'I couldn't get him,' said the Doctor. 'Or his answer machine.'

Jo looked alarmed. 'What's happened to him?'

'I don't think anything's actually happened to him. But I think something's wrong with his phone. I got some very peculiar chap's voice coming down the line, telling me about a railway carriage that's appeared out of nowhere.'

Tom laughed. 'Call the United Nations!'

'Who was it?' asked Jo.

Then she saw that Iris and the Doctor were looking at each other rather intently.

This was it. This was the adventure all four of them had been secretly expecting to flare up at any moment.

Iris set down the serving spoon. 'Do you want to go and have a look now?'

The Doctor shook his head. 'The morning will be soon enough.'

It seemed to Tom that he was barely asleep before the boy's voice came back to him.

He lay down with alcohol fumes knocking in his skull.

Iris hadn't been happy until the Doctor produced a bottle of whisky and they'd all toasted together the dawn of a new venture...

Now the dark house was still.

The others had retired to their separate corners of the redbrick mansion and Tom lay awake with his room teetering, threatening to spin.

He listened to the creaking of the old timbers as they settled in for the night and fancied he was on a great ship, bound for the darkness.

And then he felt as if he was tethered to the mast and the thought gave him heart palpitations.

He switched on his lamp, snatched up his glasses and cigarettes and went to the window.

Outside, a yellow grey mist was seeping under the stiff centurion skirts of the fir trees.

It crept and slid like a great unctuous cat towards the house, as if trapping it.

In the waxy light of the moon it almost had a greenish cast.

'When the morning comes,' said the boy's voice, tickling at the nape of Tom's neck and making his shaved hair bristle. 'When the morning comes you will be brought closer to us. Every step you take from now on will bring you closer to the other Children of Destiny.'

Tom took the cigarette from his mouth and whirled around.

He was reeling.

He gazed angrily at the dark, shadowed corners of his room, as if he would see the boy himself there.

'Who are you?' he said, the clarity of his voice shocking him.

'Keep your voice low,' his invisible companion urged. 'No one is to know of our communication. Especially not the Doctor.'

'Last night you said he isn't what he seems...'

'Don't you feel that to be true? He is an evil prince from a forgotten, cursed realm. He is here to make chaos come again on Earth. It is up to you and I, Tom, and the other of Destiny's Children to prevent him.'

'He's evil?'

'To the core. To the pit of both his black hearts.'

Tom stubbed out his cigarette on the window frame and it seemed for a moment that the chalky, seductive voice had left him.

He watched the fallen ashes of his fag burn themselves out from orange to black.

Then he was gazing again at the encroaching mist.

'Tomorrow morning,' said the voice, growing fainter. 'You will be brought much closer to us.'

As he stared, it seemed that he saw a boy standing there, on the gravel of the drive, shrouded in the mist.

He was wearing some kind of silver-white outfit, all in one, and his hair was long and grown over his collar.

As Tom watched the boy raised a hand in salute and his body was suffused in an eerie tinselling glow.

He was starting to vanish.

'Wait!' Tom said and found that he was echoing the word inside his head, as the boy had done. 'What is your name?'

'Kevin.'

And then he was gone.

A chill went right through Tom as he saw the night reclaim the garden and he crept back to bed.

Chapter Three
A Mysterious Carriage

From the journals of Ms Iris Wildthyme.

Good morning!

You'll have to excuse my handwriting, Space Chums... it's your old Aunty Iris here and she's balancing her journal on her ample lap as we speed along the country roads in the Doctor's good old vintage roadster, Bessie.

Nevertheless, spidery scrawl or no, here's your roving reporter actually on the scene again and taking notes as she goes!

So what's it like to be in the yellow car as it lurches and careers towards the site of a new investigation by UNIT's mysterious scientific adviser?

As Bessie eats up the gravel on these deserted twining roads and the Doctor hunches over her wheel with his hair streaming, I have to admit: it's all quite thrilling.

So here I am... back in the past!

With perfect access to the Doctor as he was then.

A gentler time, perhaps; a more innocent time.

Here the timelines are intact, causality is unimpeached and one historical event follows another in strict chronological order.

What bliss to be seated in the car with the Doctor and Jo and Tom in an era before canon-death!

Before everything was altered.

It seems almost unfair to warn the Doctor of what will happen years hence from now...

Jo is fiddling with the tea service on the back seat. She

produces a small tray of cakes to fill us up as we go.

She's pouring tea in china cups with saucers and a golden trim.

Innocent times!

Yet even with my being here, out of sequence, out of capriciousness, I'm wedging open a slice of alternity in the Doctor's life.

Without me here he might perhaps be having a quiet week; a restful, forgettable week of holiday.

But here I am goading him into filling up his time... I'm just one of the many forces feeding back and looping round on the Doctor's established past...

Changing it for ever and giving him extra interesting times...

Of course the Doctor reaches elegantly for his china cup of tea with one hand and doesn't spill a drop, even intent as he is on his driving.

Jo passes mine and I've barely taken a sip when we lurch over a bump in the road and my cup and saucer are flung over the windscreen and into a ditch.

The little pastries and cream cakes go a similar way.

Every now and then the Doctor stops the car and checks his map, the snarl of blue lines, his grid referencing. Jo asks him impatiently why he won't trust her with the map-reading and he gives her what is almost a withering glance and I think, aha! Small sticky bone of contention here. And indeed he mutters something about what happened once when they were en route to Devil's End... but maybe I misheard that bit. So we go on and the Doctor is in charge of the map and the countryside around us is becoming hillier, wilder, more overgrown with these stumpy, lopped-off trees tangled in parasitic vines.

The trees look as if they've been startled in the process of pulling on their clothes; they stand frozen with their jumpers of foliage and vine half over their faces.

Did I ever tell you about my fear of trees?

There was once a planet of living trees, trees with faces and witchy fingers and I had to go there to...

Ah – we've arrived.

Bessie screeches to a peremptory stop, causing Tom to swear loudly and both my hearts to fly up into my mouth.

The Doctor flings himself out of the car and rushes to a gate into a wide, swaying field of corn and he's got his hands on his hips, gazing implacably at the sun-browned prospect.

Jo hops out and totters after him on her platforms and Tom, looking oddly troubled this morning, it has to be said, pursues at a more respectable pace.

Something is troubling my young companion... something besides carsickness.

I must stop here.

'Where is everyone, Doctor?'

Jo stared at the empty expanse of the field.

She had been on these trips before and, when Bessie pulled up at the scene of investigation, it was usually in the midst of a whirl of activity.

Land Rovers, jeeps, lorries stuffed with scientific equipment.

Soldiers would be busying about and the air chattering with helicopters swooping and snooping overhead.

Today there was nothing. Nothing but the hoarse complaints of crows as the small party started to walk across the field of corn.

The Doctor was thoughtful.

'Where's the Brigadier?' asked Jo.

No answer was forthcoming.

Iris was struggling to keep up with the Doctor's long strides. 'We haven't all got UNIT passes,' she was saying. 'Does that mean they'll throw us off the site?'

Then she was hunting through her handbag. 'Oh, hang on... here's my old one...'

The Doctor stopped in his tracks and wheeled round, thrusting his beaky nose in her face. 'You've got a UNIT pass?'

Iris blanched. 'Well, yes...'

'And how exactly did you come by that?'

Tom could see that Iris was hiding something.

'Oh,' she said, with mock-breeziness. 'These things are easy enough to fake. I thought it might come in handy...'

The Doctor narrowed his eyes. 'You play some dangerous games, Iris.'

She smiled and batted her eyelashes, as if she'd been paid a compliment.

Then Jo's scream cut through the air.

'Look!'

At the brow of the hill, almost obscured by the rippling corn, there was a railway carriage.

Its green paintwork had blistered and its windowpanes were dark with streaky dirt.

'There aren't any tracks,' said Tom, leading the way. 'How could it just arrive in the middle of a field?'

'It's materialised there,' said Iris firmly.

'But why would anyone want to do that?'

'Some people,' she said darkly, 'do some very funny things.'

'Indeed,' said the Doctor stiffly. 'The voice on the phone last night said that we would be interested in what was inside the carriage.'

'That was helpful of them,' said Jo.

Iris started scuttling forwards. 'What are we waiting for?'

Jo grasped the Doctor's arm. 'Warn her, Doctor! It's bound to be booby-trapped.'

Jo had learned a thing or two in the last couple of years.

'She can look after herself,' he said.

Iris was pressing her ear up against the side of the carriage.

'It isn't electrified or anything,' she called to them, pressing her palms to the metal. 'And it didn't explode when I touched it.' She drew a hair pin from under her hat and stared at it. 'And it's only mildly radioactive. It's very chilly, though.'

She started to walk round to the door at the end. 'What do we think it is?'

The Doctor led the others towards her. 'Why don't you break in and tell us?' He sounded almost surly.

Tom muttered to Jo, 'He's making poor Iris do all the work.'

Jo touched his arm. 'Don't worry. If the Doctor thought there was anything really dangerous in that thing, he wouldn't let her go first. He'd go in by himself.'

The Doctor looked at her and laughed. 'I most certainly would not. I'm only too happy to let her take the brunt.'

Iris was rattling the heavy door handle.

She grunted and shouted at them, 'I can see shapes inside…'

She gave the door a good wrench and it flew open.

'Well done!' Tom shouted and hurried round to see.

A chilling breeze issued from the open carriage.

The four of them stood, baffled and battered by it, in the few seconds till it died away and they were left staring at the still, dark interior.

While the others were concerned with what lay inside the mysterious carriage, Tom was distracted.

He felt a sudden burning sensation against the skin of his stomach.

He lifted his T-shirt slightly and gazed down to see his belt buckle glowing.

It was glistening with a somewhat uncomfortable heat and, as he stared, it was tingling.

He gulped and pulled his T-shirt back down.

The Doctor had shouldered Iris aside and he was peering into the freezing gloom.

Iris tiptoed to look over his shoulder and gasped.

'They're all asleep!'

Every seat in the carriage was occupied and each bulky figure was quite still. They weren't, however, slumped or reclining.

Each sat bolt upright, staring dead ahead; disconcertingly, straight at those who had broken in.

'It looks like a tomb,' breathed Jo as she followed the Doctor and Iris a few steps down the gangway, the ground underfoot crackling with frost.

The Doctor was examining the first few passengers he came to. 'There's a faint pulse.'

He glanced at Iris. 'What do you make of their dress?'

The first few passengers were in hooped and elaborate crinolines.

The young woman the Doctor had looked at was in a short-sleeved dress, with yards of frozen silk bunched up around her in the small space. She had a high forehead and her hair was up in ringlets.

Her expression was completely serene.

'Their dress?' asked Iris. 'I think it's fabulous.'

'Which era?' he said, testily.

'Eighteenth century, definitely,' she said. 'Some time then.'

'I thought so.'

Jo gasped. 'They've travelled in time?'

'But then the train doesn't fit,' said the Doctor softly. 'It's too modern.'

'What we've got here,' Iris said, 'is a mystery.' She looked round. 'Tom?'

He was silhouetted in the doorway of the carriage. 'I'm here.'

'Bless him,' Iris told the others. 'He gets scared.'

The Doctor tutted.

'There are soldiers as well,' Jo said, looking further down the carriage. 'In their red coats and everything. And look at this old man with his whiskers…'

'I don't like this,' said Iris.

The Doctor became decisive. 'We need some help. Something is obviously very wrong with these poor people.'

'Are they in comas?' asked Tom.

'Something like it.'

The Doctor was trying to prise open the eyes of the old gent Jo had pointed to.

When he looked down he saw that the man's hand was frozen solid; holding out a fob watch.

The Doctor squinted at the crazed and cracked face of the watch and saw that it had apparently stopped at five minutes to thirteen.

'We need to get them to a hospital,' he said.

There was a sudden cry from Tom.

'What is it?' Jo asked him.

'Nothing,' he stammered. 'I slipped on something.'

Iris told the Doctor, 'He's always doing that.'

'We'll drive out to that town a few miles back,' the Doctor was saying. 'We can alert the authorities from there. Get the local bobbies and ambulance services going...'

'Authorities,' said Iris scathingly.

'What do you expect me to do?' the Doctor snapped. 'I can't do very much for them without my TARDIS, can I? And without Lethbridge-Stewart here...'

'Don't get worked up,' she said. 'Let's get back to the town, then.'

'Jo, Tom...' the Doctor began, turning round. 'You two wait here and keep an eye on...'

But Jo and Tom had gone.

Jo was pursuing Tom through the lashing stalks of corn.

'What is it? What's the matter with you?'

Tom found he had no choice but to run.

It was as if his will was no longer his own.

The sun was quite high now in the brilliant blue of the sky and he could feel it beating down on him, sending coloured lights to crowd in on his vision.

His head was spinning and the belt buckle was burning into his skin.

But he couldn't take it off.

At the very top of the hill, in the middle of the field, he staggered and swayed.

Jo caught up. 'Tom?'

He pointed into the spread mass of corn before them.

His finger shook.

There, in the field, stood two figures.

Jo squinted.

They were both in white outfits. A boy and a girl. They were staring back at Tom and Jo.

'I know them…' Tom said. 'They're coming for me.'

Jo gripped his arm and stared as the two strangers flickered with a nimbus of orange light and slowly faded away.

Tom slumped against her.

Chapter Four
Children of the Revolution

Wanda had never known anything like this.

In all her twenty-four years on the job, she had never known anything like it at all.

Usually her job was fairly straightforward.

The locals of the town didn't tend to suffer from anything too outlandish.

Dr Prendergast came every couple of weeks, circulating himself around the countryside and tending to the region's mostly elderly population, and most of the time Wanda was left in charge.

The surgery was small and spotless and she was the no-nonsense nurse in charge.

She administered jabs and pills and set anything broken in a cast with skill and aplomb.

Winter was the toughest time here; when the narrow country roads and the cobbled streets were treacherous with frost and hazardous for shaky old bones.

The summer months tended, in Wanda's experience, to be slack.

This morning, though, there was a phone call and a curious, flat voice alerting her to an emergency somewhere out in the countryside.

Her surgery was the closest one.

She would be receiving an influx of mysteriously ailing rail passengers.

But there isn't a railway anywhere near here, she wanted to say, as the caller rang off the line.

Their station had been closed down over twenty years ago

and the tracks were overgrown and choked with weeds.

This had to be a put-on. Nevertheless, her nursing instincts kicked in and she set about readying the small ward and calling up Dr Prendergast and then she sat and fretted about what exactly was on its way.

It's some kind of practical joke, she thought and, struck by a good idea, gave the local police station a ring.

Dobbs was quick to answer.

'Oh,' he said wearily. 'It's you, Wanda.'

Wanda pursed her lips.

Dobbs always sounded a bit lax to her. He tended to have even less work to do than she did.

Today though, he sounded more weary than bored. Quickly, she told him about her tip-off.

'I had the same call!' he said agitatedly and she shuddered as she heard his moustache bristling against his receiver. She thought the policeman was the most unappealing man she had ever met. 'We don't know where it came from.'

'Have you alerted your superiors?'

'About a crank call?' She listened to him grunt with laughter. 'No, I'm waiting to see if this train full of people actually turns up.'

'Can't you go and look for them?'

'Where would we start?' he asked. 'The voice didn't give us any directions.'

The Voice, Wanda thought, shivering. She didn't like the way Dobbs had put that. It made the whole thing a good deal spookier.

Just then she became aware of a kerfuffle out in the waiting room.

Someone was coming in, slamming the door and ringing the bell again and again.

She sighed and told the policeman, 'Duty calls, Sergeant Dobbs. Would you be so good as to phone me if you hear anything further?'

He growled out his assent, but Wanda knew from experience that he'd most probably shut up shop as usual and end up down the Horse and Plough for the afternoon.

Briskly she marched out of her office and into reception.

A very dishevelled young man was propping himself on her counter, disarraying her papers.

His fair hair was tousled and he was wearing a ripped shirt and jeans. He looked filthy.

'Well,' she said, brushing down her starched apron. 'Whatever has happened to you, young man?'

'I got away,' he said and, by his voice, Wanda could see he was about to pass out.

She bustled around the counter to take hold of him.

'What's your name?' she asked.

'Mike,' he said, 'Mike Yates.'

And he promptly passed out in her arms.

As if today hasn't been bad enough already, Dobbs thought as he surveyed his own new arrivals.

A very odd pair of day-trippers had arrived at his desk in the small police station, and just when he was about to set off on one of his quiet perambulations around town.

The man was over six feet tall and talking busily as he entered the room.

He was clutching an opera cloak to him and rolling his eyes in irritation as he quarrelled with a much shorter, dumpier woman with bright purple hair and garish make-up plastered on her face.

'Iris,' the man said, breaking into her gabbling, 'I really don't think it's a good idea for me to let you investigate any of this on your own. You don't know how I work any more. There are correct channels and procedures…'

With this, he arrived at Dobbs's messy desk and slid into an easy, charming grin for the sergeant's sake. 'Isn't that right?'

'Indeed, sir,' said the flustered Dobbs, looking the new arrival up and down.

'Procedures!' Iris laughed. 'That's not how it used to be! You're just wasting time!'

She gave Dobbs a savage glance. 'How's this fat fool going to help?'

Dobbs coloured and stroked his moustache. 'Perhaps if you both calm down and tell me what's wrong…'

'Well,' said the Doctor, leaning in. 'It all started with a phone call…'

'Tom!' Jo shouted worriedly. 'That isn't the way!'

She had already found the surgery and was making her way determinedly across the street towards it but, as Jo turned round, she saw that Tom was striding off in the other direction, back towards the shops.

'Tom!'

It was curiously empty in the small village. They'd hardly seen another soul since they'd arrived. It was so quiet Jo could hear the birds up on the thatched roofs and the sound made her shiver.

Tom didn't even turn to look at her. She was concerned about him.

Ever since they had seen those mysterious teenagers in the field, ever since they had watched them drain out of existence, glowing with spangling light, Tom had been dizzy and sick.

Jo would have thought the local doctor's would have been exactly where he wanted to go.

He was acting very strangely indeed; beseeching Jo not to tell the Doctor and Iris what the two of them had seen.

Well, there'd hardly been a chance to, anyway, what with haring off in Bessie to this town, and the Doctor despatching her and Tom to tell the local hospital to prepare themselves.

And now this.

She had to prioritise. Tom was acting strangely but there was work to do. She had to get medical help for those poor people on the train.

She found the nurse in charge of the small hospital less than helpful. Nurse Wanda was gargantuan and rather truculent.

When Jo breathlessly explained the nature of their discovery in the field, the woman's eyes narrowed and her expression became hard.

'The Doctor is getting the police to ferry all of the victims here,' Jo explained. 'Is there only you here to look after them?'

'I manage very well,' said Wanda gruffly.

'I doubt you've seen anything like this before.'

'Hm,' said Wanda and reached for the kettle as it came to the boil. She was making a Cup-a-Soup for her single patient.

As she took the brimming mug through to the ward Jo pursued her. 'This is important!' she said. 'These people are in desperate need of our...'

She came to an abrupt halt at the foot of the bed.

Wanda was holding out the mug of soup to the woozy-looking figure propped up on nylon-cased pillows.

He smiled weakly, thankfully, at his nurse.

Jo's eyes were out on stalks. 'Mike?'

He fixed on her unsteadily. 'Who?'

The Doctor marched out of the station to find Iris, who was sitting happily in Bessie, having a cigarette and looking as if she had forgotten that they had an emergency.

'That fool of a police sergeant at last consented to let me use his precious telephone,' he said. 'I phoned UNIT and the Ministry and nothing.'

'Nothing?'

'Not a squeak. They've all gone to the seaside, I suppose.'

'How very odd,' said Iris and tossed her cigarette away. 'So?'

'So Sergeant Dobbs is calling in various local police forces. We're going to have to do without military help. They're bringing the passengers to the surgery here. I hope Jo's warned them.'

'Well,' said Iris, shoving up along the front seat and trying to cheer him up. 'We can do without the military this once, can't we? You don't want to go soft and all reliant, do you?'

'Soft!' he cried.

'What kind of a man are you,' she said, 'if you go calling up the Brigadier every time something goes wrong?'

The Doctor was furious. 'I do not call up the Brigadier when...'

She cackled. 'You do! Whenever your toaster needs mending, you're on that phone! And you pretend you hate him interfering in your life and getting you all involved in saving the planet and what have you. Oh, I think it's very sweet, but it doesn't fool me, old chum. You love it. You love getting all involved. What are you after, a bleeding knighthood?'

'I want you to get out of my car this moment,' said the Doctor, in a very level voice.

'What?'

'I want you to leave. I don't want to see you again all day.'

'You can't be serious! We're in this together!'

'No, we aren't.'

'It's our adventure!' she cried.

'It isn't. It's a highly sensitive and mysterious issue that needs investigation. You are not required.'

'But I am! I'm helping you!'

'You, madam,' said the Doctor, barely restraining his ire, 'are an oafish and clodhopping harridan. You cause more trouble than you're worth! How can the likes of you help me?'

Iris's voice went quiet. She sunk her chin into the fur collar of her coat. 'I saved your life in Scotland. Remember Mary, Queen of Scots? And remember the Ice Warriors on Neptune?

And the drashigs on Qon-ti-jaqir?'

The Doctor turned steely. 'No, I don't.'

Tears stood out in Iris's eyes. 'We make a fantastic team! You need me!'

The Doctor harrumphed and gunned the engine.

'Where are we going?'

'To the hospital. To await the arrival of the passengers.'

Iris's eyes lit up. 'You're letting me stay?'

They were interrupted by the burly figure of Sergeant Dobbs rushing out of the station.

'They've got them, Doctor! They're bringing them in lorries!'

The Doctor nodded. 'Hop in the back, Sergeant Dobbs. I'll need your help.'

Then he gave Iris a significant glance which, dismayed, she took to mean: even this fat idiot is more help than you are.

As Bessie sped them through the quiet town Iris resolved that she would show him.

She would prove to the Doctor just how indispensable to him she really was.

At first Tom wasn't at all sure where he was going.

This town was strange to him, as was this whole era. It was familiar but in a rather displaced manner.

It was like stepping into an old film or TV series or an alternate plane in which the 1970s never ended.

Something was driving his feet onwards. Once he had shaken off Jo, he found himself walking towards a café between a newsagent's and a bookie's.

Inside there were more people than he had seen in the town altogether.

Something was telling him he had to come here and sit at one of the Formica benches.

The air was thick with cigarette smoke.

Faces looked up at him as he hurried in and made for the counter.

As he queued and asked the thin man behind the urn for some tea, he received a quizzical glance.

'Is your name Tom?'

Tom nodded.

'That's five pee. Some friends of yours, over at that cubicle.'

The thin man nodded at the table and took Tom's money.

The belt buckle was tingling against his stomach again as he made his way over. This was it.

His confrontation with whatever destiny had in store for him. Over the crackly transistor on the counter T Rex were playing 'Children of the Revolution'.

Tom slid into the cubicle, on to the squeaking PVC of the bench.

Kevin looked up from his burger. He was eating it fastidiously, careful not to spill ketchup on his white jumpsuit.

Beside him was the girl Tom had seen him with in the field. She had jet black hair and she looked genuinely glad to see him.

'He's replied to our summons,' said Kevin, looking pleased. 'We've tested him enough, I think.'

The girl smiled. 'He's one of us,' she said. 'Welcome, Tom. I'm Marsha. And this is Kevin.'

Tom found he couldn't reply.

He watched Kevin take a massive bite out of his burger. 'Is that beef?' Tom asked.

Kevin nodded.

'I wouldn't eat that, if I were you. Not in this era.'

Marsha looked entranced. 'He really is from our future!'

'But I know you!' Jo was insisting, sitting beside Mike's bed. 'We work together. I saw you just over two weeks ago...'

The bemused young man was shaking his head. 'I've never seen you before in my life.'

They sat staring at each other for a few moments.

She wondered if she could have got it wrong. He certainly looked and sounded like Mike, but there were subtle differences. His skin was ashen and his eyes were drawn.

Even the effort of refuting her claim had seemed to wear him out.

They were trapped here now, looking at each other.

Jo started to feel as if she had made some kind of *faux pas*. Had Mike ever said he had a twin?

She realised she could probably write down everything she knew about Mike Yates on a postcard.

It was only as she tried again to remind him of who he was supposed to be, launching into it, telling him what he did for a living and reminding him which terribly hush-hush organisation he belonged to, that it came over her how little she actually knew about him.

At the UNIT Christmas party last year, he had opened up a little, spoiling it then, snatching a clumsy kiss from her in the hallway and she'd managed to divert him into talking about his unhappy childhood.

'You think I've lost all my marbles,' he said now, slumped disconsolate on viscose pillows. 'You think you know me. I don't know you, but I'm prepared to believe I've got something wrong with me.'

Suddenly it hit her: this must have something to do with the radio silence from UNIT HQ.

She had uncovered a first clue.

Mike was saying solemnly: 'There is something dreadfully wrong with me. I thought the hospital would be able to help.'

He held out one shaking hand across the bedcovers.

Jo gasped, shocked to see how pale and hairless he'd become. Mike Yates was a soldier; an out-doorsy type. Out of choice he spent weekends on Ministry training courses; the survivalist sessions that Jo had tried hard to avoid.

Now he looked wan and thin and… two-dimensional.

He wasn't just skinny, he was flattened out.

He rotated his hand before both their faces and there was even an edge to it, as if he suddenly had barely any depth at all.

It was exactly as if he was made out of cardboard.

'It's spreading,' said Mike. 'It began with one finger. Now it's both my arms.'

Jo stared in horror at her erstwhile colleague as he gathered up the bedclothes to his flattening body.

'Are you going to tell me what this is all about?' Tom asked the two teenagers.

Kevin smiled wryly and wiped his greasy fingers on his napkin. 'Not yet.'

'Why have you been contacting me? How do you know who I am?'

Marsha was smiling at him in an almost patronising manner. 'It's always like this with a new member. You're confused and becoming paranoid. I've seen this again and again.'

Tom tutted. 'Oh, yes?'

'You see,' Marsha went on. 'Kevin and I are part of a new species… and so are you.'

'Not now, Marsha,' said Kevin. 'Don't tell him everything yet. We have to be sure.'

'Oh, he's definitely the one.'

Kevin's face was serious. 'Perhaps. But we have to be certain that he will work for us.'

Tom was studying the boy's face. He found himself saying, 'What is it you want me to do?'

Marsha beamed. Kevin leaned forward and told him: 'You need to stay with the Doctor just a bit longer. We need you there with him.'

'Why?'

'You need to see what he's really like. And what he is up to.'

'Why is he so important to you?'

'You'll see.'

Tom was starting to feel rather perturbed.

He wanted to warn Iris, and then, almost as if his mind had been read, Marsha put in: 'That old woman who you travel with. You mustn't tell her everything. She is part of this, but we don't know yet just how she fits in.'

'Iris?' laughed Tom. 'She's just Iris. She wouldn't do anyone harm.'

Kevin said, 'We don't know how involved she is with the Doctor. We suspect she might be working for him.'

'She says they're very old friends...' said Tom slowly. 'She's quite evasive about the actual circumstances...'

'Exactly. She's a loose cannon.'

'She's certainly that!'

Kevin was getting up to go and taking out a scrap of paper from a pocket in the breast of his jumpsuit. There was an address scrawled on it. 'Stay with them, Tom. And when the time is right you will come to us. You will come to this location.'

Marsha was sliding out of the cubicle after Kevin. 'It won't be long,' she said. 'Then you can join us. But please, don't tell anyone. Do not betray us. You are part of us and there is so much for you to learn. There is so much waiting for you.'

Then Kevin and Marsha were gone, leaving Tom sitting alone in the café, looking at the scribbled address and listening to Suzi Quatro on the radio.

He didn't know what to believe any more.

The address was a quite complicated one, somewhere in South London.

He wanted to run after the two teenagers now and quiz them more. He wanted to follow them to London.

But the business with the Doctor and Iris was more intriguing.

Iris was his only way back to his own time.

He had to know more. He had to stick close to her.

* * *

Mike Yates had fallen silent as the process by which he was reduced to a shadow of his former self inexorably continued.

Jo found herself staring.

No one had come in to see them.

There was silence in the room; simply the slight creaking of cardboard. His bedclothes had sunk flat on the bed.

His stricken expression was etched on a face flat as the rest of him.

She reached out one hand and touched the cool smooth expanse of his torso.

It was as if she was operating in some completely separated moment, outside of time.

She found she couldn't run for help or decide on any rational plan of action.

All she knew was that here was someone whom she regarded as a friend and he was afflicted by some vile and unknown dimensional instability.

She didn't even think to run and find the Doctor. She found herself, instead, determined to take Mike to the place where she had seen him last thinking that, somehow, the root of his predicament must lie there.

She was like a girl possessed as she stood, suddenly, and unshouldered her bag. She reached for Mike and found him amazingly lightweight.

He was exactly like a silhouette cut from cardboard.

Yes, she knew what she had to do.

Jo slid him out of the bed and, pursing her lips, folded him neatly up and slipped him into her handbag.

Then she stole guiltily out of the hospital.

The lorries arrived within the hour, pulling up with a screech in the car park behind the infirmary.

The Doctor rushed out to help, to see that all was well, but Nurse Wanda took immediate charge, waving the policemen inside and making sure they carried the stretchers carefully.

'Don't they look peculiar?' said Iris, eating a banana she'd plucked from her handbag. 'I mean, in all their stiff old dresses and uniforms. That's a real mystery, that is.'

'I hope we can bring them round to solve it,' said the Doctor.

'Where are Jo and Tom?' Carefully Iris folded the banana skin back into her golden clutchbag. She didn't want to throw it down where someone would slip on it.

As they followed the bodies into the small hospital, Tom was watching from the road outside.

He was missing all the action, he thought.

Already he felt like an outsider and a spy.

What he really wanted to do was sit Iris down and explain all the mysterious things that had been happening to him. It would be such a relief to get it all off his chest.

But he couldn't. He had as good as given his word.

And it was true: somewhere deep inside himself he felt some innate, deep-rooted connection with Marsha and Kevin.

There was something about what they said that rang very true to him.

He wanted to see Kevin again.

There would be no chance of that, he somehow knew, if he spilled the beans to Iris.

Why had everything become so complex, suddenly?

His previous forays into the fantastic with Iris had been fairly straightforward, compared to this.

It was all the Doctor's fault.

His intrigues and mystery had infected them all.

Tom watched the policemen who had brought the bodies to the hospital climb into their van.

He shrank back against the tall redbrick wall as they drove out. Funny. They were so silent and businesslike.

As the van slid past, he saw that both men sitting in the cab were completely bald.

When it was gone he stepped on to the forecourt.

He was grabbed immediately by his arms.

Before his next breath someone had twisted both of his arms up his back and slammed him against the wall.

He gasped out, winded, and found he was held immobile by one of the police.

'You shouldn't be here,' he was told by an oily voice.

It spoke right into his ear and Tom knew that this wasn't usual police procedure.

'Who are you?'

Tom stared down, craning to see the hands that were gripping him.

It was an inhuman pressure he felt on his arms.

The policeman breathed right into his face – a pungent smell – but he couldn't see the man's face. He caught a glimpse of the hands, though, and they were a sheeny, rich green.

'I'm Tom,' Tom gasped. 'I'm here because my friends are here. What are you... ?'

Then he felt the pressure relent and he slid down against the wall, grazing his forehead.

When he stood again, shaking, he found that the man had gone.

He was alone in the forecourt.

None of the figures on the hospital beds was stirring. Nurse Wanda had never seen anything like it.

Beside her, the Doctor was gazing speculatively at their flouncy gowns and outdated uniforms. It was as if this was the kind of state of affairs he was quite used to.

Maybe there was an entirely rational explanation. Maybe they were a film crew. Maybe the whole cast of a Jane Austen serial had gone down with a dreadful lurgy.

One thing was for certain and that was that this Doctor was nothing like Dr Prendergast.

Instead of the reassuringly sane and dull Prendergast she had this man, who seemed some two feet taller than herself, draped in velvet and reeking of some exotic eau de Cologne.

Then, in one swift movement, he was at the side of one of the patients. A pouchy old dear encrusted in white panstick.

She was matronly and ruffled, with her limp arms spread over her ample bodice.

There was a serene expression on her face, one that never flinched as the Doctor leaned over her.

'I thought I could hear one of them starting to breathe more deeply.'

He turned swiftly to look at Wanda. 'I think she's resuscitating.'

At this point Iris came trolling in, stirring a cup of machine coffee. 'Coming round, is she? By jingo!'

Wanda didn't quite see how Iris fitted into things. The Doctor seemed to spend most of his time trying to ignore her.

He prised open the old woman's eyes and now Wanda could hear it too; the dreadful, slow sound as she filled her lungs with new air.

Then she was awake.

Her hands flew up like frightened birds and grasped the Doctor's wrists, bunching up his frilled cuffs.

'Easy now,' he said, in a doctorly tone.

The woman started to gabble. 'I have to get us all home. We're terribly late. Something awful has happened. My girls! Oh, my girls!'

'Calm yourself,' said the Doctor. 'You're quite safe here. Now, tell me your name…'

Her eyes fixed hesitantly on him. 'I need to know that my daughters are safe.'

Wanda spoke up. 'Everyone from the railway carriage is here.'

The woman sighed. 'Are they all living?'

'Was there an accident?' Wanda asked. 'Was that it?'

'No accident,' said the woman. 'We ran out of time, that is all. Do you not find that? Everything we do is against the clock, is it not?'

'Indeed,' said the Doctor gently.

He was alarmed by her heart rate as he tested it. It was all over the place. 'That's all too true, Mrs…?'

'Mrs Bennett,' she said firmly. 'There, you have my name now And perhaps you would be good enough to…'

'Just you relax,' said Wanda, deciding it was time she took charge.

'There isn't any time to relax,' said Mrs Bennett wildly. 'You must revive my poor ailing daughters with all due haste! You oughtn't to have woken me first! My life hardly matters any more, compared to theirs! You should make quite sure my daughters get home before… Well, just before. They are the priority…'

She seized up then, into a kind of spasm.

She seemed to be locked in a split second, her mouth frozen around her final word.

The Doctor jumped and touched her skin.

'What's wrong with her?' Iris cried.

'Frozen solid,' he said.

They watched then as hairline fractures appeared all over the woman's skin.

The lines crazed and cracked a fractal path up her arms, her bosom and contorted face.

They crizzled and ominously crisscrossed and ran like black wildfire.

Her flesh was breaking up before their eyes.

Wanda was paralysed with shock.

'She's dying,' said Iris. 'We're too late.'

Mrs Bennett cracked open like over-ripe fruit.

It was as if her fragile form had been dealt a deadly blow. With a puff of foul-smelling vapour her whole body sagged down into itself.

A slight gust of a breeze and her elaborate dress collapsed. In seconds the woman was reduced to almost nothing.

She left behind her nothing on the prim hospital bed but her vintage dress and a trace of fine, green, oily powder.

'Don't touch it!' the Doctor cried hoarsely, as Iris reached out one curious hand.

She swallowed hard.

Some uneasy memory was leaping up in her mind, but she couldn't snag it. 'I've seen a death like this before…'

When they turned to look at the rest of the ward, exactly the same thing had happened to the other patients.

They had been left with a roomful of theatrical costumes and a kilo or two of emerald dust.

'All her daughters…' whispered Wanda, shaken. 'They're all dead…'

At this point Tom burst into the ward.

'You're here!' he said, breathing heavily.

He was bleeding and bruised and confused.

'I can't find Jo. I thought she was here with you…'

Chapter Five
It's Only Mind Control But I Like It

From the journals of Ms Iris Wildthyme.

The poor old Doctor still wouldn't have it.

I kept telling him, on that late-afternoon drive back to his house, that surely he had to agree by now.

Surely, after all this.

If this wasn't evidence of alien malarkey and technology, what could be?

I'd helped him and Wanda use a brush pan and shovel to collect up the dusty green remains into carrier bags.

We were taking the luckless and mysterious passengers home to study them.

And it was then, as we set to work on the first glistening heap of leftovers, that we found the first of the wrist communicators, tangled up in the empty lace sleeve of Mrs Bennett's frock. It was a golden bangle studded with crimson stones and it must have been pushed right up her forearm for us not to clock it earlier.

Tom made a quick check of the other abandoned costumes and found that everyone had been wearing a similar device about their persons.

The Doctor popped each expensive-looking artefact into another carrier bag (not very scientific, I know) and he said we'd be examining those at our leisure, too.

Driving back at breakneck speed I was goading him.

'They've just got to come from another world.'

He was evasive. 'We'll just have to see.'

I didn't like this caginess in him.

Elegant and dashing he may be, this Doctor, but his previous self would have been a mite more enthusiastic. He'd have been jumping up and down: 'Oh yes! Oh, my! It must belong to some ghastly invasion force hovering over our very heads! Goodness me!'

I looked at him. 'What's the matter with you? You don't seem very excited.'

'Excited! When alien incursions occur in this time and place, my dear Ms Wildthyme, they really aren't anything to get excited about.'

I studied him as he turned back to concentrate on the road. 'You're worried about that Jo, aren't you?'

'Kindly stop referring to her as "that Jo".'

Before we set off on our return trip, he'd been striding about the small village shouting her name, at first impatiently and then with a tinge of panic in his voice.

'I bet she's always wandering off.'

'Hm,' he said. 'And it's never anywhere very safe.'

'Tom's the same,' I said, turning to look fondly at my boy, who was being bounced up and down on the back seat. He looked wan. 'Well,' I said, Jo will turn up again. She isn't completely dim. Is she?'

The Doctor glowered at me.

I added, 'She probably found something more interesting to do. Anyway, you've got me now, lovey. I'm all the help you need! We can crack this little mystery in no time!'

'I was rather hoping you would leave me to it.'

'Oh, no. You need me. You're stuck with me now till the bitter end!'

I could tell that, secretly, he was delighted by this.

It was in the way he muttered something in an archaic dialect under his breath.

I couldn't quite make it out, but I think it was an offering of thanks to the gods.

* * *

Jo was on remote control.

She walked miles that day in the blazing heat and never once felt the temptation to turn back or find her friends.

Her compulsion took her miles out of the small village and purposefully down the country lanes, where the fields were shimmering with endless heat and the hedgerows hummed and agitated with insects.

She clasped the bag that contained Mike Yates and set herself a brisk pace.

The day started to mellow and grow cool as an indigo cast took over the wide bowl of the sky.

Clouds like streaky blue bacon stole into view and common sense asserted itself enough to tell her that it was getting late.

There was no way she was ever going to be able to walk the whole distance.

Then, like a miracle, on the iron bridge she was approaching as she voiced this thought to herself, she saw a waiting taxi.

Its engine, she could hear, was still running and, as she set foot on the dusty bridge, the black cab's door swung open, ready for her. Entranced, Jo clambered gratefully aboard.

The driver half turned to look at her as she settled on the blistering upholstery, stowing her bag beside her.

His head seemed too large and it was covered in coarse grey hair. His ears stood out like trumpets and from them sprouted astonishing clumps of silver hair.

Jo caught his glance in the rear-view mirror and his eyes were livid and burning orange, almost buried under a neanderthal brow.

She took a deep breath. I've got into a taxi on a bridge in the middle of nowhere and my driver is a troll.

He wrinkled his huge nose at her and she swallowed hard.

'I'd like to go to UNIT headquarters, please,' she said, with mock brightness.

He spoke in a guttural voice, as if English wasn't his natural tone.

Watching out for strangers who spoke oddly accented English was one of the few bits of Ministry training that Jo could remember.

'That's a good few hours' journey away, miss.'

'That's all right,' she said. 'This is an emergency.'

He nodded. 'You're always having them emergencies there, aren't you?'

'Oh, yes,' she said. 'One a week, most weeks.'

She laughed as the taxi started off and it was only after a few moments that she considered the strangeness of the cabbie's question. But she was too exhausted to go into it now.

With almost obscene haste it grew dark.

Soon they were in the deepest heart of the countryside and there wasn't a star to be seen.

It was as if the troll had reached one massive hairy paw out of his taxi window, scraped them all out of the sky and stashed them in his glove compartment.

Just to keep her lost.

If he stopped the car now and sent her out to make her own way, Jo wouldn't have the first idea where to go.

Tom followed Iris into the cool stone kitchen, where she was unscrewing the lid of the gin bottle.

'The Doctor's gone straight to his laboratory with his samples.'

'He would,' she said, hacking away at a lemon.

'Aren't you going to help him?'

She shrugged. 'It's boring, faffing on with microscopes and all that. If he finds anything interesting, he'll shout.'

'Will he, though?'

'What do you mean?' Iris took a long swig and smacked her lips. 'Hm?'

'I think he'll keep quiet about it. He doesn't want you involved.'

'Doesn't want me involved!' she roared.

'He thinks you're a nuisance. I don't like him much.'

'This Doctor can be a little abrupt. I should have taken you to one of the later ones. One of the nicer ones.'

Tom sat down and she knew he was about to broach something. 'I was thinking of going to London. Would you mind?'

Iris bugged her eyes. 'You're leaving me!'

'Just for a few days.'

'You're going to run away from me! Like everyone does.'

'No I'm not…'

'You wouldn't be happy in this time, Tom. It isn't the same as yours. It might look more innocent and safe, but…'

'Only a day or two. While you're here, working with the Doctor.'

'I'll think about it,' she said sternly. 'Although I'm sure you'll wander off if you feel like it. Just you watch out though. You be safe.'

He nodded and left her then. He wanted to explore the Doctor's house a little more.

Iris sat slumped at the table, pouring herself another drink.

'Why do they always want to leave me?' she asked the kitchen at large. 'It's different for the Doctor. He can barely get rid of his companions. They even come back to see him, years later! Mine run away screaming!'

She could feel herself working herself up into a temper.

The hugely fat cat had slunk off its chair and was padding heavily into the kitchen.

It stared at Iris from the doorway and made her jump.

'Oh! Hullo, puss! Don't mind me, mithering on. I've just gone a bit maudlin…'

As if in response, the marmalade cat lumbered across the flagstones, under the table, and rubbed itself against her legs.

Its claws clicked on her thick wool tights.

'You wouldn't leave me, would you, puss?' she smiled.

Then she screamed as the cat sank its teeth into the fat meat of her calf.

Iris leapt to her feet with the cat still attached, yelling and swearing profusely.

As much as she shook her leg, it wouldn't drop off.

'Doctor!' she howled.'Tom!'

Before anyone could respond to her cries there was a tremendous clatter as every drawer and cupboard door in the kitchen shot open of their own accord.

Iris stared, the savage pain in her leg forgotten, as every single piece of gleaming silver cutlery lifted itself from the knife drawer and came hurtling through the air towards her.

The taxi driver was singing to himself.

He had a curious, crooning voice.

All Jo could make out of his peculiar song were the repeated lines:

'It isn't very good
in the dark dark wood...'

She shuddered and tried to put the words out of her mind.

Instead, she peeked inside her bag to check that Mike was okay. He seemed just the same. Neatly folded and quite lifeless.

She worried vaguely about the creases she'd put in him.

'We'll soon be there,' said the troll-driver suddenly, making her jump. 'Are you quite sure you want to go into that dark old building this time of night? You could come and stay at our house. It's quite nearby. My wife would be pleased to put you up.'

'Oh, no,' said Jo. 'I couldn't put you to any trouble.'

She was thinking about corned beef sandwiches and hot cocoa in the canteen at UNIT HQ.

There was always someone there, whatever the time of day. Mrs Hope, who always stood by the urn and who was a favourite of the Doctor's, would surely be there.

And maybe Sergeant Benton. He would be a reassuring sight to see.

The car slunk along the dark road and soon they were pulling up before the heavy iron gates.

They were forbidding, but happily familiar.

'What do I owe you?'

The troll waved her money away. 'I'm just glad you people are there, protecting us all. Making the world a safe place to go to sleep at night.'

Jo frowned.

She wasn't sure how her driver seemed to know so much about the organisation.

'You be careful, miss. It looks awfully dark in those grounds. I can't see any lights on in that building, there.'

Perhaps she had misjudged him.

It was rather sweet, the concern he was showing.

She shouldered her bag and stepped out into the road. 'I'm all right now,' she said, brightly.

'I'll wait here a few moments, miss,' he said, stolidly. 'Just in case anything is wrong. You can give me a shout.'

He wouldn't be dissuaded. The odd thing was, his face had taken on a bizarrely greenish cast.

Jo shook her head and looked for her pass-key to the gates. What could possibly go wrong once she was inside the grounds?

To her, stepping inside UNIT HQ was like stepping inside the front door of her own flat.

The Doctor's lab in his own house was better equipped than the one at UNIT HQ, but it was infinitely messier.

Yellowing papers and charts were spread out with abandon on every surface.

The floor was strewn with cracked glass and frazzled bits of circuitry and the furniture was stained with chemicals of all kinds.

He was peering at a print-out of an analysis of the mysterious green residue when Iris's frantic screams came to him from downstairs.

He groaned, dropped what he was doing, and pelted out into the hallway.

All the way down he was thinking: simple verdigris.

That's all it was. An oxidised residue from copper.

Nothing more exotic than that.

And the bracelet things they had found in the remains had told him little more. They refused to yield to analysis.

He thudded through the downstairs hall, past his TARDIS, and through the series of brightly coloured rooms to the kitchen.

As he whirled past the police box, he didn't notice that its tall door was hanging open.

From within, flattened against the humming wall, Tom was watching him fly past.

His heart was in his mouth, terrified he'd be caught snooping around.

But the Doctor had gone.

And something was wrong with Iris.

As the Doctor crashed into the kitchen, the silver utensils lost their bizarrely independent momentum and dropped to the floor.

Iris, who was pressed, sweating and screaming up against the Aga, let out a howl of relief.

In the corner the cat was tense and spitting.

As the Doctor stared at his panicking house guest he saw that three of the sharpest knives were embedded, quivering, in the wall either side of the old woman's head.

He stepped towards her.

'What on Earth is going on?' he demanded, as if it were all her fault.

She sagged forward and fell into his arms.

She forced him to embrace her and to gather her up in his velvet sleeves.

'It was terrible!' she sobbed. 'The whole kitchen came to life! All of your utensils were possessed! And the cat bit me!'

'Nonsense,' he said, gingerly stroking her hair. 'She wouldn't hurt a soul.'

'I'll need a tetanus!' Iris wailed. 'That creature is feral.'

'Sit down,' the Doctor urged. 'And tell me calmly what happened.'

'Calmly!' she said, and reached for her glass.

Outside Tom was listening.

He was satisfied that Iris was in no further danger. Her screams, coming at the precise moment he had managed to step aboard the Doctor's unlocked and perplexing craft, had jolted him badly.

Now, pulling the blue door closed behind him, he stepped inside again to investigate.

This TARDIS seemed a mite more sophisticated than Iris's.

Its white walls crackled and hummed with an alien energy and cool vitality.

The control console was a ghastly mess. It looked as if it had been taken apart again and again and none of the pieces would return neatly to their original places.

Tom stood by it, drawn by the intricate play of dials and lit controls.

As he stared he saw that the scanner – rather like Iris's in that it resembled an ancient TV set – was crackling into life.

Kevin was there, standing with his arms folded in a distinctly futuristic setting.

Behind him tubes and wires were glowing with colour.

He was whispering.

'You've got to come to London,' he hissed. 'I can't stay on this line long. Tom... we want you here. Things are going to get lively and pretty dangerous there...'

Then the screen went blank.

UNIT HQ was always bugged.

Everything that was said or done within its walls was recorded and photographed and filmed.

It was one of the first buildings to be tapped quite so comprehensively.

Within twenty years, of course, even the humblest supermarket would be graced with the same equipment, but in the early summer of 1973 and on the evening that Jo Grant stole into the building through its curiously unlocked front door, UNIT HQ was pretty much ahead of its time.

Jo knew that, with every step she advanced into the reception area, automatic lenses were squeezing themselves tighter and monitoring her progress.

She knew that every sharply drawn breath was being picked up by microphones no larger than a cat's nose.

She had seen the ten-by-twelve black and white glossies on which luckless intruders were unwittingly captured. One of her first jobs here had been filing the secret stills away.

She knew that, though the building was silent and seemingly abandoned, her visit wasn't going unnoticed.

Still One

Of the pictures remaining from this evening (much of the UNIT material having been junked in the late 1970s), the first relevant one shows this very small, very pretty, very blonde girl in her shaggy fur coat in the hallway, turning on one heel – apparently gasping in shock – as the main door slams shut behind her.

Still Two

This girl has decided to head straight for the office of Brigadier Lethbridge-Stewart.

She is framed in the open doorway.

She seems to be astonished to find, instead of the expected desk, phone, notepad and filing cabinet, a roomful of flowers.

Our still is black and white but the concentrated scent of these thousand, variegated and flaunting blooms still seems to rise off the glossy page.

Still Three

Jo in the hallway. Perplexed by a stuffed and mounted bear.

Its paws raised threateningly over her head, its jaws in a hungry rictus.

She looks as if she is saying: 'That wasn't here before.' Which, of course, it wasn't.

If we look carefully, we can see the grooves in the matted, hairy belly of the beast which, with a sharp creaking noise, suddenly breaks apart in the second after this photo was taken.

A kind of door opened in the bear's vast stomach and, to Jo's silent astonishment, out stepped a very short, mostly bald man, in a pink and grey suit.

His cravat was a salmon pink and held in place with an exquisite diamond pin.

A snippet of their conversation – his tone dry, benign and hers, baffled, almost panicked – remains on crackling audio tape.

Jo: (indistinct) better tell me what's happening here.
Pinstripe: Think of it as an exam, my dear.

Jo: (indistinct)

Pinstripe: That's right. The final stage in your training. Let's just say you aren't (indistinct) pass with flying colours now, are you?

Jo: There's no (indistinct)

Pinstripe: And would you really find it easier if the Doctor was here? You've been stuck in these places with him before. Flashing lights coming out of the ceiling, a cacophony of unearthly noise, the floor begins to spin and the walls start to swirl with colour and you, of course, my dear Jo, you succumb to some kind of hypnosis.

Jo: (indistinct)

Pinstripe: At this point, naturally, the Doctor turns to you and what does he do? What does he do to break the spell? (indistinct) He slaps you hard in the face. Tells you that you almost lost control. 'Snap out of it, Jo! It's only mind control!'

Jo: I wish he was (indistinct) here now.

Pinstripe: Perhaps you've already succumbed. Perhaps I should slap you in the face. Would that help?

Jo: (indistinct) about an exam?

Pinstripe: It's a very expensive process, training the likes of you. This is the final stage. When we strip away the façade of the UNIT Headquarters and reveal the true skull beneath the skin.
Jo: (indistinct)

Pinstripe: (indistinct)

Jo: (indistinct)

Pinstripe: No, no. UNIT itself was the illusion. It was simply another stage in your training. The Brigadier, the Doctor, even the lady who served the tea. All of them actors and illusionists. Nothing, don't you see? Nothing in the last two years of your life had any credence or truth value whatsoever (indistinct)

Jo: But why? (indistinct)

Pinstripe: You have your uncle to thank. Didn't he inveigle you into the Ministry in the first place? Use your common sense, girl! Do you really think there would be an organisation like UNIT here, in the 1970s? Pledged to protect Earth from alien life forms? Do you really think there is such a thing as life on other worlds?

Jo: There is! I do! I've been there.

Pinstripe: If you'd been a little more cynical you'd have seen through our (indistinct) inventions.

Jo: (indistinct) Daleks and spaceships and guns…

Pinstripe: Think about every alien artefact or creature you have ever seen. Weren't they always surrounded by a crackling nimbus of blue light?

Jo: Well… yes.

Pinstripe: Didn't they sometimes look a little… unconvincing?

Jo: (indistinct) That's just how things are, isn't it?

Pinstripe: They were all special effects. It's all a put-on, my dear.

Jo: But why? It's (indistinct) cruel.

Pinstripe: To test you. And you have failed.

Still Four

The malign and dwarfish pinstripe man grabbing at Jo to kiss her. She's struggling with him.

She's about to cast him off; send him toppling into the bear from which he emerged to engage her in the above, eavesdropped, worrying conversation.

The bear will explode and kill him and the whole grand staircase will open up, revealing a corridor painted Bridget Riley style.

Black and white stripes lit from an unknown source, receding into the gloomy distance.

Still Five

A shaken Jo stepping past the blackened body of her pinstriped aggressor, moving into the corridor adorned with black and white stripes.

Still Six

Jo stands transfixed before a futuristic device.

Something rather like a glitter ball.

Still Seven

Jo running down a corridor, away from the gloating, gleaming device.

Still Eight

Jo confronted by the same device. Transfixed again.

Still Nine

Jo in another corridor.
 Tearing her hair out.

Still Ten

Jo looking at the glitter ball once more.
 She can't get away from the thing.

Still Eleven

Jo in a corridor, this one covered in swirling patterns.
 She has found a note on the floor.

Note on Yellow Paper:

'The Doctor wrenched it open... ushered... female companion... hall of... high-pitched whining of the... battled for a solution... for any control... open them up! ... The door might be... ever decreasing and increasing throbs... see a carousel... floor... vibrate... the amazed duo standing below... would be instant death... touched the handle lightly... drew a smart smack across her cheek.'

Still Twelve

Jo has met another man.
 One she recognises and, in this instant, is gratefully embracing. The note has dropped to the floor.

The man has a florid complexion and a handlebar moustache. He is in a checked tweed suit. A fragment of tape exists.

Uncle: (indistinct) the result of my own nepotism. You should have gone for a job in a bank.

Jo: Why have (indistinct) can we do now?

Uncle: What he said was true. (indistinct) torture and mayhem.

Jo: (indistinct)

Uncle: Information (indistinct) protection (indistinct) Marquis de Sade (indistinct) Gothic heroines are always (indistinct) just like the *Story of O*, really (indistinct) all of us inside Bluebeard's castle…

Jo: (indistinct)

Uncle: (indistinct)

Jo: (indistinct)

Uncle: (indistinct) on your own.

Jo: You can't leave me!

Uncle: Don't believe (indistinct) true (indistinct)… that old hag, Wildthyme. The Children of Destiny (indistinct) prevail. Goodbye!

Still Thirteen

Jo by the great shimmering globe of the mirror ball again.
    She looks close to despair.

Still Fourteen

Jo backing away from the device.
  It is darker. Something is happening.

Still Fifteen

Jo crouching behind a bank of instruments as a gash opens up in the mysterious ball.

Still Sixteen

A metal ramp has extended itself out of the ball.

Still Seventeen

Jo watches. Horrified.

Still Eighteen

A sheep has emerged from the ball and has slid halfway down the ramp. It is on castors. Its eyes glow malevolently. We can see another behind it.

Still Nineteen

A sheep has emerged from the ball and has slid halfway down the ramp. It is on castors. Its eyes glow malevolently. We can see another behind it.

Still Twenty

A sheep has emerged from the ball and has slid halfway down the ramp. It is on castors. Its eyes glow malevolently.

We can see another behind it.

Stills Twenty-one to Sixty-eight

A sheep has emerged from the ball and has slid halfway down the ramp. It is on castors. Its eyes glow malevolently. We can see another behind it.

Still Sixty-nine

A column of sheep, each identical, each running on castors, emerging from the ball (which has to be bigger on the inside than on the out). In the background we can see the astonished Jo, still crouching.

Still Seventy

A queue of thirty sheep, sweeping down through the black and white corridor, eyes glowing, heading for the main door.

Still Seventy-one

Jo watches the fiftieth and final sheep emerge.
　She looks like a harried shepherdess.

Still Seventy-two

Jo, alone again, staring at the ball of mirrored glass, and the sheep-sized aperture, which remains.

Still Seventy-three

Jo grasps the sharp sides of the aperture and begins to climb inside.

Still Seventy-four

The empty room and the device, which has sealed itself up again, with Jo inside.
 She has left her bag on the polished floor of the room.
 We can just about see Mike Yates's cardboard hand sticking out, between the straps.

Still Seventy-five

And then, a curious troll-like being, who has crept into the still room, is staring at the place in amazement. He appears to have noticed the captain's fingers.

Chapter Six
Beside the Sea

In the morning Iris seemed quite like her old self.

Over breakfast with Tom she behaved as if nothing untoward had happened the night before and, he noticed, at some point in the early hours she had popped back to the bus and kitted herself out in her regulation cardigan, woollen skirt and sensible brogues.

He recognised her sudden and straightforward demeanour: Iris meant business.

What had began as an adventurous jaunt had become deadly serious because someone or something had dared to attack her.

As she ravenously dealt with her bacon and eggs she kept a beady eye out for the cat.

'Did the Doctor see you go out to the bus?' Tom asked quietly.

She shook her head. 'He's still in the laboratory, looking at those bracelets.'

She smiled at Tom's concerned expression. 'Don't worry. The door's alarmed. If he tries to steal her, I'll be the first to know.'

Tom shuddered. 'I hate being somewhere where we can't trust anyone.'

'He saved my life,' said Iris dreamily. 'I know he'd always step in to save my life. But I wouldn't trust him for a second with my bus.'

She sighed contentedly and pierced the fat yolk of her egg.

'Look what I found,' Tom said suddenly, 'Under my bed.'

Iris's eyes grew wide as Tom placed on the table two green rubber gloves.

They were covered in gleaming lizard-like scales and each finger terminated in a sharp nail.

'Goodness!' she said.

Since dawn the Doctor had been busily lashing together a device he hoped might tell him something about the artefacts.

Working by candlelight, he was weaving the bangles into a complex of wires and glowing crystals and attaching them all to a rather old-fashioned radio and a green ear trumpet.

He heard the front door bang as Iris left to fetch a new outfit from her bus and, working steadily, he ignored it.

Now he could hear his guests moving about in the kitchen downstairs.

He laboured on with the fiddly construction, toying with the shrill alien frequencies to which the bracelets were attuned.

He worked with the expert deliberation of a blind piano mender.

He was happiest when there was something like this – intricate and practical – to be getting on with.

Without this task in hand he would be going out of his mind with worry for the missing Jo and for the odd silence from the Brigadier.

His most immediate and natural gut reaction would be to comb the countryside indiscriminately; to set off by car, helicopter, hovercraft, motorbike and sweep across acres of land in search of his friends.

But the more methodical part of himself insisted that he apply himself to more pressing concerns.

The radio's dial changed colour to a gloriously warm tangerine. 'Ah,' he muttered and slowly eased the volume up a notch.

Something was coming through.

The green ear trumpet gave what sounded like a very human cough.

A quavering voice said quite distinctly: 'Gross Expectations, A Tale of Nine Cities, Hard Lines, Bleak Horse...'

As it faded out the Doctor frowned.

A deeper, gurgling voice took up the litany: 'Jude the Obscene, Pride and Permutations, Sensibility and Sense...'

'The other way round, surely,' murmured the Doctor absently.

'We are overheard!' shrieked the higher voice.

'No matter. Continue with the itinerary.'

'Vapidity Fair.'

'Check.'

'Melmoth the Wanderer.'

'Check.'

'Excuse me,' said the Doctor. 'I think I might have tapped into the wrong place. Is this some kind of intergalactic book club?'

'Ignore him,' said the first voice. 'The Turtle of Wildfell Hall.'

'Check.'

'Hullo?' said the Doctor.

'Sssh!' hissed both bibliophiles together.

At the end of the workbench, the phone gave a startling ring.

The Doctor snatched it up and watched in dismay as the orange glow faded from the radio and the voices drained away, still chanting their curious titles.

'Hullo?' he snapped, tiredly.

'... which you may want to have a look at,' said the bland, colourless voice he had heard before.

'Some of your operatives might be very intrigued by the railway carriage which has manifested itself during the night on the beach...'

'The beach? Which beach?' demanded the Doctor.

'... on the beach at Great Yarmouth,' said the dull voice, unperturbed.

The Doctor jumped as a great, resounding crash came from the supplies cupboard in the corner of the room.

There was a click as the phone line went dead.

He threw the receiver down in disgust.

Then, steeling himself, he advanced on the cupboard door.

More noises. Clattering, whimpering, stumbling noises were coming from behind the door. There was something in there!

Cautiously he took the brass doorknob in his hand. He reminded himself of Iris's ordeal with flying utensils in the kitchen.

Bracing himself, the Doctor wrenched the cupboard door fully open.

And a rather battered, exhausted Jo Grant fell out, into his astonished arms.

'Jo!' he shouted, delighted.

She had sprung from the supplies cupboard exactly as a magician's assistant would.

She squeaked at the sight of him. 'Where am I?'

She seemed to be quite disturbed.

He did his best to put her at her ease.

'You're home now, Jo. You're safe. But how did you get here? Where did you come from?'

Jo looked at him and promptly burst into tears.

When the Doctor led the shaken-looking girl into the kitchen, Iris popped the rubber hands into her handbag for later inspection.

She watched as Tom gallantly gave up his chair for Jo and rushed to brew a fresh pot of tea.

Then, stumblingly, Jo launched into the story of her adventures the night before.

'Well,' said the Doctor, pulling on his bottom lip. 'There's something very odd indeed going on, and no mistake.'

Jo looked beseeching. 'But tell me it's not true, Doctor. Tell me that UNIT *is* real. And that you're not just pretending and it's not all a test…'

He put a consoling arm around her shoulders.

'Of course it's not, my dear,' he said. 'I am as real as you like. And everything that has happened to us – however improbable – is as real as Iris and Tom sitting here now.'

Iris rolled her eyes. 'Oh, don't count on us, dearie.'

Tom said, 'But why would anyone want to make you believe that UNIT was fake? '

'To undermine her confidence,' said the Doctor sharply. 'To stop her believing in what she's seen.'

He looked very solemn all of a sudden. 'To take away her faith in me.'

He stood up and paced up and down on the flagstones.

'But look at me, Jo! I'm real! Everything I've ever told you about the universe, about all the places I've been and what I've seen… it's all quite true! You trust me, don't you?'

She nodded dumbly. 'Of course…'

'Well, then go on trusting me. You've been on other planets, in other dimensions, even back into your own history with me. Why should a little man in a madhouse put you into any doubt?'

She was nodding still.

Iris spoiled it all then. 'Mind you,' she broke in. 'The Doctor doesn't do very much to prove himself, does he? It's all hot air, really. He's stuck here on Earth. Haven't you ever thought, all that marvellous intensity of his could really be in the service of some grand and extravagant confidence trick?'

'Iris!' he said, appalled.

'I'm just playing Devil's advocate.'

'You,' said the Doctor, 'are disturbing my assistant.'

Iris pulled a face. 'Oh, pay no heed to me, lovey. The Doctor's telling the truth. Whoever it was who had you prisoner last night was just having you on.'

'I know that,' said Jo unsteadily. 'But I don't know why they wanted to torture me like that.'

Tom was looking at the Doctor curiously.

He was remembering what Kevin had said about him. The Doctor was quite insane.

The Doctor's evident fury as his ontological status was put into doubt seemed proof enough of his madness to Tom.

'We can talk about all of this in the car,' the Doctor said.

'Where are we going?' asked Iris, reaching for her bag.

'Great Yarmouth,' he said, helping Jo up. 'Another railway carriage has appeared.'

As he followed the troop out of the kitchen and towards the garage, Tom was wondering when he might make his escape to London and report back to the others.

As they drove they were mostly silent and thoughtful.

At one point Jo cried out, 'Mike!' and had to explain how she had left Mike Yates folded up in her handbag at what had once been UNIT HQ.

'Flattened out?' cried the Doctor. 'Two-dimensional?'

She nodded firmly.

'Something very odd is certainly going on,' he said, and accelerated.

The day was a cooler one, with the sky a heavy, almost lilac, grey.

The rest of the drive passed in silence.

When they could see the sea beyond the dilapidated buildings of Great Yarmouth, it was a still and gun-metal grey.

The Doctor managed to park with ease, on the promenade by the pier.

'Why's it so quiet?' asked Iris suspiciously, bundling herself out on to the road.

'It isn't quite the season yet,' said the Doctor, glancing up and down the prom.

The only noise, beside the sea itself, came from the amusement arcades; the chuntering hurdy-gurdy of the Silver Slipper arcade.

'Even so,' he said. 'There should still be more people about.'

Jo was staring at the rather large gulls as they wheeled and dipped and settled on the roofs of the Britannia Pier.

The Doctor suggested that they climb down to the beach itself to look for the mysterious carriage.

Iris led the way down to the damp, greyish sand.

'I'm going up on the pier,' Tom told them, surprising himself with his sudden decision. 'I might get a better view from there.'

The Doctor nodded and watched him go.

'He'll be all right,' Iris told him.

You could steal the car, Tom told himself as he walked along the boards of the pier, glancing nervously down the wide gaps that showed the sea beneath him.

You could dash back to that ridiculous yellow car and be in London in a couple of hours.

You could nick it while the others' backs were turned.

They all seemed obsessed with checking out these railway carriages as they appeared.

Tom knew that these vehicles and their enigmatic freights of passengers weren't the real issue here.

Somehow he knew they were just a distraction.

He leaned on the railing and glared out at the beach, picking out the stumbling figures of his companions as they trudged on the sand.

Slowly he withdrew his hand from his pocket to inspect the bangle he had picked up yesterday.

The Doctor hadn't even missed it. Something had told Tom to pick one up and stow it away.

Something had suggested this to him; he assumed it was his belt buckle, buzzing away against his skin.

He blinked as the crimson jewels set in the gold shone in the mild sunlight.

As he looked, they seemed to pulse with an energy of their own. He jumped then, hearing voices behind him.

Someone was coming out of the amusement arcade at his back.

He was so used to the idea of this place being utterly deserted that simply the sounds of others could startle him.

He turned to see a middle-aged woman in a ratty anorak bustling out of the building, calling after two children.

She was getting them away from the slot machines, wanting them to have a go on the mechanical grabber outside the arcade. She was telling them to spend their money on something where they might actually win.

The breeze was whipping up her stringy dark hair and the two children – a girl and a boy – were pressing their noses to the glass, staring at the pincers of the grabber and the shabby-looking gonks and bears inside.

It put Tom in mind of being a kid. His mother used to take him to Blackpool, with all his aunties at the end of the season, to see the lights.

She would want to go on everything; try out every ride and chance her luck on every gambling machine. She was fearless. They always came home on the coach penniless and queasy.

For the first time Tom was wondering where in this time his mother would be. He tried to work it out, counting backwards.

As he counted back, totting up the years with the noise of the sea and the clanging music from the arcade in his ears, he saw that the two children's attention had drifted away from the grabber machine.

Their mother was slotting in money for another go and they had wandered to the railing and were pointing and shouting at figures they could see under the pier.

They were shouting at their mother to come and see. Tom's heart jumped. He realised that they were pointing at his friends.

'Mum!' the girl was shouting. 'Look at the funny people. They're getting on the train!'

Tom craned right over the railing and saw that, indeed, his companions had found the carriage they were looking for.

It rested, lopsided, in the sludgy sand.

Iris and the Doctor were working on the rusted door, far below, as Jo hung warily back, hugging herself in her fur coat.

Tom felt curiously distant from them all. It was just as if he was watching it on TV.

'Mum!' the boy called. 'Come and see!'

'Sssh!' their mother said, concentrating on the grabber controls. 'I've almost got it…'

Tom turned to watch her and found he was holding the alien bracelet even tighter in his pocket.

It was getting warmer, almost burning his skin.

He watched the woman clumsily manipulate the controls and he saw the pincers inch arthritically towards her prize.

It was a toy double-bus, waiting patiently on a heap of fluffy stuffed toys.

The pincers quivered on the air inside the glass case and the woman was biting her lip and holding her breath.

'Mum!' shouted the girl. 'They've got inside the train now! The funny people down there…! They're inside!'

Then the girl, who was standing on the second railing, seemed to crumple up and turn rigid.

She fell backwards, with terrible slowness, on to the bleached boards of the pier.

The boy whirled around, dropping off the rails, and followed her, landing heavily beside her.

Tom was frozen.

He watched the woman let go of the machine's controls.

He saw the pincers lose their slight grip on the toy bus and the bus drop it back where it had started from.

He saw the woman scream at the sight of her children sprawled out on the deck.

He saw as she started to run towards them, her limbs moving as if she had no control over them. They moved with the jerky imprecision of the grabbing machine's pincers.

Then he saw a ragged, tense-looking figure emerge from the corner of the amusement arcade and level his handgun at the shrieking woman.

The silencer wavered once in the air and there was a noise like a swiftly indrawn breath as the stranger's finger squeezed on the trigger and the woman dropped to the boards with her children.

Tom was still rooted to the spot.

He watched the man – shabby but still with a sort of military bearing – advance on the bodies.

The killer nudged each of them with the toe of his boot.

He was wearing, now that Tom looked, a military greatcoat that was stained and patched and caked in grimy sand.

He nodded in satisfaction to himself and stood back.

The three bodies drained of colour then and, before Tom's eyes, crumbled away into dust along with their clothes as if they'd never been there. All that remained was a trace of green powder, which trickled and slid through the boards of the pier.

The stranger looked at Tom and nodded once.

Tom started backing away.

'Not you,' the stranger called. 'You're necessary, Tom.'

With that he turned away and, with unhurried steps, went to find the way down to the beach.

He's after the others, Tom thought. He's going to kill them as well.

Without a second thought, he set off after the man in the greatcoat.

He followed him to the wooden steps that led down to the shingle.

From there, he could see the stranger's stealthy progress towards the railway carriage.

It was a carriage just like the first had been. Liver brown and cream paintwork, ruined by age. The same fly-blown and darkened windows.

There was Jo, peering cautiously inside, and presumably the Doctor and Iris were already aboard...

Tom thudded down the unsteady staircase and set off at a run across the sand.

He couldn't get there first.

He couldn't warn them.

The killer was taking off at a run now, his coat tails flying out behind him.

He made hardly a sound.

'Jo!' Tom screamed, making both figures turn.

Jo's head snapped round and for a second Tom thought she'd been shot. She seemed to reel in the air and he expected her to drop at any second.

But what she did do was the last thing he expected.

As the stranger advanced on her Jo broke out in a warm grin.

'Brigadier!'

Tom halted in his tracks. The killer was bounding up to Jo. He was taking her in his arms.

She embraced him and she hadn't even noticed the weapon in his hand.

They're in this together, Tom thought. They're all killers. All of them.

In that second he knew that he had to get away.

He backed up through the sand with his mind racing.

The car. He would take the Doctor's car.

He took one last look at the carriage and saw the Doctor and Iris join those outside.

The bracelet was still burning hot in his hand.

The belt buckle was tingling like crazy now; as if it was aware of the decision he had made, to flee to London immediately and desert these people, and it approved.

Chapter Seven
Spacejacked!

The Doctor slapped the Brigadier's back.

He was always slapping his back, Jo thought.

The two of them got along with a surprising degree of heartiness and old-school-chumminess, despite their many run-ins and the fact that their separate schooldays must have been lived in quite different times and places.

Jo understood that the two of them had known each other for a fair few years; long enough, now, to trust that when one of them was in danger, the other would soon turn up to help him, though both, separately, would claim to be the more resourceful and that the other was the one who routinely got into trouble.

A constant, though, was their robust and hearty pleasure when the other turned up.

Like now, standing by the railway carriage on the grey sands of Great Yarmouth.

This moment was especially potent, Jo thought, because of the Brigadier's recent, curious silence.

They were laughing and slapping each other's backs, as if nothing untoward had even happened; as if UNIT HQ hadn't been oddly remodelled and things were just the same as they had always been.

An incongruous pair, the Doctor and the Brigadier made. The former an iconoclast, a headstrong adventurer with a raffish line in flamboyant evening wear, and the latter a stoic and practical man of action, rarely, if ever, seen out of his trim-fitting olive-green combat outfits.

Yet there was a certain overlap in sensibilities that allowed the two of them to interact; the Doctor professed and displayed a streak of military nous the Brigadier often envied, and the Brigadier himself was known as something of an eccentric in military circles.

In the regular army, his absolute belief in extraterrestrial intelligence had marked him out as a loose cannon. They had been glad to let him head up his own, peculiar outfit. And head it he did, with brisk, unflinching common sense and never looking anything less than his very best.

But he looks dreadful today, Jo thought. That old coat. He hasn't shaved.

Why, the Brigadier looks as if he's been sleeping rough.

Behind Jo, Iris was thinking the same.

This wasn't the character she'd been expecting at all.

She nudged past the Doctor and looked the new arrival up and down, an incredulous expression on her face.

'What the bloody hell happened to you?' she burst out. Jo cringed at her lack of tact.

The Brigadier gaped at her. 'Who are you?' His eyes hardened.

'He looks like he's been dragged through a hedge backwards!' she laughed. 'This old tramp's your precious Brigadier?'

The Doctor struggled to maintain some dignity. 'Iris, would you please keep your tongue still for just a moment? I'm sure Lethbridge-Stewart will bring us up to date with what's going on...'

'Who is this woman?' the Brigadier barked, with a touch of his old authority.

'Calm yourself down, old man,' the Doctor said soothingly.

He patted the Brigadier's back again and Jo could tell how worried he really was. 'This is Iris. She's a... friend of mine.'

He completed his sentence with a slight grimace but, all the same, Iris looked smug at his words.

'I'm sorry, Doctor, Miss Grant,' smiled the military man grimly. 'I've been through rather a lot just lately...'

'You can tell us all about it later,' said the Doctor. 'Right now we're examining this curious railway carriage...'

'Don't go in there!'

'Why ever not, old chap?'

The Brigadier looked stricken. 'Something evil in there. There's...'

Iris rolled her eyes. 'Thanks for the advice, lovey, but we've already been inside and it isn't that scary.'

The Brigadier narrowed his eyes at her.

His voice came out very low and threatening. 'I know you,' he said.

Then he blinked and seemed to come out of a trance. 'I suggest we get back to Headquarters immediately and rally...'

'Brigadier, we can't...' said Jo. 'I was there last night. UNIT Headquarters isn't there any more.'

He bridled. 'Isn't there? But it's huge!'

'It's been gutted inside,' she said. 'And replaced with some kind of madhouse. Your office is full of tropical flowers...'

'Flowers? I didn't put them there.'

'Quite,' said the Doctor.

Iris put in, 'Jo reckons that the whole thing is a sham. Some little fella jumped out and told her that UNIT doesn't exist, that it never did.'

'Arrant nonsense,' clipped the Brigadier. 'What have we been doing all these years?'

'Hoodwinking people,' said Iris sadly.

'You sound as if you believe it!' Jo said hotly.

'My dear, I'm only going by what you said.'

The Doctor looked at her curiously. 'The fact is, we all know UNIT is genuine. Someone must have infiltrated it and put about these wild stories...'

'Exactly,' said the Brigadier. 'And the sooner we get back to investigate, the better...'

'Look!' Jo cried, and they all whirled around on the sand.

Emerging rather grandly from the dark doorway of the carriage was a hunched figure in white.

She was draped in yards of crumbling, yellowing lace and faded flowers hung from the crackling tresses of her frock.

She gripped the doorway with two clawlike hands and, even through her tattered veil, they could see her ancient eyes balk and twinge at the mild sunlight.

She had a haughty expression and a hooked nose and she didn't look in the least pleased to see them.

'Who might you be?' she asked, in a voice dry as the pages of an old Bible.

'Madam,' said the Doctor. 'You've come round.'

He went to take her brittle and spindly arm, but she threw him off with surprising strength.

'I was never unconscious,' she snapped. 'I was awake through the whole flight. Oh, all the others fell asleep, of course. They haven't my stamina. Estella, Pip. They were out like a light. They're still in there, snoring away. But when you have endured a life like mine, nothing is difficult to weather. Least of all planetfall.'

The old woman gave a bleak, rattling laugh. 'I've been let down too hard, too many times before.'

'Pip?' said Jo. 'Estella?'

'Ha!' Iris cawed and thrust her face into the old maid's. 'Am I right in assuming then, that you would like to be known as Miss Haversham?'

The crone was startled at Iris's booming voice.

She glared at the others. 'Who is this terrible woman? Take her away from me. She's much too loud and obnoxious.'

Miss Haversham seemed to reel on the rusted steps of the carriage.

Deftly the Doctor took her arm and helped her totter down on to the crumbling sand and this time she offered no resistance. 'Pay no heed to my companion, madam…'

'Companion!' cried Iris. 'Colleague, or nothing!'

'Pay her no heed,' the Doctor continued. 'She's rather common, of course, but her hearts are in the right place.'

'Common!'

The Doctor was coaxing the frail figure of the ancient bride across the sand, towards the prom.

'Let me help you to some shade…'

Iris muttered darkly, 'The old rake has gone and copped off!'

'Iris,' hissed Jo.

The Brigadier was fishing around in his greatcoat pockets and at last retrieved his walkie-talkie. 'I'm calling in the troops. Get this carriage sorted out.'

'Do you think it's full of people?' Jo said.

'Go and have a look,' Iris suggested. She looked up and down the beach, struck by a thought. 'Where's Tom gone?'

The Brigadier was cursing at the loud static from his walkie-talkie and shouting something about greyhounds.

Jo stood in the carriage doorway. 'It *is* full! All asleep. They're all in old-fashioned clothes again…'

Iris was behind her. 'Nineteenth-century this time. *Great Expectations*. Dickens was rather later than Austen. Look, there's nasty old Magwitch, the convict.'

'Magwitch was all right in the end,' Jo reminded her.

'Oh, I never get to the end of books,' said Iris. 'It's more fun making it up yourself.'

'What are we saying?' Jo said. 'We're talking about fictional people… characters… crashlanding on Earth.'

Iris nodded. 'And this time they seem more successful. They haven't broken up into green powder straight away. Maybe if the Brigadier can get them to Headquarters, we can…'

They were interrupted by a great shout from the Doctor, further down the beach.

It was just like the noise he made when he was doing his Venusian aikido.

They all whirled round to see him being flung through the air by the wizened crone.

Not so frail now, then! Iris thought.

The Doctor had landed heavily in the sand, with a grunt, and Miss Haversham was hobbling away of her own accord.

'She's going at a fair clip!' Iris remarked dryly.

'Doctor!' yelled Jo and ran to him.

The Doctor was rubbing his neck ruefully. 'She gave me quite a wallop!'

'What did you do?' Iris said. 'Try to kiss her?'

He stood and brushed himself off. 'She must have become tired of my company.'

They stared at the retreating back of the decrepit bride.

'No wonder no one would marry her,' said Iris admiringly. 'She's a harridan.'

She clapped the Doctor on the back. 'I'll run after the old thing with you. She's heading for the road. We don't want her getting run over. She's not used to cars and things.'

They set off at a gallop across the sands.

Jo made to follow but was grasped, suddenly, by the Brigadier.

'Miss Grant,' he said, with a pained look. 'I need you to stay here with me. You need to tell me more, about what you found at Headquarters last night…'

Jo looked longingly after the Doctor and Iris as they jogged up to the prom, but she recognised where her duty lay.

She nodded.

'Thank you,' said the Brigadier wearily.

'Have you contacted them?'

'Not a dicky bird,' he said. 'That's why I need to hear what you were told.'

'You don't think it could be true, do you?' Jo looked scared. 'That the government has suddenly decided to shut UNIT down? That's what I've been thinking. And they've constructed this whole elaborate thing, to make it seem as if it was a masquerade the whole time…'

'But in that case,' the Brigadier said, 'Geneva would be able to tell us the truth. We have to talk with them…'

Jo nodded.

'I can't bear not having back-up,' said Lethbridge-Stewart miserably. 'You don't know what it's like. I'm a man who is used to being able to just phone up, on this little walkie-talkie, and to demand back-up. I can have hundreds of men sent out immediately to be at my disposal. I can have helicopters and tanks and submarines dispatched within the hour to act on my command. I can have anything blown up on a whim.'

'I know,' said Jo gently. 'And you will again, I'm sure.'

'I need back up,' he said fiercely. 'I need my men!'

'She's heading for the amusement arcade!' panted Iris. 'The Silver Slipper, look, over the road! She must be a gambler!'

Miss Haversham had skipped easily across the main road, picking up the rotted silk of her skirts.

Now she was stepping in under the glittering, tawdry awning of the arcade.

'Whatever does she want in there?' said the Doctor.

'She's playing hard to get!'

Iris and the Doctor hurried after her, towards the sound of money crashing down and cheap music.

A taxi blared its horn at them. It was one of the few vehicles besides their own they had seen that day.

'Whoops,' said Iris. 'We've forgotten our Green Cross Code.'

'Our what?' asked the Doctor crossly as they dashed into the Silver Slipper.

Inside, it was a labyrinth of flashing and tinkling machines. Iris's eyes had lit up.

'Have you got any change, Doctor? I'm a dab hand on the bandits.'

'You would be. And no, I haven't.'

He paced around the corner, to find that the hall of machines was huge.

One or two teenagers were drifting about in a desultory fashion, and others were hunched over slot machines and games.

'We'll have to split up,' he said. 'And don't start gambling.'

'What do you think she meant, about planetfall?'

'I would have thought that was obvious,' he snapped.

'She's from Outer Space,' Iris concluded, with relish.

'Hm,' grunted the Doctor.

'But is there really a world where the nineteenth-century novel took over? Some distant, alien planet that was invaded by Victorian High Realism?'

'How should I know?' he said, exasperated. 'I don't get out much, these days.'

'There she is!' Iris yelled, almost deafening him. 'She's on that racing car, look!'

On a podium, Miss Haversham was crammed into a miniature Formula One racing car and her deep-set eyes were glinting with pleasure at the screen in front of her.

She was careering down a simulated Brands Hatch as if she thought she could escape that way.

'She's bonkers, poor thing,' Iris said, as they caught up with her and stepped on to the dais beside the car.

'Madam,' coughed the Doctor politely, over the noise of the fake engine. 'Madam!'

'You always call everyone Madam,' said Iris. 'You should stop. It makes you sound obsequious.'

'There's nothing wrong with manners.'

'You sound anachronistic,' Iris told him. 'You should say, "Hey, man," or call her baby or darling or something.'

The Doctor grimaced and tapped Miss Haversham on the shoulder.

She jolted with shock and her liver-spotted hands dropped off the steering wheel.

Immediately, the screen went dull grey and the furious engine noise ceased.

'How dare you!' she roared.

Iris was staring at her hands, which lay uselessly in her lap now that her game was done.

A flash of green had caught Iris's attention. She was staring now at the bracelet that the old woman was wearing on her right wrist.

Iris nudged the Doctor significantly as he addressed Miss Haversham.

'Where were you going?' he asked pleasantly. 'We told you we would look after you.'

'I don't need any help, young man.'

For an instant the Doctor looked rather pleased at this epithet. 'But you're confused,' he said. 'The effects of planetfall, the disorientation… You need our help, believe me.'

She laughed in a curious, gurgling falsetto. 'I have been disoriented for years. I don't need you to tell me that.'

'Where were you going?'

'My house,' she said and suddenly looked stricken. 'I was told it would be here. It has been prepared for me, and I should have arrived in its grounds. It is a neglected house, miles from anywhere, in a location hidden from the common rabble. I was promised a place where no one could disturb me. I only want to live here in peace.'

'I understand,' said the Doctor.

'They have deposited me in quite the wrong place,' said the crone sadly. 'If the ordinary people discover me I will be tortured. That is what I was told. I just want to blend in and go about my life quietly.'

'Then let us help,' the Doctor smiled, winningly.

'Can you help me?'

Iris's patience snapped suddenly. She made a grab with her chubby fingers for the green bracelet on the old woman's wrist.

'Look, Doctor! She's got one of these! These... wrist communicator things!' Iris pulled at the bracelet and felt the tiny jewels burn into her flesh.

As they tussled like this, Miss Haversham started to howl.

'Don't, Iris!' the Doctor shouted, and pulled at her shoulders. 'You'll...'

The noise of rushing wind filled the Silver Slipper Amusement Arcade.

There was more noise, to counterpoint the uncontrollable shrieking of the old bride, as every machine in the place went haywire - flashing all their gaudy lights at once and disgorging every coin in the place in one tremendous crash.

'Don't take me back! Please don't take me back!' screamed Miss Haversham.

Then the thrashing, spindly hag, the astonished Iris and the furious Doctor all vanished from the place in a shimmer of gold and green.

And silence fell quickly in the Silver Slipper.

The Brigadier was inside the carriage now, examining the face of Magwitch the convict which, even in repose, looked malevolent.

Jo hovered uncertainly in the doorway.

'I don't think we should disturb them,' she said, as the Brigadier tried to prise open the big man's eyelids. 'We should wait until the Doctor gets back.'

The Brigadier looked at her and said gruffly, 'You don't think I can do anything without the Doctor, do you?'

'I never said that! I just...'

'You're like the rest,' he spat, and started moving towards her. 'You think I'm a joke. You think I'm just some barking old fool, utterly dependent on that extraterrestrial fop. Let me tell you, Miss Grant, if it wasn't for me, the Doctor would have been dead a hundred times already. The planet would be overrun by now by nightmarish creatures you can't even conceive of!'

She looked shocked by his outburst. 'I...'

'Oh, don't give me that. I've heard you giggle behind my back. You and the others. You don't think I've got feelings. You think I'm an overbearing, pompous old fool who...'

'Brigadier!' she cried as he roughly seized her arm.

'You never see the real man,' he said, more gently, his grip hardening on her.

'I...'

'You never see under this brittle exterior...'

He moved towards her then and, for one awful instant, Jo thought he was about to kiss her.

She reached up swiftly with her free hand to push his face away.

His skin was soft and pliable.

It ripped easily under her nails.

He was laughing at her.

Jo screamed as the flesh of his face peeled neatly away and he shook his head to help the revelation along.

She gazed in horror at his true face, the scream dying in her throat.

His hair was slicked neatly back and his mouth sneered in contempt.

He jabbed his newly revealed pointed beard at her.

'The Master...' she gasped.

Then he did kiss her, stifling the sobs as she ceased struggling and a familiar wheezing-vworping-groaning noise began.

In the first mad instant Jo thought the noise came from within his body, but then she felt the interior of the carriage vibrate with alien energy.

Outside, Great Yarmouth was dematerialising.

The Master threw her roughly away, against the wall and spat, rather succinctly, on the shabby carpet.

'My apologies for kissing you, Miss Grant. It seemed the right thing to do. It had the appropriate chilling effect, I suppose. But I didn't enjoy doing it much, did you?'

Jo watched the vortex heaving and swirling outside the carriage. She held on to the wall.

'Where are you taking me?'

'Oh, hush now. While I concentrate.'

Miss Haversham woke first. She sat up on cold concrete and, with as much dignity as she could muster, hauled herself to her feet on the station platform, cursing her brittle old bones.

All around her trains were boarding and preparing to leave the station.

Optimistic groups of travellers were rushing aboard and finding their places.

Hasty goodbyes were being said and tears were being shed.

She glared around imperiously, yet no one had seemed to notice her sudden arrival in all their excitable hurly-burly.

No one had even noticed the Doctor and Iris, lying bundled on the ground.

A muffled tannoy voice was announcing the late departure of the next carriage.

On a nearby platform there were shrieks and guffaws.

Miss Haversham looked sadly at the terminus and the vast aperture through which the carriage would depart. She blinked at the shining blue arc of the Earth.

'I've missed my chance again,' she said, turning, and then she tottered off down the platform, clutching her skirts about her.

The tannoy announcements continued, alerting more and more passengers to their imminent departure.

There were scuffles breaking out as queues broke up.

People were stepping over the prostrate newcomers, and it was as one particularly bulky traveller trod on Iris's hand that she flew awake and turned to shove the Doctor.

'It looks like Paddington!' she gasped, as he helped her up.

'Actually,' he said, with exactly the sort of pedantry that exasperated her, 'it looks rather more like St Pancras.'

'You're so parochial,' she said, with a toss of her head. Then she started to look, with a practised eye, at the mish-mash of anachronistic travelling outfits. 'Some of these people seem familiar,' she said.

'Where's Miss Haversham?' the Doctor asked.

'Gone,' said Iris sadly.

Then the Doctor was haring off to a booth, across the marble floor of the station. He pushed past the milling crowd and Iris had to struggle to keep up.

'We're going to ask at Information,' he said.

There was no queue here.

Behind the smutty glass partition there sat a suspicious-looking rabbit with gleaming white fur and pink, narrowed eyes.

'Which carriage are you on?' he asked, in a high-pitched and condescending voice.

He took out a pocket watch, flipped it open and tutted. 'Whichever it is, you're bound to be late. Well? Have you forgotten?'

'Yes,' said Iris, shouting as the tannoy cut in again indistinctly. 'Could you tell us where to go?'

'Judging by your outfits,' the white rabbit said, in a bored voice, 'I'd say Thackeray, though I'm no expert. I'm only here to tell people when they should go, not how. And you're late, at any rate. Try *Vanity Fair*. You look as if you'd fit in there.'

'Look here,' snapped the Doctor. 'I don't know what you're talking about. My friend and I have just arrived against our wills and we don't...'

'Doctor!' said Iris shrilly.

She had just noticed the gleaming curve of the Earth's atmosphere beyond the mouth of the station.

'We're in outer bloody space!'

'I know,' he said tersely. 'Can't you tell by how thin the atmosphere is?'

Iris nodded, reached into her golden bag for her inhaler, gave herself a blast, took out her cigarettes and promptly lit one up. She sighed deeply.

The white rabbit was preening himself with his dapper little paws. 'Are you saying,' he snarled, 'that you oughtn't to be here?'

The Doctor nodded. 'That's exactly what we're saying.'

Iris shook her head, laughing. 'I can't believe you're talking to a great big bloody bunny.'

The white rabbit showed his nasty incisors and leant closer to the startled Time Lords.

'Are you saying, the two of you, that you're both... unauthorised?'

He said it like it was the worst word he knew.

'Quite!' said the Doctor.

'I see,' said the rabbit, and discreetly pushed the emergency button underneath his disarrayed desk.

Immediately there was a terrible noise of klaxons, blaring right across the dome of the station. Every passenger in the place looked up and whirled around.

An electronic voice boomed out the word, 'Unauthorised!' repeatedly, as if it were the worst word it knew.

The Doctor grabbed Iris's hand and tore off across the marble floor.

Shouts of 'There they are!' and 'Get them!' burst out, predictably, in their wake.

They scattered terrified people on their way as they hared towards the exit. Ladies with parasols screamed and flapped; moustachioed soldiers in red barked out their complaints; some rather intellectual-looking horses whinnied in horror as the Doctor and Iris fled a blue streak through the station.

At the information booth the white rabbit had become apoplectic: 'I found them! Me! Don't let those evil unauthorised freaks get away! The reward is mine! Fetch them back! Don't be late!'

Hundreds of yards away, at the exit, where a new crowd of astonished, distinct and eccentric-looking travellers were massing, the Doctor and Iris were finding that they had reached the end of the line.

They couldn't escape. A gap had opened up in the crowd and three massive, quite alien figures stood before them.

The crowd shrank back in terror at this apparition.

Even the Doctor and Iris had lost the will to run at the sight of these three, sent to retrieve the errant passengers. They stood at least twenty-foot tall. From this vantage, their faces could barely be discerned.

Each of them sat in what appeared to be shining metallic eggcups and they were raised into the disturbed air of the station by three telescopic stilts, all of burnished gold and each terminating in a hooked and vicious looking claw, which screeched nastily, with every step, against the marble.

The Doctor and Iris looked up to catch a glimpse of livid purple gazing down at them.

There was an impression of tentacles and a whiff of sulphur.

'I knew it,' Iris said. 'I knew we'd end up running into Wells's Martians. Typical us.'

'Silence!'

The triad of creatures spoke as one.

The Doctor tugged his velvet jacket and cape straight.

He smiled wryly and tapped his nose speculatively. 'I do hope you're going to say how useless our resistance would be. Because, personally, I'm rather tired and couldn't budge an inch anyway. How about you, Iris, dear?'

'Completely fagged!' she grinned. 'So just take us away, boys!'

Chapter Eight
You Live in a Perverted Future

The thing about being back in the seventies is this: I can't quite believe that many of the people I'm seeing are real.

As I drive into London, through traffic so amazingly slack you'd think a national crisis was on (a fuel shortage! An invasion by dinosaurs! Ha!) and the pedestrians I see seem like inventions.

They're wearing flares and floppy collars and fitted jackets and stack-heeled boots for the first time around. Quite naively, without a touch of retro chic or irony, they are sporting polyester and other, even more noxious, man-made fibres.

To me they look like extras out of road safety adverts or public safety broadcasts warning you of the dangers of playing too near pylons or messing about with fireworks.

Everyone looks as if they're in *Get Carter* or *Are You Being Served?*

And what this does is make me feel smug and complex.

Like I've got some special kind of interiority denied to the seventies people.

I'm more evolved. I've got the foresight; knowing, of course, all about the nasties on the way, just around the corner: Thatcher, AIDS, Global Warming, trouble in the Gulf, in the former Yugoslavia, and how the Revolution never actually came.

Twenty-seven years from now, all these trendies in day-glo hipsters will be watching *Changing Rooms* in their suburban homes and wondering how to do up their back bedrooms.

I feel like I've got the edge on these people as I muddle my way through South London (which still has a touch of the good old days about it: teeming, filthy and smelling of fish and chips.

And where's Canary Wharf? Where's the Millennium Dome? And what about that bloody great Ferris Wheel rotating absurdly on the skyline above the Thames? And then it hits me. I'm in London before it went oh-so-self-consciously Sci- Fi).

Of course, I can't help feeling it means I'm a more fully rounded person; a character with more depth and understanding, perhaps.

In this time, I could trot around like Cassandra, letting them all know what's on the way.

This is an era that hasn't even heard of Princess Diana yet. How fickle we are about choosing our icons, our symbols.

It's a wonder Iris hasn't warned me not to go around, spreading tittle-tattle about the next couple of harrowing decades. She must trust me not to.

Gary Glitter and Suzi Quatro are still big stars in this time. Punk has a couple of years before it comes slouching in.

Ziggy Stardust is still around: it's this very summer that David Bowie will kill him on stage at the Hammersmith Odeon.

I must remember that the funny looks I get as I drive into New Cross are not because people instinctively know I am strange and hail from the century's end.

I'm getting those looks because I'm sitting up and driving a vintage car, the colour of English mustard.

They actually think I'm looking curiously old-fashioned.

Best not to think about it now (though I'm dying to go to the shops and enquire after the price of things: a bottle of milk, a bottle of gin, a packet of fags. The exchange rate between my time and this will undoubtedly be fantastic), and I should try to remember that I left that dishevelled killer at large on the beach.

Iris could be dead because you turned and ran.

But Iris can look after herself.

You thought it best to escape; to find the Children of Destiny and to let them help you out.

There was nothing else you could do in Great Yarmouth.
You had to come away to London to find out the truth.
Pull in here.
Check the address on the card you were given.
The snooker hall, its name printed in tiny letters below the buzzer.
Its windows dark, protected by rusting wire. Charming.
Time to integrate myself fully into the early seventies, and what better way than to get myself in with a gang of super-powered space-hopping teenagers?
I've come to join the gang.
Buzz the buzzer.
Let them let me in.
It's just hit me: in 1973, no one has even heard of Abba.
What kind of time is that?

Inside the gloom of the snooker hall the single table's baize was ripped and faded.
Tom ran his finger along the edge as he went by and tutted at the dust.
'So you came.'
The voice made him jump.
He was lighting a cigarette and singed his finger as he heard the voice and felt it bristling at the nape of his neck.
He whirled round to see, in the dingiest corner of the room, a small window with a grille.
It was like a cloakroom and Kevin's face was pressed up to it, like an attendant's, or a bouncer's, watching him, smiling slightly. Again Tom found himself drawn to those eyes.
As he moved towards the window his feet seemed too loud on the bare boards, his heart was banging in his chest and his belt buckle was tingling like crazy.
'You've come to join us.'
Tom nodded. His mouth was dry. 'I stole the Doctor's car.'

Kevin laughed. 'You'll need to hand over your belt before I let you in. Just a precaution. Just in case you're not entirely friendly.'

Tom blushed. 'But my mother gave me that!'

'You'll get it back.' The metal grille slid aside and Kevin's hand shot out. 'Hurry up.' Tom undid the buckle and unthreaded the belt and, with a jangle, handed it over, wordlessly.

'Good.' He heard Kevin stowing it away in a drawer. 'Golly, it's burning hot! You really are one of us, aren't you?'

Tom licked his lips. 'I don't know yet. I can't be sure.'

Kevin's eyebrows twitched into a frown. 'You've had no previous telepathic episodes?'

'Never.'

'You've never popped up somewhere spontaneously, somewhere you didn't expect to be?'

'No... Yes! I mean, I don't know...'

Kevin smiled slowly. 'Well, never mind. We'll have Simon check you out.'

'Simon?'

'Our electronic mentor.'

Then the wooden wall with the grille and the smutty window pane was shunting to one side, to reveal a dark corridor lined with transparent tubes, pulsing with green light. And, standing in his trim-fitting one-piece suit, Kevin urged his new friend on.

'Time to go down to Headquarters. This is all extremely secret, mind you. The others are keen to meet you.'

Tom followed warily, thinking that Kevin sounded almost nervous of him. He was over-eager to impress Tom with this underground hideout.

Glowing tunnels, a clanking escalator and finally a cramped lift in which Kevin brushed against Tom and said a hurried 'Excuse me'.

And then the door swished open and they were standing in a room that seemed to be the size of Liverpool Street Station, only darker and marginally more cheesily futuristic.

Quickly Tom took in the staggering sight of teleportation tubes, dinky little space-walking outfits, a vast viewing screen and one or two high-topped tables, of the kind he hadn't seen outside of the swankiest cappuccino bars.

At one of these sat Marsha, the girl he had already met, in a lilac outfit with a short cape. She was sucking at a milkshake and waving happily at them as they stepped into the echoing chamber.

Above her, Tom suddenly saw, the ceiling was a mass of pulsating cables and, taking up much of the space, was a glowing electronic brain-like device: all coruscating colour and bright sparks.

That had to be Simon.

'You came!' cried Marsha as they joined her. 'Simon, another milkshake for our new friend, Tom.'

'Actually, would he run to a gin and tonic?' said Tom. He was used to gadding about with Iris.

He hoped these new companions weren't too squeaky clean.

A high-pitched voice jabbed from the ceiling.

'The Children of Destiny do not partake of alcohol.'

A glass of lemonade shimmered into existence on the table before Tom.

'They believe it impairs their multiple psychic powers. Nor do they smoke.'

Tom, who was looking for an ashtray to put out his fag, blinked, drank down his lemonade in one gulp, and put the cigarette out in the glass.

He could feel an air of haughty disapproval bearing down on him.

'We need to know what the Doctor is up to right now,' said Kevin briskly.

'Oh Kevin,' said Marsha, giving Tom's hand a protective squeeze. 'Give the boy time to settle in. He has to meet the others and get himself kitted out with a proper Destiny's Children outfit first…'

'Hm,' said Kevin. 'All right. But we are in the middle of an emergency, Marsha. This isn't just a game.'

Marsha flicked her hair out of her face and rolled her eyes.

'Simon,' said Kevin, 'where are the others?'

'Mary and Peter,' warbled the disembodied voice, as the colourful brain pulsed in time, 'are paying a call on the Galactic Federation at Galactic Federation Headquarters in Deep Space, to appraise our delegate of the situation here. The Federation is taking this whole thing extremely seriously. They had thought that the Earth was a dingy backwater, interesting only because of the advent of you special people.'

Kevin looked rather pleased at this.

Simon went on, 'But now they realise that there are other alien intelligences at work here and this increases the stakes many times over. If we do not deal with the Doctor issue, Earth's entrance into the glorious union of the Galactic Federation could be badly retarded.'

'What is that?' Tom piped up. 'Some kind of EU thing with single currency and no duty-free?'

'The Galactic Federation,' said Simon wearily, giving the distinct impression that he wasn't at all impressed by their visitor from the future, 'is an almost mystic union, an harmonious telepathic gestalt comprised of the most evolved and advanced members of races from across the galaxy. The Children of Destiny, as Earth's superior beings, are pushing for Earth's inclusion. But if what we suspect of the Doctor turns out to be true, our chances are ruined.'

Tom frowned. 'Superior beings? Isn't that a bit fascistic?'

Kevin looked blank. 'Every race evolves in this way. We are simply the first children to be born with the faculties that will lead the human species into a golden age. If they listen to us.'

'I don't know,' said Tom. 'It sounds a bit dodgy to me. What exactly marks you lot out as special?'

'Lots of things!' said Marsha brightly.

'Such as?'

'Telepathy,' she said. Then she thought for a bit and said, 'And we can pop up anywhere in a flash. Just by using the powers of our minds.'

'Well, that's all very nice,' said Tom. 'But how does that make you the future of the human race?'

There was an awkward silence. Kevin was blushing.

'He'll learn,' Marsha put in hastily. 'He'll see what we mean. Tom's just tired. He's driven all the way down from Great Yarmouth.'

Kevin was looking at him strangely. 'I hope Tom will come to understand what it means when we say our duty is to civilise the Earth.'

'I'm sure it's all very well-intentioned,' Tom said. 'But I'm not sure that's how things happen. Remember, I come from the future and...'

'Enough!' cried Simon from above, quite shrilly. 'We will not have a debate on Federation politics today, thank you. There are more important things to attend to.'

Tom agreed. 'I left my friend, Iris, in what I think might be terrible danger. I need you to tell me exactly what the score is, with the Doctor and UNIT and everything. You've been oblique up till now. As far as Iris is concerned, they're as well-meaning as you claim to be. They're simply protecting the world from the invading alien horde and doing a splendid, if occasionally cack-handed, job. You've all made out it's more sinister.'

'And it is!' boomed Simon sagely.

'How?'

'Behold!'

The huge screen before them lit up and started whizzing through a selection of faded press clippings.

Simon's voice gave its patient commentary:

'Although the activities of the organisation known as UNIT are supposedly top secret, in the past five years of its existence a number of stories have appeared in the national press.'

Tom took in a bewildering blur of headlines and muzzy photos.

The *Guardian*: Home Secretary Says: 'What Robot Army in Sewers? We Didn't Put it There.'

The *Financial Times*: Southern England Meteorite Shower: Stock Market Responds with Alarm.'

The *Daily Mail*: These Daffodils Can Kill!

The *Sun*: My Yeti Hell!

'So?' said Tom. 'Doesn't that back up what UNIT claims?'

'Fakes,' said Kevin simply.

Beside the screen (which still showed the front page of the *Sun*: a model in a bikini hugging a vast, featureless creature covered in fur) a wall panel slid open and Kevin and Marsha went over to pull out a host of improbable objects.

Tom gasped.

'That's a Dalek!'

Iris had been showing him her scrapbooks and the very sight of the thing in the titanium flesh made him jump, though it was rather smaller than he had expected.

Kevin and Marsha wheeled the object out for his inspection. It was a cone-shaped thing, studded with what looked like tennis balls, painted gunmetal grey and black.

Its protuberances hung down, disconsolately.

'Is it dead?' Tom asked.

'It was never alive,' Marsha said, almost sadly and, grasping the top half of the odd but malevolent-looking thing, wrenched it open like a salt cellar.

The top flipped back and Tom found himself staring into a dark, empty interior.

'If you look right down,' said Kevin helpfully, 'you'll see there are little pedals at the bottom, and a seat, for the actor inside.'

'The actor?'

'As I said, fakes. The UNIT files put about this story that these creatures are actually a deadly invasion force from the future, come to colonise Earth.'

Simon added, 'As if.'

'Where did you get these things?' asked Tom, turning to look at an admittedly not-very-realistic-looking vegetable creature, covered in roots and tubers and bright orange in complexion.

He touched it and found it was made of rubber.

'In a warehouse,' said Kevin. 'In Clapham.'

Tom shook his head. 'But who would go to all this trouble? Why would they want to make it seem that Earth was under such a dubious threat from outer space?'

Marsha took up the tale. 'That's what we need to find out. Imagine our delight when we discovered that you, our anticipated fifth member, was coming to us via a curious connection with the UNIT organisation. When we found that you were linked to Iris and Iris was linked to the Doctor, we became very excited.'

'What's Iris's connection to this?'

'We can't be sure if she's a party to the fake or not,' said Kevin. 'According to our sources, it's absolutely impossible to tell how much of a liar and vagabond the woman actually is.'

'Quite,' agreed Tom.

But all the while he was thinking: I've been in space with Iris. I've seen the monsters and aliens she comes up against.

He decided to keep mum about those.

Then another thought struck him.

'I found a pair of fake monster hands in the Doctor's house. Part of a lizard person. Iris was as shocked to see them as I was.'

'Oh yes,' burst Simon excitedly. 'They would have been from when the Doctor and UNIT were trying to convince Whitehall that a race of prehistoric reptile men were living underneath Derbyshire and wanted to reclaim the world. Well, I saw the reports. They looked rubbish. And as for those so-called Sea Devils...' Simon gave a brisk tsk-ing noise. 'I've seen more frightening kippers.'

'Quite,' said Kevin. He looked imploringly at Tom.

Tom looked back, and tried not to glance down at Kevin's belt buckle, which was pulsing with energy in a quite familiar manner.

'Do you see, Tom? Do you see why we need your help?'

'Not entirely,' Tom said. 'Even if you're right and UNIT is a fake and the Doctor is a terrible fraud, what difference does it make to you?'

'We are forging real alliances with the genuine inhabitants of the outer worlds,' Marsha said, her voice full of pride. 'We can't have others putting about ghastly stories about who's up there. It's terribly embarrassing for us when we make first contacts. No one wants to invade the Earth, really. Why bother? We've not got much they'd want. They look at our media and all they see is rampant paranoia and nasty, unconvincing alien fakes.'

'More importantly,' said Simon, 'the genuine alien powers are perturbed by the source of these frauds. And this we have found to be the machinations of this self-aggrandising madman known as the Doctor. His hoaxes are losing us vital credibility with the Galactic Federation. We can only assume that he knows this and seeks to prevent our union with the galactic powers-that-be. He is, single-handedly, preventing the next stage in the glorious evolution of mankind!'

Tom was incredulous. 'Just through a few practical jokes?'

'These are very sensitive times,' Kevin said. 'We can't afford to have practical jokers around. And there is more to the Doctor than just a bit of fun. He's deliberately hampering the progress of Destiny's Children.'

Tom seriously doubted the Doctor would even know who they were, but he didn't say anything.

Marsha said sadly, 'He's trying to make us look like frauds, too.'

Tom's heart went out to her. 'Well, I'm sure you're not. I'm very glad to have met you.'

'And to join us!' cried Kevin. 'It's time we found you a jumpsuit all of your own and then you can properly be one of the Children of Destiny! We have to see what we can do about stretching your latent faculties!'

Tom wasn't quite sure if he liked the sound of that.

Kevin's face had taken on a messianic gleam and he appeared to have gained a suspicious bulge in the lower half of his own jumpsuit.

On balance, Tom was glad to play along for a while.

Another thought struck him, 'If you're worried about the Doctor preventing Earth's entry into the Galactic Federation...'

'Yes?' snapped Kevin, jolting out of his moment of rapture.

'I'm already from the future,' said Tom. 'I already know. I know for a fact that, in the year 2000, Earth isn't in any kind of galactic union. No one's ever heard of such a thing in my time.'

He expected their faces to drop in abject disappointment.

He was telling them that the things they fervently hoped for were doomed to failure.

But: 'See?' Kevin said, his face shining again. 'That's precisely because the Doctor has been allowed to intervene in your history. You live in a perverted future, Tom.'

'Oh, cheers,' he said.

'And your coming back into the past allows us to restore destiny to its proper track. The Children of Destiny could provide ourselves, and everyone else on Earth, with a rightful and fitting end to this century, if only it wasn't for that meddling Doctor!'

There was a split second before a very familiar noise crashed in waves upon the gloomy, echoing chamber.

It was the rasping hurdy-gurdy of a TARDIS materialising.

Tom was shocked, but the others looked complacent as they turned to see, in an uncluttered corner of the room, a rusting railway carriage shade into being.

Tom recognised it instantly as the one from the beach at Great Yarmouth.

'He's back,' Marsha smiled.

As the door opened and two figures struggled out – one svelte in black, keeping tight hold of one dishevelled in miniskirt and furry coat – Tom burst out with: 'Jo!'

The man in black glared at him. 'She can't hear you.'

'Who are you?' Tom demanded. 'What are you doing with Jo?'

Kevin interposed himself to explain. 'He is our Master. He's brought this girl here to help us build a trap for the Doctor. The Master is just as concerned as we are to take the Doctor to the Galactic Federation and to make him explain himself.'

Tom gazed at the wildly staring but somehow powerless Jo Grant. 'Have you hurt her?'

The Master stroked her golden hair and chuckled. 'Oh, my dear. I think you've got a young admirer here, in young Tom.'

Tom flushed. 'I care about what happens to her.'

Kevin looked piqued. 'You care for this young woman?'

'Not in that way!' said Tom hotly.

'Enough of this!' roared the Master and started to drag Jo

towards an alcove. She flapped feebly in protest.

Simon's tinny voice blared out, over them all. 'I have had a communication from the Galactic Federation.'

'Put it on screen,' the Master snarled.

Tom frowned as the screen shimmered and refocused itself to show a creature formed of some fleshy, toffee-coloured substance. Its body was thick and rotund and its eyes were out on hair-like stalks that flapped and whipped about in agitation as it addressed them from across the universe.

'It's High Councillor Borges!' gasped Marsha.

The High Councillor's shaggy eyebrows bristled and met in barely repressed fury.

It was the most unlifelike creature that Tom had ever seen.

'Children of Destiny!' squawked the creature on the screen. 'I am commanding you to proceed in your investigations with the utmost care. You must approach the Doctor and Iris Wildthyme with extreme caution. Our spies have learned that they are aboard the spacecraft of an alien race they are currently exhorting to invade the planet Earth!'

'What?' cried Tom.

The Master rolled his eyes.

High Councillor Borges thrashed his eyestalks into a terrible frenzy.

That must really hurt, Tom found himself thinking.

The creature raged: 'Also, something dreadful has happened. We have learned that the woman, Iris Wildthyme, has kidnapped one of the members of the High Council of the Galactic Federation! She has him hostage, about her person, and will kill him if we interfere with her terrible plans!'

'But that's impossible,' said Kevin.

'No, indeed, young man. It is both possible and true. The Doctor and Iris are far more of a threat to us than we ever believed! They not only know about us and all our projects... they are taking deliberate steps to destroy us all!'

Chapter Nine
The House of Fiction

From the journals of Ms Iris Wildthyme, Lady Adventurer and All Round Good Egg.

I am sure you will all be frightfully pleased to hear that the Doctor and I are in the most awful danger.

And, not to put too fine a point on it, I am frantic with pleasure at our predicament.

Oh, you'll think, what a perverse woman she is, to relish scrapes like this and to extol the bliss to be squeezed from romps in the sublimely hazardous.

But I do!

I adore being thrust on to a sea of mischance and uncertainty; especially with the Doctor by my side, and especially in this incarnation of his; booted and velvet-suited, his white hair bright as an everlasting lightbulb and his face all creased up in wonderful concentration.

Here we are again, in space, aboard an enemy craft, surrounded by ghastly beings intent on perfidy and trauma.

We're actually on a ship that has portals set into its walls, so you can look out at the gleaming shell of the Earth and count down those precious moments till the apotheosis of its horrible imperilment.

What marks this ship out as unique is its lack of gleaming metal corridors.

Oh, there are miles of corridors, sure enough, and we've been led through them all, to our inevitable place of incarceration, but the interesting thing about these infinite passageways is that they have all been fitted with shelves.

Unique the alien invaders who take the trouble to make their gangways and thoroughfares easy on the eye!

The Doctor has been plainly fascinated by the shelves and their colossal freight of ancient books.

Jam-packed and squashed haphazardly into place, with hardly a gap left for a single pamphlet or chapbook more.

And all in no discernible order: a nightmare of a library, floating inexorably through space, in which every book has no natural link, neither alphabetical nor thematic, to its neighbour, so that Thomas Hardy rubs himself suggestively against Jilly Cooper and Geoffrey Chaucer seems wary, slid in alongside Christine Brooke-Rose.

'All of them come from Earth,' said the Doctor. 'With a bias towards English and... have you noticed, Iris? They are all fictional texts.'

To be honest, I hadn't noticed anything much besides my own transport of joy at finding myself up in space again, even chivvied along, as we were, by those hideous beings on metal, clawed stilts.

'I wonder where they got them all from,' said the Doctor, doing that lovely, thoughtful thing where he rubs his chin.

'You can get anything from the Internet,' I suggested.

'Too early for that,' he said. 'Not in 1973. Well, only a little bit,' he added darkly.

'I adore the Net,' I said. 'I think it's very sweet of them. Have you tried putting in your name?'

'Certainly not!'

'I did. And the things they say about me!'

He frowned then, and seemed about to launch into another telling off.

He thinks I impose myself too much on cultures, wherever I go. If he only knew the half of it!

But we were interrupted by those foul-looking beings on the stilts and shoved into a somewhat poky cell.

'A darling little prison!' I said. 'Now we feel completely at home, don't we, Doctor?'

He thought I was being sarcastic.

He went in first, with a groan at the sight of the single straw pallet and the graffitied walls.

'We will need to talk to you quite soon,' said the first of the alien beings, rather politely.

I nodded. We had already ascertained that this hideous aspect was the aliens' true one.

It wasn't just one more disguise, like Miss Haversham or Mrs Bennett.

At first, I thought this tripod business was their aping H. G. Wells, as one naturally would, but it turns out that they really are like this and Wells was cleverer than he thought.

There's no accounting for evolution.

'Right!' I beamed. 'Well, there's no need to hurry, dears. The Doctor and I don't mind waiting alone in close, confined quarters. We are extremely old friends.'

With that I popped into the cell and the small door clanged shut behind me.

Outside, we heard the creatures perambulate heavily away again.

Odd thing is, the only thing to read in the cell was the graffiti which, to be frank, was all Greek to me.

So here we are. Together at last.

Awaiting our interrogation and the invasion of the world.

Fabulous.

The Doctor is hunkered down on the little futon affair, with his head in his hands.

He thinks he's got first dibs on the comfy bed, evidently, but, come sundown, there'll be no holding Iris back.

These old bones need a proper lie down and he's welcome to share if he so desires, but he'll have to bunk up, the old rake.

I squash myself down beside him – and look!

Look at him flare his elegant nostrils at my proximity! Oh, he loves me really.

'Don't look so upset, ducky.'

I'm hunting through my clutch bag for ciggies. 'We can be out in a jiffy. You've got your sonic whatsit, haven't you?'

'No.'

'Well... we can simply pretend I'm having a hearts attack or an attack of the vapours, we can yell a lot and get the guard to come... and then we can overpower him and...'

'They haven't left a guard outside,' he said. 'All three of them went off. Didn't you hear?'

Curse his hypersensitivity!

'Then there must be a ventilation shaft we can shimmy up... or we could fan noxious fumes up it and put them all to sleep...'

'There's not,' he said, 'a ventilation shaft to be had for love nor money.'

'You're not giving up!' I burst.

'Certainly not. But before we break out of here I think we should think over what we are going to do, once we do free ourselves.'

'That's obvious,' I smiled.

'Would you mind not smoking in here, Iris? I'm getting something of a headache.'

'That's stress,' I said. 'I'll give you a massage.'

He glared at me. 'You will most certainly not.'

'Anyway,' I went on, 'it's quite obvious, what we have to do. Find out what they're up to, disguising themselves as characters from novels, and put a stop to it. We can't have fictional characters wandering about all over the place, it's ever so confusing. There would be chaos!'

'An ontological nightmare,' the Doctor agreed. 'It's bad enough, in the last quarter of the twentieth century, as it is.'

'You would know,' I couldn't help saying. 'What's it really

like, Doctor? Being stuck in one time? Being unable to shoot forward or back and to have to live every moment as it comes, one after the next, in the correct, chronological order?'

He looked at me dolefully. 'It's ghastly.'

'I thought it might be.'

'Imagine if someone took all of those books out there,' he gestured grandly with one arm, 'and put them in strict order of publication. And then they made you sit down, for the rest of your life, and forced you to read them all in that order. You couldn't skip ahead, you couldn't radically juxtapose. Just imagine if you weren't free to pick up what you wanted, having to adhere, instead, to the humdrum, plodding, prosaic march of accurate chronology. It's like being a hamster on a wheel.'

'Bless your hearts,' I said, as sympathetically as I could. He never believes me when I'm being sincere. 'I could take you away from it all, you know.'

Suddenly his eyes had a little gleam in them. 'You would?'

'I told you years ago, dearie. You're welcome any time to join me on the bus.'

His face darkened. 'At what cost? Abandoning my own poor ship?'

And the unspoken subtext there, too, I thought: having to sleep with me! The old rake!

'I could take you to Gallifrey,' I said. 'I could plead your case. We could both talk to Them, tell them how the universe is better off with you gadding about... just like it is with me gadding about!'

He shook his head woefully.

'I've tried to speak with Them. They won't listen to a word I say. Why would They ever listen to you?'

Now, this stung my feelings a little.

'If you're going to be rude about it...'

'Face it, Iris,' he said, not unkindly. 'You aren't even a proper Time Lady. They don't even know who you are. Where did you come from? The New Towns under the Capitol. The slums, as far as the High Council is concerned. If they found out about you, they'd do the same to you as they did to me. Worse, perhaps. You should never have been allowed to even get a whiff of a TARDIS, let alone borrow one. They'd wipe you out of history. You'd be an abomination to them.'

My throat had gone dry.

'I never borrowed my bus. I found it, when They had left it to die in the mountains. They had abandoned it; a wasted experiment I coaxed it back to life, I taught it the things it needed to know, and fed it and helped it evolve. I disguised it and it was the bus, the bus itself, that in turn, told me what I should do with my life.'

'I know,' he said softly.

'You don't know half of it, Doctor,' I said. 'You rant and rail about what a rotten deal you got from the Time Lords, but at least you're posh! At least They think it worthwhile to exile you and impound your ship! They wouldn't dare atomise you or pretend you didn't exist. Not like me. I'm a freak. I'm... what did you call me? I'm common. Common as muck.'

'I'm sure I'm not as important to Them as all that,' he said.

I tossed my head. 'You underestimate how much They know about you. They know you're not just some simple renegade. They know more about your past lives than you even think.'

'More about my past lives...?' He looked completely baffled.

'Oh, you know. All that... You know... The stuff that's meant to be secret. Your past. That's why They've just bunged you away on some backwater. They know you've got a history and a destiny to fulfil.'

'My dear,' he said, licking his lips. 'I'm sure I don't know what you're talking about.'

'Oh,' I said. 'Bugger.' I think I'd spoken out of turn. I'm always doing that. Swiftly, I tried to change the subject. 'Whatever happened to that snooty-looking bird you used to knock about with? She had her claws right in you, she did. Now, she was a proper Time Lady, she was. Of the first rank. Did you give her the push?'

He looked blank. 'Who on Earth are you talking about?'

'You know. She had a silly bloody long name. She really used to come it. Couldn't abide me. She thought I was common as well, while she was just the bee's knees, of course. All fur coat and no knickers. Now, if we could contact her, she could help us out of here. What was she called? It was round about the time you used to drag along that whatsit – that daft robot dog of yours. And what an obnoxious piece of tat that was!'

'Robot dog?' said the Doctor, incredulously. 'What the Dickens would I want with a robot dog?'

I felt myself blushing then.

I did a quick sum on my fingers. 'I am sorry. I'm being clumsy and messing it all up. I'm being anachronistic again. Getting ahead of myself.'

I put on a very genteel voice, speaking deliberately, so as to mollify my seething companion. The scarlet feather in my hat nodded a gentle accompaniment as I vowed: 'I will endeavour to keep myself in strictly chronological order while I'm with you, and try not to tell you anything of your own personal future.'

The Doctor's eyes grew wide. 'My own...?'

Suddenly he was on his feet and hauling me up to mine.

Oh, he was rough with me, the beast!

I grunted decorously and felt unsteady on my pins.

Then he was shaking me by my shoulders and my teeth were starting to rattle.

'Tell me, Iris! When does my exile end? Does it ever end? When do I get my freedom back?'

For a fleeting second I was going to kick him in the balls and see how he liked that; shaking a poor old lady about and dragging the truth out of her but, before I could even get my knee into position, the door shot open and one of those long-legged beasties was peering in at us. It blinked its purple eyes in shock as if it had walked in on us doing something rather rude.

Immediately the Doctor let go of me and I sagged – like a sack of bloody potatoes – back on to the futon.

'Our commander will speak to you now,' the creature said and I couldn't help thinking that it looked a mite embarrassed.

Perhaps, in its universe, a tussle like mine and the Doctor's counted as foreplay.

I wish it did in mine.

Tugging our clothes straight, we followed the alien, relieved, into the booklined, musty corridor.

The Doctor gave me a beady glance, as if to say, 'I'll get the truth out of you later,' but I ignored him.

Silly old sod.

As a control room, as a hive of activity at the centre of operations, as the complex nexus of information at the heart of the invasion, as the brain's trust for an alien attack, it was somewhat dull.

Iris and the Doctor were led into a room with a domed ceiling that glowed a gentle green.

It was like being in a fishtank.

Their guard lumbered across to stand with its two fellows, who glared down from their tripods in some suspicion.

On a smart, padded chair sat the being responsible for the entire invasion force.

It was obvious that the leadership was hers.

She looked imperious, even though she was quite small.

She wore a bright scarlet cape and, resting at her feet, were a small basket of goodies and an entirely prostrate wolf.

As the girl addressed her captives, the wolf stared up adoringly at her and twitched his huge ears as if he longed to have them scratched.

'Welcome, Doctor, Iris,' said the girl.

'This has got to stop,' said the Doctor. 'Iris and I demand an explanation as to what you are all up to. You can't go dropping fictional people on to the Earth! They are suggestible enough as it is, down there!'

In their eggcup-like devices, the three grotesque creatures bridled and rippled at the Doctor's words.

The little girl coughed and said, 'Our sensors have detected a certain ripple of ontological doubt in the culture of this world at this point in its history. They have called it postmodernity, Doctor. These people expect – and what's more entirely deserve – to have their cognitive barriers disrupted. They all believe that referentiality has collapsed and there is no discrete gateway between the Real and their Imaginary. We've read all about what they think. You should take a peek at what their psychoanalytical people are saying down there!'

'I know, I know,' said the Doctor, shaking his head. 'But referentiality is one thing. Turning up on Earth claiming to be Banquo's ghost or Grendel's Mother and expecting the council to give you a flat is quite another!'

Iris put in, 'What kind of deluded nincompoops ever believed that they could invade the Earth posing as fictional characters? Are you all bonkers?'

'In a postmodern age...' began Little Red Riding Hood, 'When the paradigm shift means that the epistemological dominant has been replaced by...'

'Bollocks,' said Iris. 'That's just retrospective justification.

You've buggered it up, haven't you? You've made a mistake and you've invented this theory just to justify all your poncing about in crinolines and soldiers' outfits. You thought these disguises would make you look like real people on the Earth!'

Iris cackled with glee. 'You thought you were going to blend in!'

The wolf on the shiny floor gave a hopeless groan. 'It's all quite true.'

He looked up dolefully at his mistress and she looked as if she were about to kick him. 'We ourselves invented those ludicrous categories of "postmodernity" and "self-referentiality" and "metatextuality" just to cover up our silly mistake. Of course we thought we were going to look realistic. But we don't and we had to infiltrate your culture with something as silly as postmodern theory just to get a look in.'

At this the little girl really did dig her size fives into the wolf's shaggy pelt and he yelped.

'But that's monstrous!' the Doctor bellowed. 'You have infected the Earth with an epistemological quandary that will leave them stymied and perplexed for a century or more!'

Iris put in, 'It's the kind of cultural nightmare that filters down in the form of dreadful, interminable plays where no one knows what's going on and everyone climbs into a fridge at the end! And allows awful people with the know-how to take over the world with things like the Internet because everyone thinks it's smart to have communications networks that are all style and no content! You've turned Earth into a vapid, smugly self-referential abortion of a world just because of your own foolishness!'

'I thought you liked the Internet,' said the Doctor.

'I like the bits about me,' Iris said. 'But I'd rather have a culture with integrity and a kind of organic wholesomeness about it; one that had nice, unreconstructed grand narratives and ideas about progress and goodness and everything was still simple!'

The Doctor looked at her. 'No, you wouldn't. You like everything to be as fickle and trivial as you are.'

'Bugger you, Doctor! This is bloody rhetoric, all right?'

But Little Red Riding Hood had tears coursing down her cheeks. 'Oh, you're right. We've caused more damage than we ever meant to. We've left the narrow path and wandered into the wild woods of uncertainty and cognitive hazard.'

She let out a thick sob and an unflattering dribble appeared out of one nostril. 'Yes, we made a mistake. We only wanted to live in peace on a fairly advanced world, once our own had been shattered and destroyed by the evil Valceans from the Obverse dimension.'

'From where?' asked the Doctor.

'Let her finish,' said Iris hastily.

'We only wanted to slip on to the Earth with none of its inhabitants knowing. So we sent on a spy, to work for forty-five years in one of your greatest libraries. He worked during some great war you had and was in charge of taking all of the books deep underground, beneath a city you know as London. He took them to safety on a little railway, deep inside secret catacombs, and he was supposed to place the treasured volumes on secret shelves. But he sent them all here, to our mothership, so we could duplicate them and research the best ways of blending in.'

'But he got it wrong, didn't he?' said the Doctor, coaxingly.

Iris was staring at the girl's tears and the smear of snot across her face.

She started hunting around in her handbag for a handkerchief she could offer the poor, distressed girl.

'Yes,' sighed Little Red Riding Hood. 'Blast that Leonard Bast! We all thought he was doing such a good job as our chief researcher and librarian. In the end, before his mission was complete, a vast bookshelf fell on him and squashed him flat; dead. We had to make do with what he'd sent us.'

'Which,' said Iris, still poking around in her bag, 'was quite a lot, judging by all the volumes we saw stuffed away in your corridors.'

'But...!' gasped the girl, with her wolf moaning piteously in sympathy. 'He'd only stolen from the fiction shelves! We hadn't realised! He'd given us these things and we copied them – with our cloning machines – down to the last letter, assuming they were gospel.'

'What a ridiculous mistake to make,' said the Doctor. 'Didn't you suspect?'

She frowned. 'When we got as far as *Moby Dick*, we did start to wonder. Moby's still in the hold. He's demented.'

'You shouldn't try to blend in with alien cultures anyway,' said Iris. 'It's not nice. You should find somewhere for yourself, somewhere plain and simple and far from anyone. The Earth has its own destiny to fulfil.'

'Quite,' said the Doctor. He couldn't help thinking that, if Iris wasn't here, he could do more of his share of the talking.

'What empty worlds are there?' burst Little Red Riding Hood. 'Do you have any idea how difficult it is to find somewhere to settle down? We'd give anything to be free of this rootless existence! We just want a home! We're not a warlike race. We've seen enough of war, after the Enclave and the Obverse and all that. We only wanted to come in peace and all get little houses somewhere and forget about our past. We'd have given anything to find an empty world...'

The Doctor's eyes lit up brightly. 'Then I believe I can help you...'

Iris took out her hanky and waved it under the little girl's nose. 'That's right, lovey. We're here to help you. Now, you just blow your nose and...'

They were interrupted by a shriek from one of the monstrous creatures, high atop his tripod.

'What is that?'

'It's a hanky,' stammered Iris, frightened out of her wits by the sudden screech.

'No, that!'

One of the being's telescopic arms shot out, to point, with some alarm, at Iris's handbag, which she had hooked over her arm.

In the green light it glittered a dull, inscrutable gold.

'What?' she said. 'That's just my handbag. It's…'

All of sudden, and with a tremendous clatter, all three of the tripods dropped to their spindly knees.

They began to chant and to moan.

Little Red Riding Hood's eyes were out on stalks and the wolf at her feet was busily prostrating himself even flatter.

'What the devil are you all doing?' Iris demanded to know. The tripod creatures howled in terror and obeisance and there was no getting any sense out of them.

Iris held her handbag up before them all.

'It's only a handbag!'

The Doctor touched her arm. 'Be careful, Iris… They're…'

Little Red Riding Hood gasped out a few words: 'You have possession of the Revenant… You had it with you the whole time! You are taunting us…'

Iris was starting to get seriously worried by now. Still holding her bag aloft, she turned to the Doctor. 'What are they on about? Have they all gone crackers, or what?'

Grimly, he shook his head. 'They are worshipping your handbag, Iris. To them it is…' He looked ashen-faced, 'some kind of god.'

Chapter Ten
Night

All night there is the sound of the trains.

Our heroes – in two distinct camps: one beneath London, the other, far above – both lie awake in the same night and they can all hear the rumbling hiss and screeching of trains.

The kind of noise that keeps you awake at night because you think yourself tied to those tracks by a moustache-twiddling villain.

In his own sumptuous pad, the most luxurious room in the secret lair of Destiny's Children – all black sheets and zebra flock wallpaper – even the Master has this thought.

The hideout underneath New Cross shakes, rattles and rolls with the distant reverberations of tube trains.

During the night the Master decides to contact his own Master. He needs a little boost; he needs a chance to show off what he has accomplished so far. And so he pulls back the red curtains that cover his viewscreen in the corner of his room and activates the machine, tuning into the bristling, malevolent thought waves of the man who has set him upon this mission.

When the screen clears all that can be seen is a dark silhouette in a smoky room.

'Yeees?' asks the silhouette.

'Master,' says the Master, with a tight bow and then draws himself up to report on progress thus far.

The figure on the screen nods contentedly throughout and when his servant is finished, though he is not excessive with his praise. Then he starts to give his creature further instructions and the Master starts nodding in turn.

What a relief, to have someone telling you what to do!

'Soon,' says that dark shadow on the screen, 'the Doctor will have nowhere to go! He will be forced to leave this world... for ever!'

And both figures laugh for an appropriate length of time, at the end of which the Master clicks off the viewscreen and returns to bed.

Outside, in the main room, Simon is working in the night – totting up new figures and probabilities, the bright sparks dancing in his massive, lucent brain – and he curses the trains for their impact on his sums.

The glasses left on the tables by the Children before they went to bed tinkle and crash against each other.

Jo Grant lies on the settee in the main room, right beneath the pulsing mind of Simon, and at last she re-gathers her wits enough to realise that the Master has tied her up with silk handkerchiefs.

Now she is out of her spell and free to wonder at this new environment: a brand-new lair in which she has been trapped, another nightmare location.

She is wondering at the Master's place in recent events; no one she knows has heard much from him recently. Not since the last UNIT Christmas party, in fact.

The Doctor believed his old foe was off-Earth at last, and up to his business elsewhere, having grown bored with the humdrum doings of Terrans.

Jo is convinced that it is the Master who has interfered with the proper running of UNIT and this, curiously, comes as some relief to her. If it is only the Master behind all of this, then things are practically back to normal.

But where is she?

And what is Iris's young friend Tom doing, acting so friendly with these strange children?

She remembers two of them from that field the other day. They vanished in a flash and here they were, at home.

Just before bedtime Jo had seen two more teenagers arrive, a black girl and a blond boy.

Woozy as she had been, Jo had eavesdropped on them discussing the affairs of the Galactic Federation, how very concerned the Council were.

It almost made Jo laugh, to hear people as young as this talking like ambassadors. It made a change from feeling young and inexperienced as she did in many of the situations she found herself in. She was old enough to be aunty to this lot.

She lay on the settee, bound and gagged, and none of Destiny's Children even seemed to notice her.

Before he slipped off to the room they had provided him with, Tom sneaked away to whisper in her ear: 'I have to play along, Jo. I can't free you now. Just wait it out a bit, eh?'

Then he was gone.

Jo was alone as the lights dimmed imperceptibly and the only lumination came from Simon's constant, flickering cogitations.

At one point, in the middle of the night, she saw the oldest of the teenagers, Kevin, leave his room, slip blithely across the centre of the floor in his dressing gown, and into Tom's room.

Jo struggled feebly against her bonds. If Tom was in trouble, she would help him out – even if he didn't feel he could help her yet. But to no avail.

She couldn't budge.

She lay back on the settee and listened worriedly for any signs of struggle from Tom's room.

Across the hall, Marsha was sitting awake and chanting to block out the noise of the trains.

In her mind, she was trying to recapture the exact appearance of Councillor Borges. She was trying to imagine how he felt; exactly what he would be like in the flesh.

Almost guiltily, the girl fixed her thoughts on his alien majesty and urged on the day that would see her transported at last, for the very first time, to Galactic Federation Central.

How she envied Peter and Mary, who went up there and hobnobbed with ambassadors without turning a hair.

Marsha would die when she got to go there in person. When she could confront the dashing Borges and confess her desire for him.

She chanted on through the night; slipping in a little prayer that perhaps, just perhaps, this current adventure might necessitate a trip to Central.

Jo could hear her chanting increase its pitch and intensity and she feared something ghastly and magical was going on, behind closed doors.

She tried to put those muffled incantations out of her head; they brought back too many dreadful Dennis Wheatley-type memories of being laid out on a slab of rock (again bound and gagged by the Master) and almost sacrificed to some pagan god or other.

She jumped, slightly, as there came a thump from Tom's room.

She concentrated her thoughts on the Doctor.

Once, far from here, when they had been sent, ineluctably, across space and time by the Doctor's mysterious superiors, the Time Lords, he had taken her hands in his and said: 'Sometimes it will be enough, if you need my help, just to think of me, very hard, in the direction you last saw me. I'll come running, Jo.'

At the time they had been stuck on a ramshackle boat in a blue, blue swamp. Her clothes had been encrusted in purple mud. He was going out in a dinghy for help, leaving her alone on the boat and wasn't sure when he'd be back.

But he had come back. She could always rely on him in the end. He would always be the same.

The Brigadier, of course, said he'd been different at the start, when he'd first known him. But Jo didn't believe a word of it.

The Doctor was one of the great, still rocks in the universe. Everything else changed about him.

But where was he now?

Jo Grant had no inkling of the ship that revolved in orbit like a discreet and preposterous thought in the mind of someone serene but bonkers.

High above London and its crust of smog, stretched tall above the soapy atmosphere of the Earth, was a ship the size and exact shape of St Pancras.

It was a great salmon-pink edifice, maternal and grand, disgorging carriages all night and winking in satisfaction as they hurtled, spewing frozen steam, towards the planet's surface.

Back in their cell, the Doctor and Iris sat awake, listening to the trains.

'The fools,' he railed for a while. 'They're still sending their people down.'

Dimly they could make out the tannoy voice, telling the mother ship's occupants that *Droll Stories*, the Bible and *The Devil Rides Out* were ready for departure.

'You tried to tell them,' said Iris gloomily.

She was hunched on the mattress with her granny specs on, a sure sign that she was feeling distressed and at least some of her uncountable years.

She was also feeling the loss of her handbag, that antique treasure so revered by their hosts, the Meercocks (as, the two of them had discovered, they called themselves).

'With every carriage they send to the Earth, they are losing more of their people,' said the Doctor. 'Are they doing it on purpose? They know that the experiment is a failure anyway.

And we've seen it! Within minutes, hours, of their touching down in their new environment, they are reduced to green powder. Their essence can't hold their new forms long enough. Their recall bracelets don't do them any good at all. Why are they still bothering?'

'It's a funny thing, bloody-mindedness,' said Iris. 'When you know something's doomed to failure and yet you still go on, hoping to effect a change through… the sheer force of your personality, or your will.'

The Doctor gave her a curious look.

'You must help me convince them to let me find them a new world. I think I have one in mind. We must get them away from the Earth.'

She nodded. 'I want to know why they wanted my handbag.'

'Maybe they'll explain tomorrow.'

'I need some sleep,' she said. 'Do you mind if I have the futon?'

He shook his head absently. 'I won't sleep tonight. I've got to think.'

'Oh, come on, Doctor. You must rest'

'I haven't slept, not properly, in two and a half years.'

'That isn't right.'

He shrugged. 'I don't like the dreams I have.'

'You could cuddle up on here, with me, if you like.'

'No thanks.' He started to pace around the room, in his usual, restless way.

'What difference would it make? We're old pals. We've got nothing to…'

'I don't want to cuddle up anywhere. Thank you, Iris.'

She narrowed her eyes at him. 'What if I said it was me who needed a bit of comfort and warmth?'

He looked defeated. 'Then I still couldn't help you.'

'You're so cold.'

'Perhaps.'

She lay down on the futon and turned her back. 'Good night then.'

'Hm.'

There was silence for a moment and the tension between them jangled on Iris's nerves as much as the noise of the trains did.

'Doctor?'

'Go to sleep, Iris.'

'I have to tell you.'

'What?'

'In the end, you know..., it is all right. You don't stay on Earth for ever.'

She listened for a response – pleased, excited, cynical – but none came from the Doctor.

Chapter Eleven
Bargains

The girl in the red cloak couldn't sleep a wink, either.

She knew that her two prisoners were talking about her.

She knew they would be telling each other what a rotten invasion she had in store for the Earth, how it was doomed to disaster and she was consigning her hapless people to doom.

She had kept the green powder a secret from those under her charge. They were too excited and optimistic to even listen.

If she was to tell them: this is what you'll be reduced to, when you arrive on the Earth in your new, inappropriate guises, what would they do to her?

At best, the girl might just be ignored; at worst, they might lynch her or toss her out into space.

The girl knew that it didn't do, to be the bearer of bad news. The last Queen of the Meercocks had been her grandmother, ripped to shreds by the assembled hordes on the fateful evening when she had to tell them that their homeworld had been utterly destroyed.

This night, the girl in the red cloak patrolled the booklined passageways of her ship almost half-asleep, rigid with dread and impotent fury.

The wolf slunk along quietly beside her, doing his best to keep quiet and not disturb her, and yet making sure he was there, in case she needed him.

Occasionally, in her darkest moments, Red Riding Hood sought council from the wolf. She trusted him, even if she was fond of administering a hearty kick to his flanks whenever she felt like it, just to show who was boss.

* * *

Sometimes the wolf wondered what she would ever do if she were to find out that it was he who had orchestrated the killing of her grandmother. He who had done the final gobbling-up that necessitated the crowning of a new queen.

She would have me executed, he thought gloomily, his belly sagging and dragging on the dusty floor of the corridor as he moped along.

And yet I only did it for her. So she could be queen and lead us to a new land.

Her Granny was dead set on attacking our enemies, the Glass Men of Valcea, which would have been suicide, of course.

This way, it's better. My beloved still has a chance to save us all.

He looked up at her as they walked along, a whimper of lupine query – piteous, coaxing – in his throat.

She even gave him a tight smile in response.

Surely she couldn't send everyone down to the Earth? Surely she couldn't go on with the masquerade and let them all die? For the sake of saving face?

The wolf looked at her again as her mind went roving over the same old problems.

Perhaps she had more of her prideful, kamikaze granny in her than he'd at first thought.

Perhaps (and here the grey, brindled wolf swallowed his horror) he would be forced to deal brutally with his beloved as well.

They came to the room where the three last Meercocks in their natural forms had taken the golden evening bag they had seized from the possession of Iris Wildthyme.

The girl and her wolf stood frozen in the doorway of the great chamber, unnoticed.

The empty room had been hastily converted into a chapel and a vast quantity of reverential, worshipful hush had been dutifully imported to weigh upon the space; to fill every nook and cranny and to drape itself, like incense, around the plinth on which the golden bag rested.

Before it, the three natural Meercocks were abasing themselves, with their golden telescopic legs folded up, kneeling awkwardly on the ground.

Their hydraulic joints' hissing and sparking was the only sound to be heard.

They had been joined by others, who were likewise prostrated in the presence of the relic.

The girl could pick out a few she recognised from her reading of the terrestrial texts: Bluebeard with his scimitar sheathed in his belt, Grendel's Mother hunched over and oozing slime on the polished floor.

'They are gaining followers,' the wolf whispered in her ear. She couldn't abide the rank blast of his breath, but didn't say anything. 'Do you think they will be a problem?' he asked.

'My grandmother didn't say anything about religion,' she hissed back. 'It hasn't been a problem for our people for hundreds of years. Not since the last of the ancient relics was unearthed from the palace.'

'Best off without it,' the wolf shuddered.

'I thought,' she said sadly, 'that was the only good thing about the death of the homeworld. There would be no more relics. No more religious wars.'

'But where has this thing come from?' asked the wolf, gazing at the bag. 'How did that strange woman come by it?'

'We must find out.' Then a thought seemed to strike the girl. 'Perhaps she has been to some other world, where our ancestors also visited. Perhaps there is another place, inhabited by people like us.'

The wolf didn't look too keen on this idea. 'This relic is the most perfect one that has ever been seen. No wonder the fanatics have prostrated themselves.'

The girl looked worried. 'Do you think it could still be alive?'

'Who's to tell?' said the wolf.

'Come on,' she said. 'Let's talk to the prisoners.'

As they crept away from the makeshift crypt, they thought their going was unremarked by those busily worshipping.

But Bluebeard raised his shaggy head to watch them go.

Iris was wondering if she'd left her spare packet of cigarettes in the inside compartment of her bag.

There was a miniature bottle of rum in there too, which might have come in handy during this long, lonely night.

She supposed they were being worshipped, along with her handbag.

'Doctor?' she asked, into the dark.

He was standing against the wall, deep in thought. 'Hm?'

'What do you suppose that bag represents to them?'

There was a pause before he answered her. 'Possibly it has activated some atavistic memory.'

'I thought as much. I wish I'd brought my carpet bag instead.' She sat up lumpily and tried to focus on him. 'What kind of society worships accessories?'

Even in the gloom she could feel his suspicious eyes on her. 'Iris, where did you get that bag?'

She giggled and jumped up. She sang, loudly:

'Where did you get that bag?
Where did you get that style?
Isn't it a natty one?
I wish it was one of mine.
I would like to have one, just the same as that;
Wherever I'd go people would shout: hello!
Where did you get that bag?'

Then she laughed long and loud at him. 'Fancy us, fighting over handbags, Doctor!'

'Iris,' he warned, in a low voice.

'Oh, all right.' Now she remembered, this Doctor could be rather humourless when he wanted. 'It was given to me as a present, I think, some time ago. By a friend.'

'Who?'

'Oh, I can't remember.'

'Perhaps you should put your mind to it. If they decide you've been blaspheming their god by trolling around with it...'

She gulped.

And then the door slid open, spilling light from the book-lined corridor outside.

Red Riding Hood and the Wolf glared in at their blinking captives.

'How nice to see you again,' said the Doctor. 'Even if it is the middle of the night.'

Iris was outraged at their peremptory visit. 'We could have been doing anything!'

The girl, however, was studiously ignoring the sacrilegious old woman. She addressed the Doctor in a regal tone.

'You talked about an empty world that my people might go to...'

He nodded, pleased that the girl seemed to be seeing sense at last. 'I can find you one. If you'll stop trying to infiltrate Earthspace and fiddling around with 1973, I'll do everything I can to get you safe passage to the empty world.'

The wolf snickered. 'Why should we trust you? You could deposit us anywhere.'

The Doctor fixed him with a hard stare. 'We'll all have to trust each other then, won't we?'

Iris was pushing her hair back into shape with her fingertips, and searching around for her feathered hat. 'That's easier said than done.'

Then she saw that the Doctor was looking at her. He had an unmistakable look. He needed something from her.

'You'll have to help me,' he said.

'How?'

'Obviously, my TARDIS will be no use at all in helping these good people out. All of my time charts and everything have been tampered with by the High Council. If I could just use yours, and then if we could...'

Iris shook her head firmly. 'Absolutely not.'

Everyone gasped. The little girl looked furious. 'You are refusing to help us? Do you want our whole race to perish?'

The wolf set up a low growl, deep in his throat.

'I'd like to help, sweetheart,' Iris told her. 'But I'm not as foolhardy as the Doctor here. My bus is a very fragile, precious thing. If his was working, the old fool wouldn't think twice about giving your mother ship a tow across half the galaxy to some godforsaken place you could colonise. Me, I'm not as selfless as that, I'm afraid. I'm not risking it.'

'Iris!' said the Doctor. 'I thought you were pledged to help those in need!'

Her eyes went wide. 'When did I ever say that?'

He frowned. 'Well, maybe you didn't. But I did.' He drew himself up to his full impressive height and, despite herself, Iris was thrilled by his gravitas. 'I shall commandeer your bus myself and effect the required rescue operation.'

'Like buggery you will!'

Red Riding Hood looked her up and down scornfully. 'You would stand against the Doctor and the combined might of the Meercocks, old woman?'

'Too bloody right I would!' She was bursting with temper by now. 'Can't you see? The Doctor has his own, secret agenda going here. He's dying to get his hands on my bust... bus, sorry. He's been salivating over it ever since I arrived in this awful time and place. He won't rest until it's his and he can slip away and be free. Can't you see? Once he's got his freedom back, he won't give two figs for your predicament.

He'll be away!'

'Is this true, Doctor?' the girl thundered.

'Madam,' said the Doctor, in a very dignified tone. 'I have given my word. If Iris condescends to let me borrow the bus, I will do all I can for you and your people.'

'But he'll keep the bus!' moaned Iris. 'Once he's done with you lot, he'll never give my TARDIS back!' She looked around for support and found none from anyone present. 'You've already taken my bag! Don't take my bus as well!'

The wolf, she realised, was sneering at her, and licking its liquorice-black lips speculatively.

'Come with us, Doctor,' said the girl and turned smartly on her heel. The wolf whipped around and, in one fluid movement, trotted along behind her.

The Doctor went striding after them. He didn't even look at Iris.

She clutched her hat. 'What about me? Doctor? Doctor!'

But the cell door crashed shut on her and she was left, trapped inside, alone.

Chapter Twelve
Reading the Signals

At dawn the Master nimbly leapt out of his black silk sheets and prepared himself meticulously for the day ahead.

He slipped out to find that Jo Grant was asleep on the sofa in the room outside, still bound and gagged.

So the Doctor hadn't managed to rescue her already.

That was a good sign.

Then he stood by the gleaming chrome mirror beside the teleportation tubes and gazed into his own eyes, telling himself that he was the Master, he was the Master and he must bow down before his own magnificent will.

He stroked his beard till it was impeccably neat.

What burning eyes I have, he thought.

He went into a meeting with Simon – a fleeting, harmonious meeting of minds – and between them they thrashed out plans for the day.

Things had to move on apace.

Simon saw to it that each of the Children of Destiny received their alarm calls an hour or two early and, used to obeying their electronic mentor, the teenagers hauled themselves out of bed and were ready to do his bidding.

Kevin was back in his own room when the call came.

He had been there several hours.

He was awake and headachy, mulling over what to do about Tom.

He isn't a real Child of Destiny, he was thinking.

Tom has none of our faculties. Last night I tried to check him out and test him and there was nothing of our latency in him. None of the others know this yet.

Do I keep them in the dark? Simon must know that Tom has no talents; that he isn't a superior being like us, and yet Simon is still determined that Tom join with us on this mission.

There must be more to this than meets the eye.

Some masterplan we can't be told of yet.

Kevin wasn't at all pleased with this state of affairs.

He rolled out of bed and into the shower.

In his own room, Tom was cross and exhausted and the whining klaxon Simon had set off did nothing to improve his mood. He still didn't know what Kevin had been up to last night.

He had come tripping in, anxious for no one else to hear, and he'd sat on the end of Tom's bed, quizzing him about whether he had the same powers as the others in the gang.

Tom really couldn't have cared less about the powers. They didn't seem all that exciting anyway.

But Kevin sitting there, going on about it all, a glimmer of zeal in his eyes as he talked, had driven Tom mad.

He had fixed his gaze on the white flash of collar bone showing where Kevin's dressing gown had fallen open.

The boy's words had fallen on deaf ears as Tom clutched the duvet up to himself and wondered where this was going to end.

'Someone is using us all as pawns,' Kevin had said, resignedly and ominously, getting up to go at last.

'Kevin...' Tom said, sitting up further.

The Child of Destiny looked at him as if he hardly knew who he was. 'What?'

'You didn't really come here to talk to me about the Galactic Federation and telepathic powers and everything, did you?'

Kevin frowned. 'Yes I did.'

Tom shook his head. 'It was all a pretext. Come on, admit it. You just wanted to get in here, with me, while the others were asleep. That's what this has all been about.'

Kevin looked completely mystified and Tom faltered for a moment, thinking he might have read the signals wrong.

'I think I'd better go back to my room,' Kevin said.

'Oh, grow up,' Tom said. 'What are you, nineteen? You go around, talking about the future destiny of the world like a precocious ten-year-old. And the whole time you've been giving me the glad eye. That's why you've got me here.'

Kevin stammered and blushed. 'Simon wouldn't like this.'

Tom rolled his eyes. 'He's a machine!'

'He's our leader. He tells us what to do.'

'I thought the Master did that.'

Now Kevin looked weary and worried. 'The Master has only been around for a week or two. But Simon defers to him in everything. I don't know much about this Master. I don't like him much.'

'Can't say I do, either.' Tom had got up and walked across to the boy by now. 'Are you sure you're going? You're not going to stay?'

Kevin shook his head briskly. 'You've read the signals all wrong, mate. I'm just doing my job.'

Then he was gone, the electronic door sliding shut behind him. Tom thumped it hard.

And now, at dawn the next morning, with the Children of Destiny up and ready like a well-drilled patrol, Tom was reeling with embarrassment and hardly dared face them all.

He was sure he hadn't read Kevin wrong, though.

Out in the main hall of the headquarters, the Master was untying Jo and warning her what would happen if she even thought about running away.

She was glaring at everyone as if they were all to blame for her incarceration.

'Morning, Jo,' said Tom breezily.

He decided that breezy was the only way to overcome the curious tensions in the air that morning.

He cast a curious glance at Kevin (in a silver outfit this morning) and Kevin looked away.

Marsha looked a bit drawn, as if she'd been up all night, and they had been joined by the black girl, Mary, and the blond boy, Peter, in red and white outfits respectively.

This was the first chance Tom had had to meet them.

'I've heard a lot about you, Tom,' said Mary, in a seemingly genuinely friendly way, extending a graceful hand for him to shake.

He found himself smiling.

Then something hit him.

There was something strikingly familiar about this girl. She was about his own age and carried herself with a certain dignity and calm, which belied her vocation as ambassador to the Galactic Federation.

'Is something the matter, Tom?' she asked kindly, looking straight into his eyes.

He met that stare and swallowed, hard. He knew his hands were shaking.

She continued, 'I suppose it all must be a shock to you still, travelling here from the future. But you will overcome it, I expect.' She lowered her voice. 'You're a good boy, Tom.'

Then she swept away, to talk to the Master.

Jo joined Tom. 'What's wrong with you? You look like you've seen a ghost.'

Tom jumped at Jo's voice. 'Mary...' he said. 'That's my mother.'

'How can she be?' burst Jo. 'She's too young... Oh, I see.'

'I've met my own mother before I was born!' Now Tom was really messed up.

Before they could go on in their whispered conference, the Master addressed them all, rather grandly, relishing every word.

'Simon and I have decided that we must move on apace and step up our plans to put paid to the Doctor's vile schemes.'

'Vile schemes!' said Jo. 'If you only knew the half of it!' She turned to the Children, beseechingly. 'You can't listen to this madman. He's utterly ruthless and evil. You have to meet the Doctor and see him for yourself. He's the kindest, gentlest...'

'Oh, spare us the toadying nonsense, Miss Grant.' The Master sighed heavily. 'Poor, deluded Josephine has spent the last two years in thrall to this meddling tyrant. She is entranced, I fear, beyond all repair. We must be kind to her and give the appearance of listening to her but she is, I fear, stuffed with Ministry doublethink.'

As the Children of Destiny looked Jo pityingly up and down Tom actually found himself wondering if it could be true.

'Anyway,' said the Master quickly, 'I thought the best thing we could do today would be to travel straight to the Doctor's house while he is away... elsewhere.'

'Elsewhere?' gasped Jo. 'Where have you taken him?'

She was ignored. 'We should repair to the countryside immediately and discover what vileness he has been perpetrating there, hidden away in his rural retreat.'

The Master led them smartly to the waiting, gleaming teleport tubes.

Iris wasn't alone in the cell for long.

She had just finished cursing the Doctor with every filthy epithet she could conjure, when the door shot open again and she was confronted by the bulky spectacle of a man with a bristling beard the size of a small dog, a scarlet greatcoat and an unsheathed scimitar.

'Bluebeard!' she gasped, jumping up.

He growled out his words quietly and with care. 'The newly elected Keepers require your presence. You are Iris Wildthyme, are you not?'

She nodded dumbly.

'We need to know how you came by the holy of holies,' he

ground out through square, yellowed teeth. 'We have to weigh up your story and come to a decision whether you are indeed an abomination or not.'

'Well!' gasped Iris hotly, as she was hustled out of the cell. 'Does your queen know about this?'

He was marching her along at a rattling pace.

'Her Majesty does not need to know about this. It is a religious matter and she has made her feelings plain about such things. Besides,' he added darkly, his purplish beard rustling with menace, 'she will not be queen for very much longer.'

Iris looked shocked. 'You're going to replace her with my handbag?'

Here we must bow to convention.

In the cause of setting up a general air of menace, suspense and a better sense of context, we must leave our principals for a moment and slip into the dark, dark undergrowth and concentrate, for a moment, on somebody else.

An extra: expendable and innocent, tramping in the woods at dawn in the countryside quite near to the Doctor's home.

A gamekeeper, perhaps, or a poacher.

A brace of pheasants, say, strung up on his belt and a warm rifle slung over his shoulder.

Or maybe a tramp, crashing through the bracken and drunkenly making an unholy row as the light comes creeping through the stirring trees.

Something of that ilk, anyway, I think, is the convention.

So for a while we watch this somewhat tipsy, ragged poacher amble through the long grass, come out of the woods, sniff the air, and push off into a field. His old boots skid on the dewy grass as he comes down the hill.

Then we've got to ask, what became of the sheep Jo Grant saw, leaving the former UNIT HQ *en masse*?

She – especially in her current, befuddled state – would swear blind they were an illusion, of a particularly bizarre sort.

She saw scores of them emerge malevolently from a large electronic egg and trundle in formation, their scarlet eyes blazing, out of the building.

The truth is, they had fanned out across the landscape, for a whole day and night, gunning down anyone they come across. Quite unstoppable.

Old Ted (our convention, our stand-by, our fall-guy) frowns as he smells something unfamiliar. He can't know that what he smells is the acrid oil-and-grease of the metal sheep's gears, or the hissing and sparking of their joints.

He can smell burning, too, as they use their laser eyes to raze to the ground any obstacles they come across as they sweep up the hill towards him.

Old Ted drops his rifle in fright as the sheep bear down upon him.

Because their eyes glow so deeply crimson he thinks they have come from the devil to get him for the crime of nicking other people's birds.

He makes a feeble grasp for the gun, but the sheep surround him, each of them making a terrible giggling noise.

He stares at them all as their eyes blaze and discharge their baleful energy. Then, he's gone.

The sheep mow over the ashy remnants of Old Ted and his illegal brace of birds and then they're off, into the woods, felling trees as they go, implacably heading towards the village.

What a joke, Iris thought. Having to snatch back my own handbag.

But, as she watched the cult all bowing down in the grand chamber and making curious, complicated gestures of worship in the direction of her erstwhile belonging, she was overcome by a determination to have the thing back.

The cult had more than tripled its size.

Many of the worshippers had forsaken their places on the carriages headed for Earth to come here, Bluebeard explained to her.

They knew as well as he did that they stood a far better shot at deliverance in the service of the relic, than if they foisted themselves upon the world.

Iris recognised a number of characters from D. H. Lawrence and Thomas Hardy, all prostrating themselves before the handbag.

'What do you want from me?' she asked suspiciously.

And then, in one bound, the wolf was at the door.

Bluebeard rounded on him in fury.

'You dare to disturb the sanctity of this place?'

'Until yesterday night,' said the wolf, laconically, 'this used to be a canteen.'

'Tell us what you have been sent to tell us, and go,' growled Bluebeard.

'The Queen is most displeased at your holding up the schedules for planetfall. Many of you should already be down on the Earth, starting your new lives.'

'New lives!' cried Ursula Brangwen, from Lawrence's *The Rainbow*. 'There's no such thing!'

She was joined by Tess of the D'Urbervilles, hauling herself off the shiny floor and flicking her hair out of her face. 'Everyone who arrives on Earth dies, within a few hours of arrival. That's what you've been keeping from us.'

Iris was shocked then, to see what appeared to be Kafka's Gregor Samsen, semi-transformed into a beetle, joining their litany of subversion. He was lying on his back with his limbs twitching arthritically in the air. 'None of us is going! We have entrusted our fates instead to the protection of the holy relic!'

The wolf looked concerned. 'Who told you these lies about the fate of our people on the Earth?'

While they were busy among themselves in this way, Iris burst into action.

Clamping her hat to her head, she made one fantastic leap through the gaggle of quibbling characters.

She felt herself barrelling rather heavily, elbows thrust outwards to do the maximum damage, into a Macbeth witch and a Tolkien orc, but the room was already in uproar as the maddened worshippers shouted at and rounded on the wolf.

Iris, meanwhile, found it fairly easy to slip up to the podium and snatch up her handbag.

She stowed its reassuring shape under one arm, and pelted from the room in a blur of wool and tweed.

The wolf's ears pricked up.

'She's taken it!'

'I don't understand,' the Doctor was telling the girl in the scarlet cape, 'why you can't just send me back down with one of those bracelet affairs?'

He was staring into the cramped confines of the lifepod she had opened for him. He looked at it gloomily, as if at a rather unpromising second-hand car he was being offered.

Red Riding Hood shook her head. 'The bracelets are dangerous, Doctor. I accept that now. Our people have died after any contact with them. For too long I ignored the very obvious result of what we hoped would be our salvation.'

'Hm,' he said. 'Where did the bracelets come from in the first place? They don't seem to be part of your technology.'

'Indeed not.' She looked stricken. 'They were a gift, of sorts. From a well-wisher.'

'A well-wisher?'

'The green man gave us them. He said they would bring us to Earth and save our people.'

'The green man?'

* * *

Iris was pelting down the library corridors as fast as she could.

She could hear the crowd behind her; all howling for the loss of their god.

Both hearts were pounding something chronic.

How do I get myself into things like this?

'What's all that noise?' the Doctor asked.

The girl was urging him into the lifepod.

'My people have found religion again. A very dangerous mix. You have, albeit unknowingly, taken us back into our dark past, when we worshipped those creatures who came from the stars...'

'Creatures who looked just like that relic?'

'Exactly like that, Doctor. My people hope that, through their prayers, they can wake this one up and seek its advice, as in the old days.'

'But it's a handbag!'

'Enough,' she said regally, taking his elbow. 'We have very little time. I fear my people may execute me before you can carry out this mission.'

'Come with me, then, to Earth...'

'I cannot leave them. No, Doctor. You must return to your home and there you must take possession of the machine that belongs to Iris. Then I trust you to find us a new world and help me lead my people there.'

He looked at her kindly. 'You are a very brave young woman.'

He started to bundle his lanky form into the waiting lifepod. 'What about Iris, though?'

Suddenly the Doctor felt a pang of conscience.

He was leaving the old bat on a shipful of religious maniacs and he was nipping off to steal her bus.

If the shoe had been on the other foot, he'd have been livid.

'I will make sure no harm comes to the old woman...'

The Doctor looked into the girl's eyes and didn't believe a word of it.

But by then the noise of the crowd had come very much closer.

And, closest of all, came Iris – screaming and squawking at the top of her voice, charging towards the Doctor and the queen, with the golden bag hidden safely up her jumper.

'Are we off?' she cried, thundering up the pounding floor.

'Yes!' the Doctor replied, beaming.

The girl in the red cloak stepped back and Iris hurled herself bodily into the tiny pod.

There was a shout of pain from the Doctor, but no time to check that nothing had been broken under the impact of the fugitive Iris.

The queen set her strength behind the lifepod door and wedged it heavily shut.

There was a clang and, as she activated the controls, a great hiss and pop... as the capsule was dispatched towards Earth.

She watched it hurtle away, rather sadly.

That was the mother ship's only escape pod.

It was meant for her, as queen.

Now she stood ready and waiting as her newly converted people came bursting into the room, ravenous for the blood of Iris.

Planetfall took several hours and it was dislocating and disorienting, so the two of them weren't quite sure how much time was passing as they tumbled and twirled and banged into each other.

Sound was peculiar too.

Iris's voice was distorted as she howled: 'Look! I got my bag back! It's mine again! Mine!'

In the tiny space, she tried to turn cartwheels and the handbag floated out on its golden straps.

The Doctor was feeling somewhat seasick as they careered towards the south of England and they warmed up dreadfully as they breasted the atmosphere; the capsule tossed into the broiling mass like a stone plopped into the sea.

'Unhand me, madam!'

The Doctor's outraged voice, bursting out in the lofty air as their plummet continued inexorably and he just couldn't agree with Iris that their best bet for not breaking any bones was to squeeze together as close as possible and brace themselves for impact.

'Unhand me, madam!' he yelled again, as the familiar geography rose up, fresh green, to claim them.

Chapter Thirteen
The Order of Things

'But don't you remember exactly what your mother is like?' Jo asked. 'How can you be sure if this is her or not?'

Tom was terribly confused and Jo, though she was trying to be helpful, was making it worse.

They were locked inside the blue room of the Doctor's mansion, with the new daylight coming in rather bleakly through the soft muslin of the draped curtains.

Elsewhere in the house could be heard muffled bangs and curses and cries as the Children of Destiny and the Master went about their business.

The room was a dull blue, a whale blue, and Jo and Tom found themselves swallowed up in it; caught in the must and dust of a house that felt, oddly, as if no one had lived there for decades, and yet it was only a day since its occupants had left, joyfully, excitedly, for their new adventure in their yellow car.

As if a tremendous slice of time had come down, wedging and separating them all.

'When I left my own time,' said Tom, 'something happened to my memory. Iris tried to explain it to me. It was to do with being removed from your own chronological progression through the life of your own world. In actually leaving your time, you become almost someone else. Remade on the spot. Or, rather, you are a kind of frozen version of yourself, but one that will age and die supposedly naturally, but without the input of your own people and your own place.'

He was sitting with his back against the grand golden chair, fingering the purple plush of its cushions and frowning.

He looked, to Jo, much older than his years.

She admitted, 'Well, I've never really gone into the ins and outs of travelling with the Doctor... of what it all might mean...' she gave a self-deprecating chuckle. 'But I wouldn't, would I? I'm usually running about, screaming blue murder because something horrible is happening.'

'But you must feel different,' he insisted, 'to how you felt before. Dislocated, like me. So that your family and friends, the very place you grew up in, all seem distant and only partly familiar to you.'

She bit her lip. 'A little bit, perhaps. Every time I come back to the present day with the Doctor, and realise that we're out of sync again – maybe three months of our time, four days of theirs – then I have a funny reaction. And as for my family... I've hardly ever seen them these last few years.' She shuddered though, as she remembered the spectre of her uncle she had encountered. 'And my friends. I have little to say to Tara when I see her now. She kept finding me staring abstractedly, into space.'

Tom nodded. 'I'm finding I can't tell what's real and what's a nightmare. Are your dreams very vivid, too?'

She nodded firmly.

Tom said slowly, 'The Doctor and Iris have both changed us irrevocably, you know. I don't know if they realise it, but we can never be the same people again. Because of them. I don't think human beings were meant to travel in time. We care too much about the order of things. About being sure of what has really happened and what hasn't. We get insecure if someone shows us other alternatives.'

'If Mary really is your mother,' said Jo, 'would that disturb you?'

'In all likelihood,' said Tom. 'She is. I looked at her face and thought I recognised her from photos of my mother before she gave birth to me. There was a flash of recognition. She even looked amused.'

And, thought Tom; the clincher. The belt his mother had given him when he was a child. She had known all along where he was going to go, and that his journey away from home wouldn't simply end in London.

'The best thing I can do,' said Tom, 'is try and forget about it. Think about Mary on her own terms, unrelated to me. She doesn't know who I am yet. But one day, she will.'

Jo gasped then, as the fat cat made itself apparent, slinking into the room and glaring at them.

'How did it get in here?' she asked. 'They locked both sets of doors on us, didn't they?'

The cat ambled over to Tom and nudged his hand with its oddly dry nose.

Tom snatched his hand back, remembering how the creature had attacked Iris.

The cat coughed and hacked and retched.

Its eyes squinted shut with effort and it coughed again and, at last, spat out a long, copper-coloured key.

Tom blinked. 'That's disgusting!' He turned to Jo in alarm.

Jo snatched the key up. 'On our side after all, puss!'

'How did he do that?' Tom asked.

'The Doctor's been training him,' Jo said happily. 'To get us out of scrapes. He didn't think it had worked, but look!'

'He trained the cat to vomit keys?'

Jo nodded.

'What's wrong with a good old-fashioned sonic screwdriver?'

'I hate all this subterfuge,' the blond boy, Peter, was complaining to Kevin.

In the Doctor's messy laboratory, they were planting evidence.

Laying out cool, expensive, fussy-looking tools.

Setting out the clunky, workmanlike components.

Laying ready the sinister carcasses of half-assembled electronic sheep.

Two completed specimens, lifeless but with their eyes blazing red, stood to attention by the laboratory door.

Peter went on, anxiously, 'I feel like we're doing something wrong. Planting all this ridiculous stuff. It's not the way we do things.'

Kevin found himself defending the Master's plan. 'It's all necessary, Peter.'

'But what do we do usually? Hop right into the villain's den of operations and sort it out. We don't go in for… spying and trickery, like this. I hate the Master making us do things like this. Everything's changed, now.'

'It's a better way of doing things,' Kevin said flatly. 'Surely you can see that? The Doctor is a tricky customer and he'd easily slip through any of our usual traps. The Master has explained it all. We have to be even more subtle and sly than the Doctor is.'

'But these creatures…' Peter looked at the assembled sheep. 'And the ones he's set free to roam the countryside… ridiculous as they are, they're dangerous, aren't they? How can we be sure we're not making it worse?'

Kevin stood back from the bench and surveyed their handiwork. 'Of course we're not. We're just using our psi powers to discredit the Doctor. It's all a great illusion.'

Peter didn't look mollified in the slightest. 'It used to be different. With Destiny's Children, it used to be really clear and obvious who were the good guys and who were the villains. And what about that Tom? You've got him, supposedly joining us, but I haven't noticed anything special about him. He hasn't got the same kind of powers as us at all, has he?'

'There's…' Kevin faltered. 'There's something about him. We need him on this mission, Peter. That's all I can say.'

Peter looked disgusted. 'You're getting as bad as him. The Master. Inscrutable. Telling us what to do.'

Kevin was heading out of the room. 'Let's go and get the girls.'

Marsha was busy with the television in the kitchen.

It was an ancient set, black and white and almost as big as the fridge.

From a pouch in her belt she was producing an alarming array of alien tools and tinkering with the set's tuning.

She was covered in dust and cursing.

Marsha was the team's electronics expert and on a number of occasions she had been responsible for saving their lives – notably in situations when some kind of incendiary device needed disarming and there were only seconds left in which the Children of Destiny could escape from captivity.

Her team-mates were used to taking a back seat when Marsha started on with her tools and, as she hummed away to herself, they knew better than to ask what she was up to.

Mary couldn't contain herself, however.

'The Master seems to need our help. We must hurry.'

Marsha gave the top of the TV set a resounding bang.

She didn't like the way that Mary seemed to be utterly enamoured of that man. Ever since he had arrived in their lives, only weeks ago, Mary had been the one pushing to let him lead them.

'What's he doing?' Marsha asked, running a hand through her hair.

'Half-assembling experiments, all over the house. That fluid silicon creature we picked up on Naxon Four, that's come in useful. It's in a closet on the ground floor, right where it can be found. And the robot Yeti is under the stairs, the Dalek thing in the dining room.'

'He's having a whale of a time, isn't he?'

Mary looked serious. 'He's only doing what's necessary. The Earth authorities need to know the truth about the Doctor's meddling in the course of Earth's evolution. All we're doing is... exaggerating his activities somewhat.'

She looked satisfied at that. Marsha turned away from the buzzing and crackling of the ancient TV set and looked at her friend. She seemed almost like another person.

'I'm not so sure. What do we really know about the Master?'

Mary's mouth twitched into a tired smile. 'He's going to show me the galaxy, he says.'

Marsha tutted. 'You can already see it. You can go anywhere. You're an ambassador to the Federation!'

'He can take me places I've never dreamed of, he said. He's right. What are we? Just children. We've barely imagined the places we could go, or the things we could do out there. We're too busy running around after the Federation to even properly explore...'

'Mary!' Marsha was shocked. Her friend shrugged.

'Anyway, what are you doing to that telly?'

Marsha gave it another thump. 'While we're here and we know for a fact that Iris Wildthyme was here, I'm getting on with a little investigative work for the Federation.'

'You mean, for your precious Ambassador Borges.'

Marsha blushed. 'I'm trying to track down the missing, kidnapped Ambassador. If we can retrace Iris's steps...'

'I don't know how you can fancy that Borges,' Mary shuddered. 'Those protuberances of his...'

'I don't fancy him...'

'You go all funny, every time he comes on that screen.'

'I'm just doing my duty for the Federation,' said Marsha. 'That's all any of us are meant to be doing,' she added, pointedly.

Then, in a burst of static, an image appeared on the screen. Iris was in the kitchen, talking with Tom.

Marsha made a noise of satisfaction and the two girls watched as the speed of the images increased, winding backwards through time.

The fast-moving figures on the screen were ghostly and insubstantial.

'Telepathic traces,' Marsha explained. 'I've tuned into the house itself and I'm trying to go far enough back, through the hours, to see where Iris came from in the first place…'

'Oh, don't give me one of your scientific explanations,' Mary said.

Then they were watching Tom and Iris arriving for the first time in the Doctor's house, moving backwards out of the jemmied French windows, then purposefully tramping down the gravel drive.

Through trees and bushes they were walking backwards and eventually they arrived back in a woven corridor of cedars, not far away, in which waited a double-decker bus.

'Her TARDIS,' grinned Marsha. 'We've found it. That's where the Ambassador will be.'

Mary stepped away. 'We must tell the Master.'

Jo gave a squeal of fright when they walked into the dining room and there was a Dalek waiting there.

'It's fake,' Tom told her. 'Look.'

'But they're real!' she burst out. 'I've seen them!'

Tom shrugged. 'Why are they putting all this junk in here?'

They heard a low voice then, speaking in the hall. They crept towards the open doorway to hear.

'That's Kevin,' hissed Tom.

They listened harder.

'He's phoning the police,' Jo realised.

'It's a tip-off,' said Tom.

By the time Tom was out in the hall, confronting Kevin, the phone call was finished.

Kevin blanched at the sight of the two of them. 'You've got out.'

'What are you doing?' Jo demanded.

At this point the Master emerged from the Doctor's TARDIS, brushing his hands down his immaculate uniform.

'And what are you doing in there?' she shouted.

The Master raised an eyebrow. 'It's filthy in there. A real dog's dinner. Tell me, Miss Grant, have you really flown about the place in that death trap?'

'Why are you bringing the police here?'

'Tell them, Kevin,' said the Master.

'The Doctor has been conducting a number of dangerous experiments over the past few years. We feel that the public ought to be aware of his activities.'

'But...' said Jo. 'He hasn't...'

'Oh, Miss Grant,' said the Master smoothly. 'How can you know that's the truth? You yourself have seen him getting up to all sorts of experiments. Can you really know what he has in his cupboard under the stairs?'

'Shall we show her?' Kevin urged, smiling.

'I think so.' The Master took the handle of the door under the stairs. 'Stand well back. Not you, Miss Grant, or Tom. I want you both to see what the Doctor has under here.'

With that he thrust open the small door.

Inside the small, dark space Jo could make out racks of jars; the kind that people ferment wine in.

An organ floated in each; she caught a glimpse of clawed hands, hearts and brains.

Each was pulsing and flexing with terrible life.

The Master tutted. 'All of this is outlawed by the Federation. The Doctor has been terribly naughty.'

He reached forward gingerly and unstoppered the largest of the jars. There came a crackling of energy from within. One snaky, pale tendril waved out of the lip of the glass.

'With the police on their way,' the Master mused, 'I think it would be interesting, for them and us, to demonstrate exactly how dangerous the Doctor has made his home, stuffing it full of this kind of nasty, nasty paraphernalia.'

As if on cue, the viscous creature flowed out of the jar and began to expand.

It was an evil yellow colour and was accompanied by a poisonous chemical smell.

It was growing before their eyes, its arms flailing and making lunging slashes in the air at Tom and Jo.

Jo screamed.

'Delicious,' said the Master, backing away down the hall. 'I knew you'd scream just then.'

He paused to watch the creature's misshapen head touch the ceiling and press Jo and Tom against the far wall so they were trapped beneath its crackling bulk.

Kevin, his assistant, was pinned behind the cupboard door.

The creature howled in quivering mirth and seemed to gain more control of its many stinking appendages.

As Jo screamed again – somewhat muffled this time – the Master let out a shout of glee and hurried away, outside.

Chapter Fourteen
Space Pods and Cephalopods

How long had it been?

A few years now, at any rate.

Sally had seen some funny old things round here and today was going to be no exception.

Every time there was something funny going on, the Doctor was always involved. He'd come dashing into her shop, all of a flurry and warn her to hide in her cellar or in her attic.

She'd be selling him his paper or putting stamps on a parcel for him and he'd be going on, in all seriousness, about some dreadful catastrophe about to overwhelm the world.

Oh, he was a card all right. He knew she could take a joke, otherwise he wouldn't go telling a poor old woman things that would scare her, would he?

'Honestly, Sally,' he would say. 'I'm only telling you because if the whole place needs evacuating, I know you'd need a little longer to mobilise yourself.'

'Oh, yes?' she'd say. 'And what else was it? A quarter of strawberry bon-bons?'

'Yes, please. You see, I'm actually an alien, exiled to Earth and my presence near your charming little village attracts all kinds of unwarranted attention from the less neighbourly species patrolling this sector of space. I wouldn't like to cause some kind of disaster and not give you fair warning.'

'Uh-huh,' she said. 'Right you are, Doctor. Do you want to take your *Radio Times* now, or shall I send it out with the papers?'

'Oh, just with the papers. Do you see, Sally?'

'You mean, about you working for the United Nations and messing about with alien creatures and all? Oh, yes. Of course.'

Every time he went into her shop he seemed to try his hardest to prove his oddity to her. 'Remember when I was that other chap? The short one with the dark hair?'

She chuckled. 'The little Doctor? The first one who came here?' She shook her head. 'Don't you take the mickey out of an old lady, Doctor. He explained to me what was going on. He said, one day he'd go away and another Doctor would take his place. His brother, or something, that's who you are, aren't you?'

Still and all, this one was a dashing, charming gentleman and it cheered Sally up to have someone so refined coming into the place and chatting her up.

And he was always got up so nicely. He made a real effort dressing up. Not like some round here.

It was flattering to Sally, to have him come in and pass the time of day.

Besides, it gave the other women in the shop something to talk about.

Today was pension day and she had quite a queue at the post office counter.

She was rather hoping that the Doctor would turn up and pass the time with his usual brand of nonsense. Give the old dears something to cluck about.

Once she had asked him, 'And say that all this is true, isn't it all top secret? Why do you warn me and tell me all your secrets, Doctor?' She titivated her hair as she asked this.

'Because...' He smiled. 'Because... perhaps you remind me a little of my mother.'

This hadn't gone down well at all with Sally.

'Well, you cheeky devil! How old do you think I am? I'm only sixty-seven this March! You can't be much younger than that!'

Sally had been scandalised and the Doctor had beaten a hasty retreat out of her shop.

That had been the last time he'd visited, taking milk and newspapers and his usual sweets.

She supposed he was off on one of his hush-hush jaunts, fighting alien monsters and so on.

He was harmless enough and she missed him popping in. They said he had a rather grand old house. She hadn't seen it. An eccentric millionaire, he was.

Quite a catch, really.

The pension queue was even more animated than usual this morning.

When she asked Dolly, who was first, as usual, what was wrong with everyone, she heard the tale of Old Ted, found dead in the woods this morning.

There was something out there, the old people were saying, something unnatural.

Actually, Sally thought, she'd not seen the paper boy, Matthew, yet. He hadn't come back for the rest of the papers. He should have been back hours ago.

The old people were muttering darkly.

Dolly said, 'There's a funny old atmosphere about out there today, Sally. There's definitely something afoot.'

Then she was gone, banging the door to, setting the small bell a-jingle.

Maud, next in queue, slapped her pension book down and declared: 'Old Ned was found burned to a crisp. He was on the Doctor's land. You know. Him. Your fancy man.'

Sally blushed. She knew the old women had taken note of the amount of time the Doctor spent gossiping over the counter with her.

They were interrupted by a squawk of fright from the street.

'Dolly!' someone screamed. The old people jostled and hurried over to stare out of the shop's window.

'It's only sheep,' Maud said gruffly.

But outside, in the quiet street, Dolly was clutching her shopping bag and backing away from the neat column of sheep as they approached her.

There was something altogether too neat about that column of animals.

They moved with deliberate, sinister purpose, and their eyes were glinting a livid red.

'They aren't natural,' gasped one of the old people.

Dolly screamed again, but no one moved to save her.

The sheep closest to her stopped in its tracks.

A bolt of red fire leapt from its eyes and dazzled the spectators for a second.

Then, they could see Dolly in flames and crumpling to the ground.

'It shot her!'

'It fried her on the spot!'

'But it's a sheep!'

They cowered in the shop window as the sheep glided through the village street, turning their evil heads this way and that, moving steadily, sweeping straight over the charred remains of Dolly.

'There's about thirty of them!' gasped Sally.

'They're on castors!'

The Doctor, thought Sally. This is something to do with him. He was right!

The sheep had passed out of sight, by now.

The street was empty apart from what was left of Dolly. Curiously, her pension book lay, hardly singed, on the ground beside her.

Sally opened the door and stepped out into the street.

'You can't go out there!' the pensioners cried.

She shushed them, and cocked her head. There was a heavy silence in the small village.

And then, a whining. Almost like an aeroplane.

Sally looked up to see an arc in the sky.

A white smear against the morning blue. A ragged strip of cloud, through which something was descending at great speed. The noise was getting louder.

'Something's going to crash!' came a scream from behind her.

'Lord love us!'

Sally stared up at the sky and watched as the object came closer.

There was a tremendous roar as it skimmed the rooftops of the village. Everyone clapped their hands to their ears.

And a massive crash as it hit home, at last, on top of the old cinema.

'It's a doodlebug!'

'It's gone right into the bloody picture house!'

'No more bingo!'

Old Arthur had hold of Sally's arm. 'What was it?'

She pulled away and, leaving her shop still open and full of customers, set off at a trot across the village to see.

Whatever it was had punched a hole the size of her whole house into the side of the cinema.

The touch of the creature was surprisingly clammy and cold.

'It's the Blob!' Tom gasped, pressed hard against the wall. 'He's actually unleashed the frigging Blob!'

Kevin grunted, weighed down behind the door as the tentacled thing thrashed and heaved. 'He left me to it! The bastard actually abandoned me!'

'Of course he did,' shouted Jo angrily, with much effort. 'He always does! Can't you see the Master is evil? You're just another pawn, another…'

She screamed again as a tentacle lashed against her face.

'Peter!' Kevin shouted, suddenly struck with inspiration. 'He can help us!' He shouted louder. 'Both of you! Shout for him!'

* * *

On the gravel driveway, pausing between the mildewed statues of a gryphon and a unicorn, the Master looked up at the sky with a frown.

He too had seen the small craft crash-land in the village.

This was unforeseen. Someone was meddling and it wasn't him.

Still, he had work to do.

The small phial, in his jacket pocket. An outlawed unguent he had picked up some time ago. One he knew would come in useful.

He held it up so it glittered against the sun and, as he twisted it round, he thought he could see the colours of the moon. It was a life form of a most peculiar sort.

When it came into contact with any insentient material it would, effectively, bring it to life.

The Master actually despised clichéd metaphors of this kind, but in the case of this rare and terribly useful life form, these phrases were quite apt.

He shrugged and poured a tiny amount on to the knee of the unicorn, the chest of the gryphon.

Anything to keep the police busy when they arrived.

He didn't even wait to see the spell begin its work. He made towards the trees, where he sprinkled some more of his miraculous potion.

And here he bumped straight into the two Earth girls.

'Master!' cried Mary and, he had to admit, there was something rather pleasing in the way she addressed him. 'We've found it!'

'You've found what, my dear?' He wasn't sure if he was quite as pleased with the way that events were unfolding out of his control.

'The bus belonging to that awful old woman! It isn't far from here!'

The Master's eyes glittered.

* * *

The bus was precisely where Iris had left it.

A reassuring, oblong, cherry-red shape, nestled in the heart of the woodlands.

'I wonder,' said the Master, 'whether my key will work?'

He made for the doors.

'Oh, do hurry,' said Marsha. 'The Ambassador might be trapped aboard! She might even have killed him already!'

The doors whooshed gently open under the Master's gentle command.

The atmospheric lighting aboard clicked on and the air filled with a hum of activity.

The Master stepped aboard.

'You'd think this place had been bombed!'

Already a small crowd had gathered around the cinema. Sally found herself pushing through to the front, glad that the police hadn't arrived yet to erect barriers.

The whole front of the building had been demolished. Whatever the object from the sky had been, it had flown straight in through the front.

Chunks of rubble and masonry littered the street.

The glowing sign advertising *The Exorcist* in its thirtieth week and Thursday bingo lay on the path, hissing and sparking and shorting out.

Sally skirted carefully around it and, taking her life in both her trembling hands, stepped inside the perilous wreck of the picture house.

She remembered coming here in the war, watching newsreels of the Blitz and seeing wreckage of exactly this type.

This had always been a quiet village then, even in the war.

She had a sudden premonition that she was going to die in this building. What was she even doing here?

In the auditorium: a tremendous, ponderous silence.

Like the calm before the storm.

There was a creaking and groaning, as if the roof was wondering whether to cave in, once and for all.

The seats were strewn, ripped out of their sockets. It was a wasteland of cushions and plush.

The massive screen was rent in two.

On the remains of the stage was a steaming, egg-shaped object. It wasn't quite as big as Sally had been expecting. But it was big enough.

Gouts of steam were rising off it. She hoped it wasn't a bomb.

Somehow she knew, though, as she hobbled through the ruined auditorium towards the stage area, that it wasn't a bomb.

She knew what it was, and her heart lifted up at the confirmation of all his wild tales.

A hatchway, dark and mysterious, slid open in the side of the egg.

'Doctor?' asked Sally hesitantly. Then she said, with more confidence: 'Doctor... is that you?'

From the wreckage he jumped up unscathed.

He was standing there on top of the capsule, his velvet cape streaming out behind him.

'Sally?' he asked. 'I've just landed from space.'

He was joined by an elderly woman, who looked rather more shaken than he did. The feather in her hat was broken and hanging askew.

'I always knew you were telling the truth, Doctor,' said Sally.

'I've made rather a mess of the place, haven't I?' he grinned ruefully.

Then he came hurrying over the rubble and the broken-back chairs. He put an arm around Sally.

'Let's get out of this place, shall we, my dear? Before it all falls down around our ears?'

Sally was gazing up at him. 'I knew you were real! I just knew it!'

They headed for the exit.

Behind them, Iris was beside herself with anger. 'Will one of you bloody well help me down, please?'

Peter came down the staircase at a run, saw what was going on downstairs and turned white.

'Help us!' yelled Kevin. 'Those guns we put in the bathroom! Fetch one!'

'Guns!' cried Jo, and yelped as the creature pushed her even further back against the wall.

There was a loud banging on the door, down the hall.

'It's the police!' came a gruff voice.

'Christ,' said Tom.

Peter reappeared on the stairs with a rather bulky, futuristic-looking device. Jo was shocked.

'You were planting that thing in the Doctor's bathroom?' she accused Kevin.

Peter activated the device and the creature was suffused with a deadly orange glow. It screamed fit to burst.

Its flailed and sent out tentacles to grab the weapon from Peter's grasp.

'It's working!' cried Kevin as the hefty bulk of the creature retreated and shrivelled, concentrating its energies on wresting the weapon from the grasp of the boy on the stairs. 'Keep firing, Peter!'

Sweating, Peter kept his finger down on the trigger and tried to ignore the screams and the globular arms reaching out for him. It was pulsing with energy.

'It really is going to burst!' Jo shouted.

'Police!' came the cry at the door again.

'Down!' Tom yelled, dragging Jo and Kevin with him as the noise and the pulsating light reached maximum pitch.

There was a blinding flash, in which they buried their heads in the rucked-up Turkish carpet.

When they looked up again, in silence, the creature, the staircase and Peter himself had all been burned to ashes.

'Peter!' gasped Kevin. 'What have we done?'

'They've killed each other,' Tom said quietly.

'But that's never happened before! Destiny's Children can't die! It just doesn't happen!'

Jo was bitterly practical. 'It has now, Kevin.'

She rounded on him. 'Do you see, now, what it means to be working for the Master? He doesn't care about any of you. He's only interested in his own ends.'

The door caved in then, splintering and crashing under external pressure.

The police came storming in, armed and booted, led by the flustered, heavily panting figure of Sergeant Dobbs.

He regained his bearings and fixed his beady eye on Jo.

'You lot again!' he moaned.

The Master was carefully examining the dashboard of the bus.

When he reached out to prise open a particular panel, a small electric shock caught him by surprise. He cursed and sucked his fingers.

'Touchy,' he coaxingly addressed the bus. 'Now, you don't only answer to Iris, do you?'

There came a low growl, from the very fabric of the driver's cab itself, as if to tell him that was exactly what the bus did.

Mary and Marsha came thudding down the stairwell.

'There's no one up there,' Mary informed him.

'It's just a load of old junk,' Marsha added. 'Old furniture and racks of clothes and lots of old books.'

'Old books, hm?' asked the Master distractedly. 'Those will be Iris's journals. You could find out an awful lot about the cosmos from those, you know. She's been everywhere.'

Mary looked smug. 'I don't need to, do I? You're going to show me the universe, aren't you?'

He dismissed her with a look. 'There are more important things to attend to here. We now have possession of the old hag's TARDIS. Don't you see what that means?'

'It's just an old bus,' said Marsha.

'Hang on a second,' said Mary. 'You promised me! You said, when all this was over and we were through doing the dirty on the Doctor, you would take me away from Earth... you'd show me the whole galaxy... I would join you aboard your TARDIS and...'

The Master strolled leisurely up the gangway towards the furious Mary and placed his hands on her shoulders.

He stroked her hair and Marsha hardly knew how Mary could stand it.

'I haven't got a TARDIS,' he said gently. 'Not of my own. That's why I was so pleased to get into this one.'

'But you said you had!' cried Mary. 'You're the Master! Of course you've got a TARDIS! You're a Time Lord from Gallifrey, just the same as the Doctor, and...'

The Master shook his head sadly. 'I am awfully sorry to disillusion you, my dear. That isn't who I am at all.'

Marsha was backing away. 'Who are you, then?'

The Master threw back his head and filled the bus with the reverberations of a chilling, guttural laugh. As he did so, all the flesh on his body seemed to wither and melt away.

The two girls stared in horror as he was left standing, naked, his flesh turned a livid, metallic green.

His head was almost featureless, impassive; a statue's unfinished face.

A slit of a mouth through which that ghastly, mirthless laugh still echoed and two horrible emerald, burning eyes.

'I am Verdigris,' the figure said, and didn't elaborate.

Chapter Fifteen
In the Forest!

The crowd outside the ruined cinema was too good an opportunity for the sheep to miss.

Between them they had very little sentience or volition. They certainly had no conscience. All they had had programmed into their limited brains was a desire to cause as much havoc as possible.

That was all their master had allotted them.

Fuelled by this malicious desire and propelled by the collective psionic force borrowed from Destiny's Children, the sheep had been unleashed upon the unsuspecting, drowsy countryside to create a certain amount of mayhem.

Their instructions were to cause a great big fuss and then return, *en masse*, to the Doctor's house, in time for the police to put two and two together.

The crowd outside the cinema lured them and it wasn't long before the sheep were mowing hysterical bystanders down.

They wheeled implacably, squealing away, into the heart of the crowd, frazzling villagers on the spot.

When the Doctor, Iris and Sally emerged blinking from the wreckage, into the square, it was into a scene of sheepish carnage.

'Jehosaphat!' cried the Doctor.

'Beelzebub!' cursed Iris.

She balked at the sight of those thin black faces and their crimson eyes. 'Jo wasn't talking rubbish after all! There really are such things as robot sheep!'

Sally was moaning. 'They're killing everyone! They murdered Dolly and now they're getting everyone!'

'They killed Dolly?' cried the Doctor. He'd been rather fond of the ill-tempered spinster from the bookie's.

'What are we going to do?' Iris asked.

'Run!' And with that the Doctor urged them into a street, into an area through which the sheep had already made a clean sweep.

'I can't run!' Sally gasped, hanging on to his cloak. 'I haven't got the legs for running any more!'

She was hanging on to the pair of them, holding them back.

Ahead, among the scores of scorched bodies of villagers, the sheep were suddenly getting wind of the escapees.

They swivelled around and glowered malevolently. One of them even pawed the ground with its castor as it made ready to charge. The tiny wheel squeaked horribly.

Iris swore profusely. 'Give the old bag a piggyback, Doctor!'

Sally found herself being heaved over his shoulder as they set off, full pelt again, up a side street.

'They're following!' she gasped, feeling she was being jogged to death, craning round her spindly neck to see the black-faced horrors coming up the cobbled lane after them.

They had the faces of the very devil himself!

The Doctor wheezed: 'If we can get into the woods, we can probably shake them off. I know my way round pretty well, there. We can get back to the house and...'

Iris put on a new burst of speed. 'They're gaining on us!'

Downstairs, the Doctor's house was in uproar.

Sergeant Dobbs had placed the three youngsters under immediate arrest.

In a whispered aside, Kevin let it be known to the other two that he could transport himself away in the blink of an eye, and it was only out of consideration for them that he stuck around.

Tom could see, though, how shocked he still was at Peter's death. Suddenly all bets were off.

The universe that the Children of Destiny lived in was no longer a sure and relatively safe place to be.

Dobbs had his notebook out and was huffing and puffing at them rather pompously. 'We've had reports of all sorts going on round here. If you three are at all involved in the activities we suspect of occurring on these premises then I would advise you all to behave very, very advisedly just now.'

'What?' Tom asked.

'He means, shut up and keep still,' Jo said. 'Policemen always talk like that.'

Dobbs glared at her. 'Pretty girl like you. What are you doing messing about with the likes of this Doctor, eh?'

She played dumb and glared back at him. Then a thought struck her and she said, 'What are you doing here anyway? Your village is miles from here. You aren't the local bobby.'

'Oh,' said Dobbs. 'I had my suspicions about your Doctor before, when he came running into my station over that odd business with the railway carriages. I've made it my business to follow up this particular line of enquiry. At first I just thought he was a bit touched in the head, but it's all a lot more serious than that now, isn't it? Eh? What's he been up to, this strange old fella, eh? You can tell me.'

Jo pulled a face. Dobbs revolted her. 'I'd rather get locked up than say anything to you.'

He tugged on his horrible moustache. 'What about your boyfriend here, then?'

'Boyfriend!' said Tom.

'Are you going to spill the beans, my son?'

'Go to hell,' Tom said.

'Sarge!' One of the officers who had been checking out the other rooms came thudding back into the hallway. 'You'd better come and look at what we found.'

'Ah,' said Dobbs in triumph.

'It's a regular house of horrors, Sarge.'

Dobbs nodded and took a deep breath. 'Then you'd better hurry up and find some ladders, hadn't you, lad, and see what the old devil's got upstairs, eh?'

'Verdigris?' Marsha asked. 'But who... what are you?'

The tall, impassive figure surveyed her coolly. 'You needn't worry. This isn't just one more disguise. This is the real me. Underneath all of the costumes. This is the face of the person you have been helping.'

Mary looked stricken. 'All this time... you were just some ghastly alien...'

Verdigris looked almost amused. 'Ghastly alien? Is that any way for an ambassador to the Federation to talk?'

'Probably not,' said Marsha, giving Mary a look. Then she remembered something. 'What did you mean, anyway, about knowing that the Master had a TARDIS and was a Time Lord, the same as the Doctor?'

Mary sighed heavily. 'They both are. Well, the Doctor is.'

'But you said he was a human! A madman! A liar.'

Mary shrugged and folded her arms.

'So what the Doctor is doing... isn't wrong?' gasped Marsha. 'He was in the right all along?'

Mary shrugged again as if to say, 'It isn't worth discussing now'.

'What have we done?' shouted Marsha. 'What have you made us do? All along we've been helping this... thing!'

Verdigris reached out with one cold, massive hand and seized her wrist as she pointed at him. She gasped out in pain.

'You two are boring me.'

He grabbed Mary likewise and, dragging both girls together like rag dolls, flung them out of the bus.

They landed heavily on the rough road.

'Out into the woods, you go,' he said, a dry, green tongue licking over the lipless edge of his gash of a mouth. 'Go and see what's out there waiting for you.'

As Mary and Marsha heaved themselves to their feet, the bus's hydraulic doors folded shut.

At the top of the hill, where the woods began, the Doctor paused for a much-needed breather.

Iris was already haring pell-mell into the close confines of the dark trees.

'I think we've shaken them off,' Sally said.

'Wait for us, Iris,' the Doctor barked.

'The trees look... gloomier somehow...' Sally murmured. 'Darker and bigger and...'

The Doctor nodded. 'I thought that, too.'

From ahead, Iris gave a horrible scream.

'Iris!'

They caught up with her, to find her flailing in the grasp of black, rattling branches. She was caught up in their witches' fingers and struggling hard.

'We've got to tell the others,' Marsha said, limping along through the woods.

Mary was leading the way back to the house.

'You have to, Mary! You have to tell them all that what we were doing was wrong!'

'Was it so wrong?' Mary rounded on her fiercely, making Marsha jump.

'Of course it was! Nothing was what it seemed! It was Verdigris the whole time, whoever he was... making us do things... abusing our telepathic powers!'

'Perhaps the Doctor really does need bringing down,' Mary said. 'Perhaps that bit was true.'

Marsha tried to put her weight on her ankle, which she'd hurt being flung out of the bus. She gasped. 'Didn't you sense the evil in Verdigris? Could you really have trusted him if you'd known that at the beginning?'

'Evil?' Mary asked. She looked like she was going to laugh. 'Don't tell me you believe in "evil" as some kind of abstract, intractable quality that can possess a whole person or being?'

'What?'

'Don't you just believe in acts and attributes? Or in vastly generalised insensate qualities?'

'I'm not having a debate about relativism now! Get a grip, Mary. Look, the sky has gone dark!'

Mary looked around and seemed, for the first time, to be a little afraid. The branches about them rattled and twitched.

'The whole place has come to life,' Marsha said. 'As if something terrible has woken up…'

'Come on.' With surprising strength Mary took hold of her friend and dragged her through the undergrowth until they came within sight of the large house. Both girls stopped dead at the sight of the creatures guarding the entrance to the mansion.

'Verdigris must have given them life!' Marsha said. 'He must have!'

There was a great battle in progress on the drive. The darkened air was alive with the crashing of stone on stone, and from the bodies of the combatants arose clouds of dust and crumbling masonry. The gryphon and the unicorn were locked in deadly battle, pounding their bodies against each other and blocking the entrance to the house.

'This is madness,' Mary said, hardly knowing what to expect next.

The main doorway opened then and the police stumbled out, seeming just as appalled at the grand spectacle.

They stared as the unicorn attempted to gore his enemy with his marble horn.

The gryphon, caught unawares, waved its massive paws feebly in the air and let out a stricken howl.

At last it fell, heavily to the ground and smashed into a thousand pieces.

The unicorn jumped up on to its hindlegs, whinnying in triumph.

Then it turned to see Dobbs and the policeman watching in the doorway.

It flared its beautifully carved nostrils, reared up once more, and charged…

'Doctor!'

Sally was caught up too, now, in the twitching arms and fingers of the trees.

The Doctor hardly knew where to turn, caught between the shrieks of the two women.

On balance he decided that Iris was the better equipped to withstand the torture for longer, so he concentrated on freeing the trapped newsagent.

'Oh, that's right!' growled Iris. 'Free your fancy woman first! Go on! Just leave me to die! Pulled apart by evil bloody trees!'

He was hunting through his pockets and at last found what he was looking for.

'What have you got?' gasped Sally, and started shrieking again, as the trees tried to pull her up into the air.

Vines clawed their way down through the crepuscular air and she felt them writhe all over her.

The more she struggled the worse it became.

'Fireworks,' said the Doctor simply. He struck neatly at his tinderbox and watched in satisfaction as the fuse caught light. 'It's been a very, very dry summer this year.'

With that he tossed the fizzing missile into the thickest, thorniest congregation of branches.

An explosion.

Showers of golden and azure sparks.

An ululating shrieking as if every tree had grown lungs, deep inside their trunks, in order to express their pain.

The Doctor's face darkened in satisfaction as he sent more

and more of the fireworks spinning into the dark of the woods.

He watched the dry wood take light and the small, then larger and brighter flames lick around the delicious wood.

The branches that held his friends whipped themselves into a frenzy of terror, causing even more damage than before.

'You'll burn us all!' Iris howled in pain. 'If they don't flail us to death first!'

Choking fumes were filling the glade as the flames rose higher.

The Doctor made a grab for Sally's arm and tried to drag her out of the mesh of branches. 'I'm stuck! I'm completely stuck!' She started to cough and cry at the same time.

Iris had been rather luckier and her branches were withdrawing themselves as the tree they belonged to gave up the ghost and relinquished itself to the blaze.

She hurried over to the Doctor and, between them, they wrenched the old woman from her cage of thorned branches.

'We have to hurry,' said the Doctor. 'Before the whole blazing thing crashes down on top of us…'

Jo couldn't believe the impact.

Once more she found herself lying on the floor of the hallway, pressing her hands to her ears.

This time she was lying among rubble and dust, as the unicorn flung itself again and again against the portico of the house, as if attempting to bring the whole edifice down, crashing down around their ears.

It would succeed, too, if it was allowed to continue.

Tom and Kevin lay beside her, shouting at each other and she could hardly hear a word.

She tried not to look at the trampled and bleeding bodies of the policemen that the stone creature had crushed.

With each new charge the unicorn was damaging them beyond all recognition.

Dobbs was cowering in the dark space where the staircase had once been.

'Call it off! Call it off!' he shrieked. 'This is your Doctor's doing! He's behind all this, isn't he?'

Jo wanted to tell him that no, the Doctor wasn't.

There had to be someone else behind this. But right now she found that consciousness was slipping away from her as the great house shook under the impact of the remorseless onslaught.

And outside, the woods had taken light and were churning great black clouds into the sky.

Chapter Sixteen
Iris Puts Out the Flames

Wooden fingers were slashing and prying blindly through the choking, fuming air as they stumbled onwards through the perilous undergrowth.

The place became more lethal than ever as the trees were consumed by flame and thrashed in their final, arboreal agonies.

Desperately the Doctor was attempting to find the road, which would be clearer, and where the two women under his charge would be safer.

Iris, however, pulled ahead and led them in a slightly different direction.

Caught up in protecting Sally, he could hardly argue, but he wanted to shout out to Iris and demand to know where she was leading them.

Here.

The bus sat calmly in the heaving chaos of the woods.

'My bus!' she bellowed through the murky air. 'We'll be safe aboard the bus!'

'A bus?' muttered Sally thickly.

'She's right,' said the Doctor. 'Come on!'

'We'll be killed aboard that! What's so safe about that? We'll be roasted like... chickens!' But Sally struggled to follow them nevertheless.

Iris stopped in her tracks as she saw the looming green figure guarding the doors to her precious vehicle.

'I am Verdigris,' he said simply. She saw that viscid green tears were coursing down his weathered, oily face.

'Verdigris?' she said, as if some memory were stirring, deep within her.

The Doctor stopped abruptly at her side. 'The green man!' he shouted hoarsely. 'The Queen of the Meercocks said that they had been misled by the green man!'

Verdigris turned to the Doctor with a curious expression. 'So, Doctor. It is you.' He sounded almost sad.

'How do you know who I am?' the Time Lord demanded.

'I have known of you for a very, very long time,' said the tall figure, and this time there was no mistaking the sorrow in his voice.

'Verdigris, Verdigris,' muttered Iris, clutching her handbag to her chest. 'Where have I heard that before?'

'No matter now,' said Verdigris.

'What is that thing?' gasped Sally.

Verdigris ignored her. 'I suppose this burning of the forest is down to you, Doctor. As resourceful as ever, I see.'

'I'm ashamed to say it was me, yes. But there was no other way.'

The creature nodded. 'I knew you wouldn't come to any harm.'

'You brought the trees to life!' burst Iris. 'You're behind this whole thing!'

Verdigris shook his head balefully at her. 'Iris. You never learn, do you?'

And with that, he drained of all life and colour.

For a moment his impressive silhouette hovered in the air as his words resounded around them: 'This has gone on for long enough. There have been too many deaths. My mission is almost complete but I have been too extreme in my methods. I fear there will be worse carnage before the day is through.'

Then he was gone.

Iris jolted into life. 'On the bus, quickly!'

The burning trees were massing at their backs. The Doctor and Sally didn't need telling twice.

* * *

Verdigris had gone and left the pawns in his game to get on with it, but his malign influence hadn't deserted the forms of the creatures he had inhabited.

The unicorn still flung itself, over and over at the front of the Doctor's house, still attempting to widen the doorway.

And the sheep were still squealing and wheeling their way home. They were crunching speedily up the drive.

Until they came within sight of the marble horse.

They paused, appraising the threat that the impossible beast represented to them.

Their limited mechanical minds ruminated briefly over their chances, but their objective was clear. They had been told to repair to this building and there await their master.

They massed then, forming a rough semi-circle around the doorway.

The unicorn paused in its act of demolition and whirled in surprise to see the creatures confront him.

As one, the sheep blazed their eyes at him.

The unicorn reared up and shrieked (a noise like falling masonry; like bombs dropping into a cinema) and glowed red in the blast from those eyes.

The sheep depleted their power packs, forcing blast upon blast into the marble horse's quivering flanks.

They narrowed their crimson eyes and gave it everything they had.

The unicorn seemed, for a second, to withstand their combined might.

Then he twitched once, his stone eyes widened fractionally and he exploded into a ton of marble dust that hung, in a white cloud, for a second.

In the hallway, Jo Grant could hardly believe her eyes.

The unicorn was gone.

But the devil sheep she had seen in what she'd thought was a dream had come after her.

They powered themselves up, snickering with satisfaction, and trundled unhurriedly towards the entranceway and the human beings within.

'Tom! Kevin!' she shrieked. 'They're here!'

Kevin scrambled through the masonry and brick dust to see what she was yelling about. Not for the first time, he went white.

'They're not meant to be doing this! They were only meant to scare people!'

Tom punched him. 'They're frigging well scaring me, for a start!'

The sheep were trundling closer.

'Stop them!' Tom yelled at Jo.

Then, suddenly, Kevin was standing up.

'She can't. But I can.'

'Kevin!' cried Jo. 'Be careful...!'

But he was staring the sheep straight in their savage, ruby eyes.

'I command you to stop,' he said in a level tone.

Iris made sure they were safely installed and stalling in the coruscating maw of the vortex before she jumped out from the driver's cab to give the Doctor a piece of her mind.

But the Doctor was staring transfixed at the undulating whorls of the purple corridor outside.

Beside him, Sally's eyes were almost popping out of her head. She sat down heavily on the chaise longue, hardly able to credit what she was seeing, nor credit what she had undergone in the last little while.

'I haven't been here for so long, Iris,' the Doctor said in a small, tired voice. 'You don't realise what it's like to be divorced from your natural element.'

'Hm,' she said.

'All of this!' he cried, throwing up his arms. 'The vortex!

That's where I belong! Not some third-rate planet in the middle of nowhere! Oh, I'm fond of the Earth and all, and I've got very good reason to be… but until now, seeing all of this again, this whole corridor of time, I hadn't really realised how I missed being free.'

'Well,' Iris said. 'That said, what are we going to do about the Earth? Hm? Something pretty dire has been unleashed.'

'Yes, well,' said the Doctor. 'All in a day's work, I expect.'

She shook her head and ran her fingers through her sooty hair. 'I can't help thinking there's something else to this. Something I'm not remembering right.'

He gave a rumpled grin. 'I'm sure it will come back to you, old thing. Now, what say we pilot this old tub of yours back to my house and see what's going on there, hm? That's as good a place to start as any.'

'Old tub?' she said, with a frown.

The Doctor started ticking things off on his fingers. 'Let's see. We've got the disappearance of all UNIT personnel, excluding the Brigadier, and Mike Yates, who has turned into a cardboard shadow of his former self, we've got a spacecraft full of very irate, handbag-worshipping aliens hovering above the planet, we've got a forest of deadly trees on fire, a mysterious green man who seems to be our sworn enemy, and, on the other hand, we've got killer robot sheep and the safety of Jo and Tom to account for. Is that a fair summary?'

Sally was staring at him in awe. The Doctor winked at her.

The old rake! Iris thought and said: 'Yes, Doctor. That seems to about cover it.'

'The thing I'm worrying about,' he said, 'is that Jo and Tom will have gone back to the house, once we… ahm… left them in Great Yarmouth. The Brigadier might be there, too. I don't like the idea of them in the middle of that conflagration, what with those deadly sheep around and everything. So shall we shake a leg and see to it, old thing?'

Then he sat back on a plump settee to enjoy the ride as Iris seethed back into the driver's cab and did as she was told.

She still hadn't managed to tell him off for not putting her safety first in all the recent hullabaloo.

Could he really prefer that raddled old hag from the village to her?

'You stopped them!' Tom breathed. 'You actually managed to stop them!'

He watched as Kevin lowered his upraised arms and cautiously opened his eyes again.

The sheep had halted in their tiny tracks and the lights in their vicious eyes had died away.

Jo felt herself start to breathe again and the panic ebbed out of her limbs. She rounded on Kevin angrily.

'You were controlling them all the time! You must have been!'

Kevin shook his head. 'Not quite, Jo. I was merely co-operating. The Master was using my telepathic powers, alongside his own, to bring life to the beasts. He couldn't have done it without my co-operation.'

'But they're lethal!' said Tom. 'You've been helping him employ deadly weapons, Kevin.'

'I can see that now.' Sadly, Kevin surveyed the wreckage of the house and the squashed and trampled remains of the policemen. 'He lied to us. He said that the Doctor was the killer. He was the one that ought to be stopped.'

'At least you've seen the way things are now,' Tom said. 'At least...'

'Kevin!' came a cry from across the lawn.

'It's Marsha and Mary,' he said, as they approached at a run.

'We've got to get away!' Marsha was yelling. 'We've got to transmat away from here! The woods are on fire!'

'We can't!' Kevin said, as the girls came running up. 'We haven't got enough power to take Tom and Jo with us.'

Marsha swore.

'Where's the Master?' asked Kevin grimly, taking charge.

'He's not the Master,' Mary said. 'Someone else. Some kind of creature. He was in disguise the whole time. I'm not even sure who we were working for.'

A quavering voice spoke from behind them, back inside the gloom of the building. 'You'd better not be working for anyone now,' it said.

They turned to see the battered, bleeding form of Sergeant Dobbs confronting them.

He was on his feet and holding some kind of futuristic-looking weapon with lights blinking on it. It was trained on them but shaking wildly in his grasp.

'He must be an alien!' Jo cried.

'Why?' asked Tom.

'That gun thing isn't from this era!'

Dobbs shook his head. 'I found this left on the telephone table.'

'Oh,' said Jo.

'Now get back in here,' Dobbs went on, 'so I can see you all.'

'Dobbs,' said Tom, 'we haven't got time to mess around. Didn't you hear? There's a forest fire out there…'

'And,' put in Marsha, 'some kind of evil green creature behind all this…'

Dobbs's voice came out rather strained and high-pitched. 'I'm not having any more of your nonsense, you lot! You just start listening to me!'

Jo stepped forward and he waggled the gun in what he hoped was a threatening manner.

He produced a filthy handkerchief and wiped his soggy brow. 'Now, don't you come any closer…'

'Sergeant Dobbs,' said Jo gently. 'We're still in a great deal of danger. We haven't got time to all make statements and what have you. You really must listen to us.'

He snarled, 'Ever since I started listening to you lot, the whole world has gone mad! Look! All my lovely boys are dead! Killed by that... that thing, whatever it was!'

'A unicorn,' said Tom helpfully.

'And those sheep!' gasped Dobbs. 'Where did they come from?'

Jo kept her voice steady and comforting, using the best of her Ministry know-how.

'I promise, Sergeant Dobbs. I really promise you – there'll be nothing more bizarre or inexplicable or frightening happening here. We just have to put our heads together and get ourselves out of danger before the house burns down.'

'Do you promise?' he asked, his voice almost like a child's. 'Do you promise that there'll be nothing more bizarre?'

She nodded and took a step forward, reaching for his gun. The others drew back.

Jo said calmly, 'I absolutely promise, Sergeant Dobbs.'

He blinked and seemed about to take her word for it.

Then, with a tremendous wheezing, groaning sound, a crimson double-decker bus manifested itself on the front lawn.

Dobbs yelped, dropped his gun and sunk to his knees. 'You promised! You promised!'

Then he lay down on the grimy, rubble-strewn floor, apparently unconscious.

Tom had set off at a run towards the bus. 'Iris!' he was shouting, delightedly.

'Wait!' Mary called. 'It might be Verdigris! He was on that bus the last time we...'

'Verdigris?' asked Kevin.

'He's the one behind this,' said Marsha.

'And he really wasn't the Master?' Jo couldn't believe it. Very rare was the humanity-threatening affair in which the Master wasn't involved.

They hurried after Tom, who was pounding on the bus doors.

The doors shot open and, dishevelled, soot-encrusted and jarred still from the impact of planetfall, out stepped Iris Wildthyme.

Her hair was wilder than ever and she was trembling ever so slightly as Tom grasped her up in a huge hug.

'Ah, bless you!' she croaked and let him whirl her about a bit. She turned to the Doctor. 'See? Some people are pleased to see me!'

The Doctor grinned. 'Hullo, Jo. Who are all your friends?'

Destiny's Children drew back in instinctive dread at the rather suave sight of their declared enemy.

'Go on,' goaded Jo. 'Tell him!'

The Doctor glanced away and at the burning treetops around his home.

'Goodness. I'd never have thought the woods would burn so quickly. What have I done?' He looked sadly at his house. 'Who on Earth has smashed the old homestead up?'

'It's a long story,' said Tom.

'It's all going to burn down,' said the Doctor. 'My house. Everything.'

But, as it happened, Iris had an idea.

She urged everyone aboard the bus. 'Honestly, I can put the whole lot out. Every single flame. Just you leave it to me!'

Jo Grant stepped aboard the bus, fully expecting to experience the usual *frisson* of stepping into a transdimensional ship.

She was waiting to hear the others gasp in amazement and dismay at the vast, glowing space of the TARDIS within the London bus shell.

But it never came.

She looked around and was rather startled to find herself aboard the interior of a London bus. It was done up quite nicely, with curtains and chintz and Art Nouveau objects, but the dimensions were still a shock to the system.

'But it's the same size on the inside as on the out!' she said.

Everyone looked at her.

The Doctor turned to Iris. 'What's your plan?'

'Ehm,' came Sally's voice as the others sat down, making her budge up. 'Who is everybody, exactly?'

'Sergeant Dobbs!' burst Kevin suddenly. 'We've left him out there! He'll get burned.'

Iris was busy at the controls. 'Honestly, no one's going to get burned up! Now, listen. In the kitchen at the back of this bus I've got a water tank with enough water in it to fill the Great Lakes of Canada!'

'But how?' asked Jo. 'How could you fit all that in…' She blinked. 'Oh. I see. Carry on.'

Iris scowled. 'Oh, anyway. I'll just get on with it. If I can just materialise over the woods and kind of whiz about a bit through the air… we can whoosh hundreds of millions of gallons of water all about the place…'

'Fantastic!' Tom grinned.

She winked at him. 'Tom, do you want to see to the immersion tank and see that the bus becomes horribly incontinent at just the right moment?'

'Aye aye, Captain Iris!' he beamed, and shoved his way through the crowd of passengers to be ready at his post.

'I'm revving her up!' Iris shouted, flinging herself into the driving seat. 'We're off to save your precious house, Doctor!'

Sergeant Dobbs came to very slowly.

Very gradually he opened his eyes on the devastated house.

He could smell smoke from burning trees. Well, that wasn't too bizarre. That was a fairly ordinary catastrophe.

Nothing he couldn't handle.

He sat up. Where had all those strange kids gone?

They'd left him alone in the middle of a burning wood!

And his men! His men were dead.

And where was that bus that had arrived mysteriously out of nowhere?

He glanced around, still fearful of what might happen next.

He had to get out. He had to get away. He had to leave before the flames came any...

And then, as if it was a sign from the heavens that everything was all right again and nothing in the least bit peculiar would ever happen to Sergeant Dobbs again, it began to rain.

Heavily. Great big drops of cold rain.

Clouds of black smoke and steam gushed from the woods as, almost immediately, the flames began to die down.

Rain! He was saved!

If it was a miracle he hoped it was a very ordinary miracle.

He was saved!

It rained harder and harder and Dobbs took off his helmet to look at the sky with gratitude.

Immediately he wished that he hadn't.

In all the clouds of smoke and steam and through the teeming rain itself he saw exactly the kind of thing he didn't want to see.

The red double-decker bus was riding the storm like winged Pegasus; bucking bronco through the stormy, turbid air above.

He stared in horror.

It seemed that the bus itself was actually causing the downpour that was saving his life.

Poor, beleaguered, oh-so-rational Sergeant Dobbs would have to live to thank a double-decker bus for saving his life.

He crashed to his knees once again.

And then the fish began to fall.

Chapter Seventeen
In the Newsagent's

The village had calmed down somewhat in the past few hours.

The cinema had been cordoned off and the inhabitants spent quite some time going over the remains of their dead. They weren't entirely sure who was who.

The few stray sheep left behind to cause havoc in the village were also quite dead.

A double-decker bus was standing parked beside Sally Northspoon's newsagent's but, so odd had the day been so far, no one really remarked on the fact.

Inside her shop, a somewhat battered and worn-out-looking Sally was pleased to be sitting at her counter again with a cup of tea, and the usual ranks of sweet jars and cigarettes displayed around her.

She looked at the company around her as they drank their tea in thoughtful quiet and supposed that the fact that they were here with her meant that the last few hours really had happened.

Outside, beyond the village, the woods were soaked and scorched black.

And, according to the Doctor and Iris, there was a spaceship the size and shape of St Pancras looming high above them all.

Still, it was nice to know that the Doctor was the real thing.

He winked at her. 'We'll have to go in a minute, Sally,' he said, pushing his cup and saucer on to a pile of her papers. He spilled some tea on to the *Daily Mirror*, but she didn't say anything. 'We've got the rest of this peculiar business to sort out. Thanks for the tea.'

'The rest of the business!' she said, raising an eyebrow. 'Haven't you had enough for one day?'

'Oh, no,' he smiled. 'Never.'

'Doctor!' said Jo, almost choking on her custard cream as she was struck by a thought. 'What about the TARDIS?'

'What about it, Jo?'

'Well, in all that chaos, do you think it's all right?'

'Oh,' he said. 'She's pretty indestructible, you know. Like me!'

Iris laughed. 'Yes, I remember you telling me how it fell off that cliff face on Peladon all the way to the bottom and... Oh.'

'That,' said the Doctor darkly, 'hasn't happened yet, Iris.'

'Sorry.'

Across the shop, Kevin was having to explain sensitively to the girls what had happened to Peter. And how it was all the fault of the creature they now knew to be Verdigris.

Mary shook her head. 'Poor Peter. This is all rather serious then, isn't it?'

The Doctor said to Jo, 'Where's the Brigadier? He ought to be here too. Where did you leave him?' The Doctor was standing up, dashing biscuit crumbs off his jacket.

Jo stared at him. 'I haven't had a chance to tell you. It wasn't the Brigadier at all! It was the Master, in disguise!'

'The Master!' gasped the Doctor.

'No!' said Marsha. 'The Master was a disguise, too! It was Verdigris!'

Mary was shaking her head sadly. 'The Master never existed. It was all a sham.'

The Doctor marched up to her. 'My dear young lady, believe me, the Master is a very real and dangerous, intergalactic criminal.'

'So it might still be him!' cried Jo.

'Have you seen him?' asked the Doctor.

'Yes,' she said, 'He took me to their hideout, and that's where I met up with Tom again and...'

'No,' Marsha said. 'We thought it was the Master too, but his face and all his clothes dropped off and it turned out to be that terrible green man.'

The Doctor rubbed his neck thoughtfully. 'Yes, we saw him, too. And he claimed to know me.' He threw up his hands. 'I suggest we all clear out of this good woman's shop and get back aboard the bus.' He opened the door with a jingle.

'Oh, don't mind me,' said Sally. 'I think it's all fascinating.'

Iris shot out of the shop first, without a backward glance. She thought Sally was a bit common. The way she threw herself at the Doctor. Pitiful old bird.

'Thanks again for the tea and biscuits,' he said and marched the others all aboard the bus. 'Come along, all you young people. Back aboard.'

Once inside he wanted to get down to business and find out what these meddling youngsters had got themselves into.

'Iris,' he commanded, 'take us back into the vortex and don't bring us out until we get some answers that I'm happy with!'

Iris glowered at him, but did as she was told.

'Now,' he said pleasantly. 'I want you lot to tell me why you were working on the side of the Master, or Verdigris, or whatever he calls himself.'

They all sat down on the faded chintz and Kevin took up the tale.

He explained to the Doctor and Iris and Jo the bits they didn't know; everything he had explained to Tom, about the Children of Destiny and how they were a team of phenomenally talented teenagers bonded together to ensure that Earth was taken into the Galactic Federation.

'I see,' said the Doctor, and Jo could see he was disturbed by something.

'We were contacted first of all by Ambassador Borges,' said Kevin. At the very name of her beloved, Marsha blushed.

'And he explained what might help or prevent Earth's entry into the blessing of the Federation.'

'It sounds like a cult!' said Jo.

'And I was almost sucked into it,' said Tom dolefully. They all looked at him and Mary caught his eye. 'And she's my mother!' he cried out suddenly, unable to keep the secret in much longer. 'She's seen to it that I'm drawn back through time! Isn't that sort of thing supposed to be outlawed by the laws of time or something?'

Iris came hurrying up the aisle. 'Your mother!' she said hotly. 'Are you sure?' She squinted into Mary's face. 'Are you?'

Mary shrugged non-committally. 'Before yesterday, I'd never seen Tom before in my life.'

'Of course you hadn't, Mum! I haven't been born yet!'

She tutted. 'Don't you call me Mum!'

The Doctor broke in. 'Time paradoxes aside for the moment, where do I come into all of this?'

Iris cackled. 'You're ever so egocentric in this body, do you know that?'

The Doctor pointedly ignored her. He still hadn't forgiven her for all the shenanigans in the lifepod. 'Tell me,' he urged the teenagers.

Gradually, the story came out: how Verdigris had exhorted the Children of Destiny to use their psionic powers to make the Doctor look like a fraud.

'But if you already believed I was a fraud, why would you need to plant things in my house? Why would you need to make it look like I was building killer sheep, for example?'

'Because,' said Kevin, 'the Master said it needed to be spectacular enough to draw the attention of the authorities to you. You needed to be completely discredited.'

'Well,' said the Doctor. 'I must say, I think you're idiots for going along with such a plan. Why didn't you just give me a ring and ask me if I was a fraud?'

'And what about UNIT?' Jo broke in impulsively, 'What's happened to UNIT? Are you behind that as well?'

Kevin nodded. 'Partly. We helped to get them out of the way. We used hypnotic suggestion to erase the memory of such an organisation from the minds of most people involved.'

'Even though you believed it to be fake anyway?' said the Doctor.

'Not fake,' said Mary. 'Dangerously misguided! You and your people go around claiming that nearly every alien species up there is evil and intent on doing the people of the Earth harm! Well, we've been up there and the alien species we've met have been generous and kind and peace-loving. You spread around the wrong kind of news, Doctor.'

'My dear young lady,' said the Doctor. 'There are indeed a great number of very peaceful and gentle races in the known universe, and I happen to be on rather good terms with a lot of them. In this part of the galaxy, however, there are indeed an awful lot of savage, beastly races that the Earth needs protecting from. You, I am afraid, are being just a little naive.'

Jo said, 'It isn't all peace and flowers in space, you know.'

'Quite,' said the Doctor.

The Children of Destiny were shaking their heads. Kevin said, 'The Galactic Federation have told us and shown us. The kind of races and things you talk about, Doctor... They simply don't exist. Daleks, Axons, Cybermen. Whatever you say, these are merely fairytale creatures used to frighten children. We know, though. We know that if we join with the Galactic Federation and see that the Earth no longer has the spurious protection of an upstart outfit like UNIT, we will be quite safe.'

Iris could hardly believe her ears. 'You bloody stupid bunch of young fools!'

The Doctor nodded. 'You've been hoodwinked. Someone has been playing a very dangerous game with you.'

Kevin was incensed. 'Don't you dare patronise us!'

'We're not patronising you...' said Jo.

'They're just telling you, Kevin,' said Tom. 'You should listen. The Doctor and Iris have seen more of what's out there than...'

Iris was up on her feet, spoiling for a fight. 'I'll tan the little bugger's hide! Patronising him, indeed! Who does he think he is?'

Mary pointed a quivering, indignant finger at Iris. 'Why should we listen to a word that old creature ever says?'

Marsha said, 'That's right! Remember the message from Ambassador Borges!'

Kevin nodded solemnly, choked up with horror, suddenly. 'She is the kidnapper! Iris has the ambassador hostage!'

'What?' said the Doctor.

'What are you talking about?' gasped Iris.

Kevin rounded on her. 'On this bus, you have Ambassador Saldis of the Galactic Federation. You kidnapped him yourself in order to hold the whole of the civilised galaxy to ransom! Deny it!'

Iris frowned. 'You lot are crackers.'

'Where is he, then?' said Tom. 'Show us. Where's she hidden this Ambassador Saldis?'

Kevin looked deflated. 'We don't know.'

Marsha said, 'We don't know what he looks like.'

Mary added, 'None of us has ever seen him. He's rather small and quiet.'

Iris mopped her brow. She had got herself all worked up over nothing it seemed. She was just returning her handkerchief to her golden handbag (already the cause of much grief during this adventure) when the thing let out an almighty howl of protest.

Everyone jumped and stared at the clutch bag dangling from Iris's arm.

'Now I think it is time I spoke!' shrilled the handbag. 'For too long I have been awaiting my chance and keeping myself ever so quiet and still!'

'Iris,' breathed Jo. 'Your handbag… it's talking to us!'

'Ssssh!'

'Yes, Jo Grant,' shrieked the bag, glittering. 'You should learn to keep your mouth shut and listen more. All too often you're screaming and complaining and you fail to pick up on the vital clues!'

Suitably admonished, Jo fell silent.

'And you, Doctor,' ranted the bag, furiously. 'What of your part in this? You've flailed around all over the place, running into danger and excitement as per usual, but it was all in order to prove your own integrity, was it not? You hated the thought that someone was trying to discredit you! And all the while, I knew that your main project was to get away from the Earth.'

The Doctor shook his head. 'If you'll let me explain…'

'Silence!' roared the bag. 'You could have left me on the mother ship of the Meercocks and I could have been revered as a sacred object for the rest of time! But, oh, no. You can't let anyone else have any fun. If you're not happy, then no one else can be happy.'

'Now hang on,' said the Doctor. 'Wasn't it Iris who stole you back from the Meercocks?'

'And,' shrieked the bag implacably, 'you left the Meercocks up there, alone, in a state of religious chaos, having rediscovered and just as soon lost their faith! What kind of state do you think they're in now? Poised on the brink of invading the Earth, how do you think they're feeling, hm? Did you think you could just leave them hanging around until you got yourself around to dealing with them?'

The Doctor gave an embarrassed cough, tugged his velvet jacket straight and shot his cuffs. 'I have been rather busy, you know. It's been a very, very wearing day. Hasn't it, Iris?'

His ploy had the desired effect. The enraged handbag turned its beady eye on the nervous woman who was holding it.

'And as for you, Iris Wildthyme… !'

'Oh,' she waved her free arm airily. 'Don't even start on me. I know how bad I am.'

The handbag simmered in its own anger for a second.

'All of you will get your just desserts!'

This interested everybody greatly.

Ambassador Saldis went on, 'You will all find out what you've got coming when you take these co-ordinates and pilot this bus to the Supreme Headquarters of the Galactic Federation!'

At this, a small strip of paper was pushed out of the bag and drifted down to the floor. Iris picked it up and read out a long string of digits. 'And what if we don't take you there?'

'Then,' thundered the handbag, 'you will find the combined might of the civilised races of the Federation coming down on your raddled, malignant head!'

Iris shrugged. She looked at the Doctor.

'Was there something funny in that tea Sally made us?'

The Doctor looked deadly serious, however.

'Iris, I really think you ought to do as Ambassador Saldis has commanded us. Would you please transport us to the Galactic Federation's Supreme Headquarters!'

Chapter Eighteen
My Bag

From the intergalactic journals of the captivating Iris Wildthyme, Adventuress.

Hullooo space chums!
It's your Aunty Iris again, twice as large as life again!
Three times as beautiful as social realism again!
Four times as stupendous as magic realism again!
Five times as marvellous as science fiction again!
Enough!
Thundering down the time/space vortex again again again in my trusty old, rusty old bus!
And the exterior shell of the bus is rattling again as we batten down the hatches and brave the temporal winds!
The timely breezes are shushing through the smutty window panes and streaming back my gorgeous lilac locks.
I'm back in my comfy old driving seat on the cushion Mary, Queen of Scots crocheted ever so beautifully for me and singing along with Shirley Bassey as we career through the hectic old continuum once more!
And hush my mouth! I shouldn't even be thinking about events out of my time stream, should I? Such as the time I met Mary, Queen of Scots in Edinburgh when I was gadding about with Sarah Jane Smith and the Doctor in his raffish, bohemian fourth incarnation. I shouldn't be thinking about that in case the Doctor I've got with me now gets wind of it and tells me off again for jumping about in my time streams like a dodgy arm on a knackered record player.
I was never very good at keeping in the grooves.

And is it any wonder with a vortex like this susurrating around me? The tinkly gold at the edges of the blue ripples and whorls? Opening out like the most extravagant of lilies to suck me in and tempt me with a million possible destinations?

Who could resist the plethora of places and times to arrive in?

Here we all are now: a full bus.

Consisting of, naturally, me, the mistress of the magical bus, the delectable, debonair Doctor in his habitual velvety evening dress, Miss Josephine Grant (the most mind-numbingly loyal assistant a sexist rake could ever desire), the gorgeous Tom (eyeing up, I notice, one of our other guests with those fabulously long eyelashes of his flapping away the whole time. Oh, stop batting them, Tom boy, and give the lad a kiss!).

And, added to our motley crew, we have the children who describe themselves as belonging to destiny itself: Kevin (object of my foolish Tom's affection), the sappy-looking Marsha and the peculiar Mary, whom Tom believes to be his mother, only from a point in time before she'd even conceived of him.

Happy families.

All courtesy of your good-old Aunty Iris.

Last but not least, of course, amid our happy throng, and sitting with an irate look about it (though how I can tell what expression it bears utterly beats me): my very own handbag.

Revealed as a highly important and eminent ambassador for the Galactic Federation.

Its querulous voice still rings in my ears. It was shocking, the way my bag declared itself disgusted and disappointed at the behaviours of all here present.

Well, as a matter of fact, I think we've all been rather diligent and good, these past few days. Me, especially. What have we been doing but rescuing hapless aliens who can't even think of a decent, hazard-free method of invading the Earth? And then dashing off to save poor pensioners from being fried up into nothing by killer sheep? And then dampening down forest fires by disgorging my water tanks from a great height?

That's a point. If anyone wants a cup of tea during this haul towards the co-ordinates that the handbag gave me and swears blind are the right ones for Galactic Central (though they look a bit suspect to me) then we're completely buggered. We haven't got a drop of water aboard the bus. We'll have to make do with booze.

I call Tom over (and he comes, bless him! Tearing himself away from the sight of his adored boy, he comes to do my bidding). I suggest to him that he cracks open the drinks cabinet and gets the whole assembled company well tanked-up before we arrive. It might be easier, dealing with the Federation, if we're all pissed out of our minds. These things often are.

Even the Doctor takes a gin. He has to go one better, of course. Opens the Bombay Sapphire and demands lime instead of lemon.

It strikes me now, of course, that I could simply misread the co-ordinates that the handbag slipped me. I could miss out a digit or add an extra one in, and then we could wind up anywhere in any time.

Wouldn't that prove to these upstart youngsters what a wanderer and expert dilettante I am?

These assembled characters could be my new crew and we could abandon this venture at this very point and get our lovely selves enwrapped and involved in a completely new one, across at the furthest edge of the galaxy.

What bliss!

And what could the handbag do?

Nothing! He could rant and rail but, really, what could my own handbag do to punish me?

And if I sabotaged and impeded our journey to the Galactic Federation's so-called Supreme Headquarters here and now, no one would even know until we arrived in some other, unknown and possibly fabulously extravagant alien place and time.

But my own handbag is looking at me rather narrowly. As if it has read my mind. Possibly, as I've been driving, gulping back the Bombay Sapphire, I've been talking out loud and giving the whole game away!

'If you even think about diverting this TARDIS and taking us anywhere else,' says the golden evening bag crossly, 'then I will send a message to the Federation to hunt you down and destroy you and your pathetic bus, Iris Wildthyme.'

'Huh,' I say. 'What could the Federation do to me?'

'Send one of our fleetest ships,' says the handbag. 'The *Nepotist*, say. We could blast you out of the skies.'

'I see,' I say.

I don't tamper with the co-ordinates after all. Who knows? Maybe the end of the adventure will be just as much fun as pissing off elsewhere. Certainly, everyone else aboard seems keen to see this thing through.

'Well,' I say. 'I've had enough of driving. The old girl can go on automatic for a while.'

With that I hop out of the cab and leave that miserable handbag to sulk by itself.

The thing is, I can't even remember where I picked that bag up. It's so hard, to make the others believe that I never knowingly kidnapped some VIP, thinking he was just another bag. I mean, I've got hundreds upstairs, in my wardrobe. Handbags are very important in the adventures I find myself having. You need all sorts of specialist equipment with you. As you know, the Doctor is very attached to his voluminous, capacious pockets, but I've found (and I've been at this business longer than the Doctor, bless him!) that you really can't beat a decent handbag.

So where did I get the one who declares himself Ambassador Saldis? It's so very hard to remember. Like the Doctor, I find it difficult, keeping track of all the lives I've lived.

I shall have to work hard to remember. I might have borrowed him off someone, or he might have been a present. I might have picked him up in some foreign bazaar, full of fruits and spices and extraordinary objects. I might have picked him up and haggled over his gold lamé hide just about anywhere.

How was I to know he was a sentient and very important being? And why didn't the silly sod say sooner?

'Where's Tom gone?' I ask the Doctor, sitting down heavily on the sofa.

Jo leans across. 'He and Kevin have gone upstairs. I think they're talking about what we might do to exonerate ourselves when we reach the Galactic Federation's Supreme Headquarters.'

'Iris,' says the Doctor suddenly. 'There's more to this business than we know about yet, and I think you are the key.'

'Me?' I say, batting my eyelashes and looking purposefully flattered. 'Are you sure?'

'Well,' he goes on, in that ever so serious way that he has, 'remember when you first saw Verdigris and he seemed to trigger some kind of locked-up memory of yours?'

'You're right,' I say, with an exaggerated nod. 'He did. I was just thinking about that though, and the whole, difficult process of memory. We can't really rely on it, can we?'

'We might have to,' says the Doctor. 'If we want to get to the bottom of this.'

'What do you want to do?'

'Hypnotise you.'

'No way, José.' I'm up on my feet. 'You dirty old beast!' I try to attract the attention of those other two girls, Marsha and Mary, but they're into the pink wine and trying not to notice. 'Have you heard this? He's trying to get me under the influence!'

'It might be our only chance!' the Doctor urges.

'Ooh, you dirty devil.' I look him up and down. 'I'm not having you perform your funny parlour games on me, on my bus! It might be all right for your precious Brigadier and your Sergeant Bentons and what-have-you, but you're not tampering with the delicate fabric of my mind, thank you very much!'

Then I stomp away from him and he sulks behind me for a while.

And, Doctor, I could have kidnapped you into new adventures elsewhere on a thousand different worlds! Not a handbag! I could have taken you! Why won't you ever let me take you?

Sitting on the carpeted stairwell I have a little go at putting myself into a trance. I mull over the word 'Verdigris' and see what comes out.

Almost straight away I am on an ancient world and can feel the hot dust through the soles of my shoes. I'm tramping through miles of desert. Certainly I'm on some kind of desperate mission, for I'm in quite a lot of discomfort, trudging across the bleak landscape like this. It must be a matter of life and death.

But when was this? Where am I?

There are twin suns rising higher in the greenish sky and the light and shadows are all to pot. I'm heading towards the ruins of a city I somehow now are beyond the brow of the next hill. I keep taking out a raggy old map to take a peek and confirm my calculations.

I stop at the wreck of an old house and peer into its broken water pipes, which emerge from the dust like veins from skin. There is a tank, full of brackish water and I'm not sure I can drink it. The pipe and tank itself were once copper. Now they're caked and scabbed in green.

'Iris?'

I come out of my self-generated trance because someone is gently shaking my shoulder. It takes a moment or two before I can open my eyes. The Doctor! He's staring into my face, full of concern.

'I've come to apologise, for demanding you submit to hypnosis,' he says. 'It was rather bullish of me. I'm afraid I'm inclined to be impatient, these days.'

I jump up and shout to confound him a bit more. 'You idiot! You meddling fool!'

Now he looks somewhat startled, to get a taste of his own medicine.

'I was in a trance just then! I was getting to the bottom of things! You broke my concentration!'

Everyone is looking over to see what we're rowing about now.

'How was I to know?' he shouts. 'I thought you were just having a nap!'

'Having a nap!' I cry. 'The fate of the world hangs in the balance, and I would have a nap?'

The bus lurches then and it appears that we are arriving.

'Doctor! Iris!' Jo calls out. 'We're coming out of the vortex!'

From upstairs there is a scrambling, as if the boys up there have also realised that it is time to face the Federation.

'Don't worry,' the Doctor winks at us. 'I'm known to the Federation of old, even in this time. I've a few friends there.

We'll be all right.'

The bus rolls out of the vortex on to a walkway high atop one of the most fantastic cities I have ever seen.

Chapter Nineteen
An Attempted Escape

They knew precisely where the bus would materialise.

A welcome party of three ambassadors – Katra, Borges and Valcino – stood waiting patiently in their robes with the guards.

Valcino, who was in essence a creature whose body consisted of a pink brain with eight feeble appendages, was sporting his new, hugely muscled, strapping body. Only recently he had gone in for this kind of augmentation and it intimidated some of his fellow ambassadors.

'Do you hope to scare off our guests, Ambassador Valcino, with your brand-new physique?' asked Katra dryly.

There was no love lost between the two of them. She was ambassador from one of the distant witchworlds, inhabited by an ancient matriarchy. She had long, tattered hair, half black, half white, and she spent much of her time at Central being dryly dismissive of her fellow members' efforts at policing the galaxy.

'They are hardly our guests,' gasped the curious-looking, multi-legged Borges. His eyebrows beetled and his mandibles twitched in his usual consternation. 'They are highly dangerous criminals! They must be, to kidnap one of us in the way they have! Imagine if it had been you, Katra, or you, Valcino, when you were simply a brain with tiny legs and you'd been kidnapped. You would have been terrified, wouldn't you?'

Valcino looked uncomfortable. In truth, it was Saldis's kidnapping that had provoked his own augmentation and the planting of his body on top of this stronger body. Better be safe than sorry, he thought.

Katra said, 'We are lucky, are we not, that none of us look like handbags?'

Borges flushed with irritation. 'The ambassador's personal appearance has nothing to do with his capture!'

'Oh, come on,' said Katra. 'The woman just picked him up, thinking he was her bag, surely. It's easily done! The Saldisians should know what to expect.'

'They should all get augmented,' said Valcino thoughtfully. He was quite proud of his own changed circumstances.

Katra confided, 'Actually, the Saldisians get on my nerves, thinking they're the be-all and end-all. Wasn't it them who used to go visiting brand-new hominid races, at the dawn of their civilisations, and land bang in the middle and declare themselves to be gods? Just for the fun of it?'

Borges sighed. 'Not since they joined the Federation, have they done that.'

'They just wanted to be carried around on little platforms being worshipped by lesser species! It was outrageous.' Katra was disgusted, just thinking about it.

'Quiet,' Valcino urged. 'They're coming out of the bus.'

The small troop of guards stood to attention and held their cattle-prod-like weapons at the ready.

Even the guards here were a motley collection of races. Katra didn't think they made a very impressive bunch, actually. They were meant to be handpicked from a variety of races that the Federation represented, but to her jaundiced eyes the Central guards always looked a little bit of a hotch-potch.

Now, give her a troop of warrior women from home, and she'd scare the pants off her prisoners.

As it was, this troop consisted of no one any taller than the height of her knee. They were all either goblin-like creatures or super-advanced mice.

She didn't think the new arrivals were going to be very scared.

All the same, Katra straightened up and, with her colleagues beside her, made the elaborate sign of the Federation with both arms as the dusty bus doors swished open and the humanoid prisoners emerged.

Jo Grant was impressed with Galactic Federation Central.

To her, it was exactly what a space city ought to be, with its gleaming ramparts and turrets and towers studded with light.

The sky around was completely black and devoid of stars. It was all very impressive, however, and as the prisoners were corralled towards the central tower she was having a good look about.

Beside her, Tom was quiet for once, and Destiny's Children followed on behind; Kevin and Marsha (who'd only ever seen pictures) were rather awed by the experience and Mary was acting as if this was home from home.

She always wanted to look more sophisticated than everyone else, Jo thought. But, after all, Mary was meant to be the ambassador from Earth and, indeed, the three strange-looking ambassadors in their high-collared robes had welcomed her cordially, as an equal, and even appeared to congratulate her on successfully bringing these criminals (criminals!) to Central to face the music.

Mary accepted their compliments graciously. Jo felt tempted to say that Mary hadn't done a thing; everyone had come here of their own free will.

The Doctor and Iris were walking ahead along the rampart, and she caught only a few words of their conversation.

'I've never been so insulted,' the Doctor was saying.

'Not everyone can recognise you,' Iris said.

'But I'm known to the Federation of old,' he complained. 'I've done lots of things for them! They could at least...'

'Perhaps it's a different Federation,' she said. 'Perhaps...'

'A different one?' he said hotly. 'How many are there?'

'Oh, lots. It's a long time since you did any travelling, isn't it? You'd be surprised. Things have changed.'

The Doctor glowered and sniffed as he looked about at the impressive surroundings.

Tom turned to Jo and said, with a grin, 'It's a proper, glitzy, sci-fi city, isn't it?'

And my mum's an ambassador here! he thought proudly. Even if she won't recognise me. But she'll see. To Tom, this all explained a great deal about the feeling he had that he belonged elsewhere, that Earth was never quite big enough for him. No wonder he ended up travelling with Iris, if this was the kind of place his mother had for a stomping ground!

The tiny mice-like, goblin-like guards were carrying Ambassador Saldis on a golden platform and the ambassador was trying to muster his dignity. He was just grateful he wouldn't ever have to be swung around again, on the arm of that dreadful old woman.

When they got into the council chamber, he was preparing to tell the worst and exaggerate it, and have Iris punished by atomisation or something even more nasty.

Katra turned to the guests as they approached the tall tower in the heart of the city.

'You must wait to meet the Supreme Council.'

The Doctor gave a stiff bow. 'We are at your disposal.'

Ambassador Borges snarled, 'Guards! Take them down to the cells!'

'We can't,' said one of the tiny guards. 'We're still holding the handbag.'

Valcino flinched at this. He reached down swiftly with one of his massive new paws, cuffed the guard about the head and stamped on him with all his might, killing him outright.

'That was hardly necessary,' said Katra, shocked.

'It was! It was!' shrieked Saldis with glee. 'Pick me up,

Ambassador Katra! You must carry me! Let the guards lead the prisoners away!'

Katra did as she was told and, as the prisoners were taken off in the other direction, only she was left looking at the remains of the squashed guard.

A new kind of barbarism had overtaken the Federation, she thought. This had worried her for some time.

Mary was left looking at her. 'The prisoners aren't really wicked, you know,' she said.

'No?' asked Katra.

'They were helping us. Destiny's Children have been terribly misled.'

'Misled? By whom?'

'I'll tell you all about it,' said Mary, leading Katra into the building.

They were placed in the same gloomy cell and the Doctor was given a yellow ticket with the number seventy-four on it.

'They must be seeing a whole load of cases today,' said Iris.

'But I haven't got time to sit around in police cells all day!' said the Doctor. 'There's that ship full of Meercocks to sort out!'

Jo went to sit down with the others.

'I can't see why they've locked us up as well,' Kevin said. 'Destiny's Children are the chosen ones! The Federation has always been very good to us.'

'Things have changed,' said Marsha disconsolately. 'Can't you feel it? Ambassador Borges isn't the same any more. He looked right through me when I arrived. Usually he has a nice word for me, at least.'

Kevin sighed.

Tom rubbed his hands briskly. 'What's it to be then, Iris? Bash the door down? Skulk through the corridors and back to the bus? Or beard the alien nasties in their den?'

'Tom!' she said, scandalised. 'We're in the heart of the civilised galaxy!'

'You could have fooled me,' he said. 'We haven't been offered as much as a cup of tea yet.'

Iris looked to the Doctor. 'What do you think?'

He sighed deeply. 'Let's wait a bit and see what they have to say.'

That was when he noticed the white rabbit in the cell next to them. He hurried over and peered through the bars and stared at the creature, with its head in his paws.

'Oh, it's you again,' said the rabbit.

'How did you get here?' asked the Doctor.

The rabbit's pink eyes were drooping. 'They blamed me for the entire Meercock invasion of Earth! Which, by the way, hasn't even happened yet!' His long ears twitched with dismay. 'Federation guards appeared in disguise at my ticket office and hauled me away to stand trial. They didn't even think to take the queen or the rest of the handbag-worshipping horde.'

'That seems very unfair,' said Iris.

The rabbit nodded, pleased that he was being indulged. 'Anyway,' he said. 'I'm digging a tunnel out. Do you want to see?'

'A tunnel!' gasped Jo.

'Of course,' said the rabbit. 'Actually, that's what I'm best at.'

'What are you going to do, if you escape?' asked Tom.

'Take the Doctor's advice to our queen,' the white rabbit said. 'There's an uninhabited world that I can lead our people to. I've learned about it since I was taken here. One of the ambassadors told me. It's called… Makorna.'

Suddenly Iris was back in the desert, tramping miles over the burning red dust.

It was getting darker and she was thinking she needed to find somewhere to rest for the night.

And, just like a miracle, there appeared a tavern before her, stuck in the middle of nowhere, with corrugated iron walls and a green tiled roof.

Inside there were prospectors and archaeologists, carousing and drinking and planning their next day's assault on the antique treasures of Makorna.

Makorna, of course! She had been there!

She had become rather drunk there; dancing about in the early hours and hearing tales of the lost treasures in the ruined city beyond the hill…

She was shoved and rudely woken by the Doctor.

'You've done it again!' she howled. 'I was just about to remember and you've gone and snapped the link again!'

The Doctor looked abashed. 'I'm sorry.'

'So you should be. I'd almost remembered the key to this whole thing. It was something to do with being on Makorna, the ancient world and getting terribly, terribly drunk…'

'And that's why you can't remember anything about it?' asked Tom. 'Because you were so drunk?'

She nodded, shamed.

'Do try to remember, Iris,' goaded the Doctor. 'It might be very important.'

She flushed. 'I know it's important! That's why I'm thinking myself back there!'

They were interrupted then at the door of the cell by Mary, who had donned her silver ambassador's robes, and Katra, who came bearing a large silver key.

'We've come to let you all out,' Mary said as Katra unlocked the doors. The Children of Destiny jumped to their feet and cheered.

'Let us out?' asked the Doctor. 'What made you change your mind?'

Katra swung the metal door open. 'There is something wrong here. I wouldn't be happy letting you go before the

Council as they are. You must return to your bus and…'

'We can't do that,' said the Doctor. 'We have to see your ambassadors together and get to the bottom of this.'

Katra shook her head. 'I think you should just leave and…'

'Don't listen to him!' the rabbit shrilled. 'You can let me out! I'll go! I'd be happy to!'

No one took any notice.

'Quickly,' Mary urged. 'Before the guards see us…'

Iris and the Doctor took the lead. They stole, with the others, through the rock-lined passages, deep under the tower.

Cries of pain were echoing up the chambers, and they were coming from a number of rooms.

'Do you have torturers now?' asked the Doctor.

Katra looked abashed. 'The Federation has branched out a little, Doctor. We now have some of the most talented torturers in the galaxy in our employ.'

Kevin looked startled. 'That's not what we were told. We thought the Federation was all about peace and harmony…'

Katra shook her head. 'Not any more.' She paused then, by a doorway and the others shrank back as guards slid by across the hallway. 'Some of us are trying to change it all from within…'

'A revolution, eh?' said the Doctor, eyes gleaming.

They almost made it up through the levels of rock corridors, to the walkway where Iris's bus was waiting. Just as they reached that surface, however, a troop of guards discovered them.

These guards were a little larger than the ones they had already seen.

They were a varied assortment, again; there was an egglike creature studded with eyes, a furred creature covered in tiger stripes, an amorphous blob and something else that no one could get the hang of looking at.

'Run!' the Doctor commanded his party.

The guards all carried their cattle-prod weapons and soon the air was cracking and smarting with rather severe discharges of electricity.

Inside the *mêlée* as the prisoners fell into a ramshackle kind of punch-up with the creatures, Jo Grant watched with horror as Marsha and Tom were smartly rendered unconscious and slid to the floor.

There was hardly any room for fighting on the rampart and she was scared that someone would end up plopping over the edge.

The Doctor, of course, was whirling into his Venusian aikido, but found himself trying it on the crystalline being, who could feel very little of the impact and brought the Doctor down with one crashing, gleaming blow of its single arm.

Iris, meanwhile, felt oddly defenceless without her handbag.

She slipped her hand into her coat pocket and produced, with a cry of triumph, a small hand blaster, which she immediately put to good use.

Slim pink blasts of radiation shot out wildly, in all directions, winging the tiger creature, the amorphous one and then, by accident, Katra, who bellowed in outrage and hexed Iris almost unconscious on the spot.

One more pink report caused the crystal being, bearing down on the Doctor, to smash into a million, sparkling fragments.

'Stop!' Jo shrieked. 'Stop fighting, all of you!'

Iris confusedly grabbed her hand. 'Come on, Jo! We've got to run for the bus...'

'She's right,' urged the Doctor, holding back the remaining guards.

Jo pointed to their unconscious friends. 'We can't just leave Tom and Marsha...'

Kevin squawked in alarm. 'Look! Coming up the ramparts! Reinforcements!'

And it was true.

Heading in their direction was the most ill-assembled rabble of fierce-looking creatures any of them had seen.

They glimpsed feathers and scaled hides; silicon and vegetable creatures; machine-like creatures; the bristling nimbuses of beings composed of pure energy; the glassy hides of aqua-beings, and things that looked like nothing anyone had ever seen before.

They had all emerged from the building to claim back the prisoners.

'We can't escape,' said Kevin, bleakly.

'What a terrible lot!' Iris exclaimed and promptly passed out.

'I'm sorry,' said Katra as the guards arrived.

Chapter Twenty
The Tunnel

Iris lay unconscious in their cell and the other captives looked down at her, willing her back to life.

Mary had gone off again, to sit among the ambassadors in their chamber upstairs and the room was starting to feel a bit chilly.

'Have you noticed,' said Tom suddenly, 'that everyone we've met here sounds... well, Welsh?'

'Welsh?' asked the Doctor.

'He's right,' said Jo. 'I think it's a lovely accent to have.'

'But isn't that a bit peculiar?' Tom went on.

Kevin was watching the rabbit digging away in the corner of his own cell.

He was a terribly good digger, scooping out mounds of blue earth with his forepaws and tossing them away into a heap with his back legs.

When he stood up for a breather his white face was filthy.

'Are you going to let us use your tunnel when it's finished?' Marsha asked him, as he got his breath back.

The rabbit looked at her narrowly. 'Well! I'm the one who's put all the work into it.'

The Doctor turned on him. 'You need me to help you find your way to Makorna. You and all your people do.'

The rabbit looked down his pink nose at him. 'Don't overestimate your importance, Doctor.'

'I wish Iris would wake up,' Jo said, bending to touch the old woman's shoulder.

'Don't touch her,' the Doctor cried. 'I think she may be having one of her flashbacks... It might be very important...'

* * *

Sacred Flame! Sacred Fire!

And then, clutching our burning brands and our tambourines, we all went dancing and skipping about in the cavern; each of us ancient novices keeping one, perfect gold-and-black painted eye attentively fixed on the rapt, ecstatic High Priestess and the gambolling fluid flames that shot out of the sacred crevice and leapt fully five feet tall into the humid gloom, thrilling us all – I can tell you – to bits.

I absolutely loved all that, back when I was in the Sisterhood of Karn. Magic, ritual, sacrifice, what-have-you.

A smattering of mysticism and arcane law pander to my more mysterious side.

Oh, you think you know all about Iris, but Mystique is far more than the scent I wear.

(And it's not, actually; I wear Shalimar.)

Who could resist donning headdresses and fabulously anachronistic Ossie Clark frocks, doping yourself silly on incense and funny brews and then taking part in all sorts of sororal rites?

Not many people know that I was, for a while, in the Sisterhood of Karn.

The Doctor doesn't. If he knew, he'd have my guts for garters. He frowns – oh so sensibly – on the Sisterhood's necromantic doings.

He had a run-in with them, later in life, on their homeworld: the ruinous, litter tray of a world where I spent a year or two.

He didn't even realise as he ran about, all adventurously, that I was there, in the back row, just another witch woman stoking the pyre at his sacrificial burning.

Sacred Flame!

Sacred Fire!

Of course, had his sacrifice gone any further, I'd have rescued him. I'm surprised he never noticed me, gallumphing around chanting, Death Death Death!

At that time he was that gangly fella with all the teeth and the cumbersome woolly scarf; impractical and demented, but in fine, revolutionary mettle.

I shouldn't have been surprised he never noticed me in the coven.

He was preoccupied with the perplexing case of the brain of Morbius (a literal case, of course, in that the pulsating green mind of the creature had been placed in a great big bloody glass case and mounted on the ugliest stitched-together body you've ever clapped eyes on!).

Silly old Doctor, slipping off and taking the Sisterhood's word for gospel, that the brain and the body had taken a fatal tumble off that cliff and been smashed to smithereens in a deep crevasse.

How careless of him, to believe us witches. Off he went, into a dazzling new trip with the redoubtable Sarah Jane Smith by his side.

He never even suspected that the Sisterhood would go back and recover that queasy but not-entirely-destroyed brain and revive it for their own purposes.

And off we went again; with Morbius the evil renegade Time Lord (mad as Cheddar, of course) calling all the shots and causing a fuss.

And that was the reason I was there, of course, inveigling myself into the witchy cult.

It was all down to treacherous Ohica, newly appointed High Priestess (oh, those mad staring eyes!) and it was she who led the wounded Morbius to the Death Zone on Gallifrey, reactivated the Time Scoop, interfered with the blessed remains of Rassilon, discovered that I was disguised as part of the coven and Time Scooped all of me – every one of my incarnations into the Death Zone and tried to put paid to all of my delightful, various selves with a series of terrifying, time-snatched monsters: Voord and Zarbi and Mechanoids and what have you.

Anyway, I sorted that little lot out and that's all a different story (be patient; my unconscious is a tricky old thing and uncovering memories takes a good bit of arduous sifting).

What happened was, mad-staring-eyes High Priestess Ohica packed me and the bus right across the galaxy, right back through the centuries, to the dusty old rusty old world of Makorna, where an ancient civilisation had once flourished and died.

It was here that I got myself dreadfully drunk with the archaeologists and – miraculously – heard from one of them what had been happening to my old pal the Doctor during my absence. The ungrateful Time Lords had intervened in his life, taken his TARDIS off him and exiled him to Earth!

Well, I was furious.

Out of sync, but fired with righteous indignation and good intentions.

But what I did next was disastrous.

The white rabbit had finished burrowing his tunnel.

He expected to emerge into some kind of spaceport, or perhaps into the walkways outside the tower. Instead he blinked in the morning light and gazed around, rather shocked.

Then he bolted back down the narrow tunnel and told the others.

'What?' cried the Doctor.

'But that's impossible!' said Kevin.

Jo said, 'I don't understand.'

That was when Marsha tried to use her teleport belt to whiz herself outside and check that the rabbit was right.

'It's not working!' she burst out. 'Kevin, is yours?'

He looked shocked. 'No, it's not. I can't teleport!'

'And my telepathy... !' said Marsha, close to tears. 'I can't hear a thing!'

Kevin rounded on the Doctor. 'All of our talents have gone.'

Tom looked at him. 'I wouldn't say that.'

'What does it mean?' Marsha asked the Doctor.

He rubbed his chin. 'I don't know.'

The rabbit burst through a hole in their floor, connecting it through to his tunnel.

'Come and see for yourselves,' he said.

Jo went first because she was smallest.

In less than ten minutes, the whole party (barring the still unconscious Iris) was out on a grassy hillside.

There was a rather pleasant breeze.

They stared at the clouds scudding gently through the sky and the green hills around them. Down in the valley there was a village.

Then they looked back at the craggy mountain they had emerged from.

'This looks like Wales,' said the Doctor.

'You mean we were never at Galactic Central?' said Marsha.

He shook his head sadly. 'I thought it looked a bit strange.'

'Then what is it?' asked Jo.

'That's what we have to go back and find out. Who's been hiding Intergalactic Headquarters inside mountains in Wales. And we have to fetch Iris, of course. She's lying down there in that cell by herself.'

The white rabbit tutted. 'This is where I leave you all, then. I'm not hanging around!'

He started away down the mountainside at a trot.

'You can't leave us!'

'What are you going to do?' asked the Doctor.

'Contact the mother ship and the queen,' he said. 'Give her the co-ordinates for Makorna...'

With that he disappeared into a hedge on the brow of the mountainside. They could see him, moments later, scurrying down into the valley.

'Will that end the Meercock menace to the Earth?' asked Jo.

'Goodness knows,' said the Doctor. 'Come on. Let's get back inside.'

They found Iris being woken by the cell guard – a skinny, evil-looking, jackal-like creature. He was pouring a bucket of water over her head.

She roused in a fury.

'I was almost there!' she shouted. 'I almost remembered!'

The jackal seemed surprised to see the rest of his prisoners emerging from a hole in the ground in the corner of their cell.

'I hope you weren't trying to escape,' he said, unsteadily.

'Who, us?' grinned the Doctor.

'Your number has come up,' the guard told them. 'I have come to take you before the Council.'

'Good,' said the Doctor, brushing himself down. 'I've got one or two things to say to them myself!'

Chapter Twenty-one
Verdigris

Wherever it was – the centre of the galaxy, or in a hollowed-out mountain in the north of Wales – the Supreme Council Chamber of the Federation was pretty impressive.

The small party were looking about with interest as they were led by the jackal into a vast room, its ceiling a translucent tangerine. It was only after they were right inside that they realised that the floor was a gigantic hand.

They were standing right on the fleshy palm and upon each of the upturned fingers, high above them, rested a number of thrones.

On the thrones sat the very impressive ambassadors to the Federation. Jo could pick out Katra, Borges, Valcino and, sitting by herself on the little finger, a little to one side, was Mary, looking somewhat glum.

On the quiet walk to this chamber the Doctor had filled Iris in on their true location. She couldn't quite take it in.

'I almost remembered, Doctor,' she said, shaking her head. 'While I was unconscious, it was all coming back to me...'

'There, there, old thing,' he said protectively.

The jackal waved his cattle-prod menacingly.

Once they were assembled along the lifeline of the gigantic, fleshy palm, there was a fanfare and the members of the Council stood up. One or two of them – notably Saldis, who simply sat on his plinth – didn't.

'Ambassadors to the Federation,' shrilled Saldis (and as he spoke Iris couldn't help missing her handbag), 'we are gathered to pass judgement on these creatures who have kidnapped a very significant member of this group. Namely, me.'

'And also,' put in Valcino, 'we are here to investigate the affairs of the being known as the Doctor, who has effectively retarded the human race's entry into the blessed Federation.'

Kevin, Tom, Jo, Marsha and Iris were all looking expectantly at the Doctor.

He coughed. 'I really feel that I have to interrupt at this point.'

He looked then, at the tallest, seated figure perched on the end of the hand's index finger. This ambassador was shrouded in darkness and he pricked the Doctor's interest.

The Doctor went on, thunderously: 'This Council can neither accuse nor try us!'

'Why?' cried Borges, appendages quivering.

'Because this whole Council is a sham!' the Doctor shouted. 'This whole Federation of yours is a pack of lies! None of it exists!'

At this each member of the Council, apart from the shadowed one, burst into furious complaint. They were all yelling at the same time, as if the Doctor had said the worst thing they could imagine.

'Be quiet!' he bellowed, for good measure.

'How dare you impugn our existence!' shrieked Saldis. 'What are you? A meddling vagabond! We are the superior beings from each of our respective races!'

Sadly, the Doctor shook his head. 'You have all been misled.'

Katra was looking strangely troubled by the Doctor's words. 'But by who? Who has misled us?'

The Doctor's hand shot out; he flung out his finger to point accusingly, unerringly at the mysterious figure cloaked in shadow.

'By him! By Verdigris! He has misled you all!'

More shouts and catcalls of consternation and the Doctor's own companions gasped and stared from him to the dark figure on the huge index finger as it lifted itself from its throne and walked into the light.

On the very tip of the finger, Verdigris revealed himself.

Everyone stared at his green, metallic form. He looked unspeakably ancient and malign. When he spoke his voice boomed out, filling every corner of the orange room.

'I am Verdigris,' he said. 'The Doctor is right.'

Ambassador Borges was unimpressed by the Doctor's accusations. He waggled his mandibles and said, 'Verdigris is our representative from the lost world of Makorna. He is the last remaining life form from his world.'

The Doctor shook his head. 'He isn't alive. He is a supernatural creature.'

Beside him, Marsha and Kevin were hanging their heads in shame. They had helped Verdigris and they could see now that they had done quite the wrong thing.

'Not alive?' shrilled Saldis. 'Whatever do you mean? Verdigris has been an invaluable member of the Council, advising us on how to deal with the inhabitants of the Earth and advising us as to their suitability...'

The Doctor nodded. 'And he told you that your best bet lay with these teenagers?' He spread his arms to indicate the worried-looking Kevin and Marsha. 'He claimed they were superior beings, didn't he?'

'That's right,' said Katra. 'He said that the less advanced humans weren't to be trusted.'

'And,' continued the Doctor, 'he told you all that I was the worst fiend on the face of the planet Earth, didn't he? And that, by any means, by any foul trickery possible, I should be prevented from protecting the Earth from alien invasion?'

'Ah yes,' said Valcino. 'He did say something about that, yes. But he didn't say you were a Time Lord. We wouldn't have interfered if we'd known you were a Time Lord.'

The Doctor changed his tack. 'And you really think that you are in the centre of space, don't you? Representing a calm and harmonious universe?'

'Certainly, we are,' said Saldis, but he was looking somewhat afraid.

'My friends,' said the Doctor grandly, 'we have been outside. You are on the planet Earth yourselves. You always were. You have less idea of the universe out there than these children do. As I say, you have been representing nothing at all. You are inside a hollowed-out mountain in Wales and have been for decades, centuries perhaps. Verdigris has misled you.'

The Council began to chatter and yell once more.

Iris said to Jo, 'Mind, it must be very disappointing for them. They've spent ages thinking they're terribly important...'

Jo nodded. 'They look flabbergasted.'

'Flabbergasted' was exactly the word for the way that the creatures on their thrones and podiums were thrashing their arms and tentacles and other protuberances.

'Enough!' Verdigris boomed at last. 'Silence, all of you!'

The Doctor wasn't to be stopped. 'Ambassador Saldis. No one kidnapped you except that man there. The green man. Somehow he planted you about the person of Iris Wildthyme who, not surprisingly, mistook you for a gold lamé handbag.'

Saldis snarled at everyone present.

'What's more, and what's worse,' the Doctor went on, 'Verdigris enlisted the ineluctable help of the last remaining Meercocks. He tried to entice them to invade the Earth using the most ridiculously impractical plan I have ever heard in my whole life. He smuggled fictional texts from the Earth and got the poor creatures to base their lives on people who never even existed!'

Jo was just about piecing the whole picture together.

'And he knew they would fail and die, but he didn't care! The Meercocks were just more pawns in his overall plan. He gave them bracelets fashioned from the same noxious material as his own unnatural hide and he knew they would be killed by using them as links to their own kind! Verdigris was prepared to sacrifice a whole race, just in order to bring me out in the open and to discredit me on the Earth! He tried his best to make the top secret organisation I work with, UNIT, appear to be a badly run, ramshackle, unprofessional team of bunglers!'

There was a resounding silence.

'Have you finished, Doctor?' asked Verdigris calmly.

'I have not, sir,' said the Doctor, in a quieter but even more dangerous tone. 'I demand to know why. Why have you been interfering in all our lives and causing all of this grief?'

Slowly, Verdigris took the narrow steps down the side of the index finger. He reached the palm and walked straight to the Doctor, where he towered over him, and all the others.

Jo, Marsha, Tom, Kevin and Iris shrank back in terror.

Verdigris looked down at the Time Lord.

'I did it all for you, Doctor.'

'Me?' The Doctor pulled a scornful face. 'Why would you do these terrible things for me?'

Now it was time for Verdigris' accusing finger to shoot out and to point unerringly at Iris.

Iris looked very surprised.

'Because she told me to!'

Chapter Twenty-two
The Manager

'Mr Benton?'

He moved smartly down the aisle, dodging past a young woman who was trying to bribe her small child to stop squealing. The woman was giving her child a packet of crisps. Alistair hoped she would remember to pay for them when she got to the checkout.

'Mr Benton?'

Alistair marched up to the burlier man, who was working slowly, clutching his back, and staring miserably at the stack of tins he was meant to be making into a pyramid shape.

'Yes, sir?' asked the shelf stacker.

The manager looked at him and sighed. 'Any sign of that shoplifter?'

'No, sir. I've been keeping a good eye out, though. But there's been nothing untoward all day.'

'Very good, Benton. Carry on.'

In the next aisle, at the deli counter, Liz Shaw had nothing to report, either. Still, there was something troubling Alistair this morning. Something he couldn't quite put his finger on.

He hoped he wasn't growing dissatisfied with his life again.

Every now and then he would wonder – in the wee small hours – whether running a supermarket was a waste of his talents. Sometimes he felt that he ought to hanker after a more… adventurous life. He supposed it was his old army training. Perhaps he should never have left the army at all.

He marched down the aisles and, as he approached each member of staff, they would stiffen and rise from their tasks, almost to attention.

It was a good, busy morning and the clanging and crashing of the cash registers rang through the place. He should be pleased, really. He tried to hum along with the muzak on the tannoy, but his heart wasn't in it.

He found himself thinking over what Mike Yates had said, the day he'd finally gone mad and come dashing out from behind the meat counter, scaring everyone in the place.

'None of it's true! We're all living a made-up life! We shouldn't be here at all!'

Well, of course Alistair had had the store detectives drag him through to the office, where he couldn't disturb anyone.

'Mike? What do you mean?'

Mike had looked as if he'd seen a ghost. 'You! You're the Brigadier! We don't work here! Not in a supermarket...'

Alistair had chuckled. 'I never made it to Brigadier, I'm afraid, old chap. Only as far as Colonel...'

Then Mike from the butcher's counter really had started to babble. 'We work together fighting creatures from outer space! We do! Don't you remember the Doctor? Someone has put us here, to keep us out of the way!' He eyes went wild and staring. 'Perhaps they're already here!'

Then he had gone running from the office and from the shop itself. Mike hadn't returned. If he'd come back, Alistair would only have been forced to fire him. Not a pleasant job, but he couldn't afford to have his staff going doolally on him and scaring all the customers. Creatures from outer space, indeed.

Still. When he thought, Alistair did think he remembered someone known only as the Doctor.

And 'Brigadier' did have a certain ring to it.

He brushed these thoughts aside and determined to get on with the morning. He'd be going barmy himself, if he carried on like this. Best get on with the day. He contented himself with the thought that soon it would be time to read out the day's specials over the tannoy. He enjoyed doing that.

Chapter Twenty-three
Iris Remembers

Iris was in tears.

From high on their podiums the members of the purported Supreme Council glared down at her.

Verdigris' emerald eyes blazed into her accusingly.

Even her friends: Tom, Jo, Kevin and Marsha, were awaiting her explanation.

And, more than anyone else, the Doctor was peering down his beaky nose, expecting her to tell all.

It had all come back.

She began to speak in a quavering, oddly timid voice.

'I went to the planet Makorna many years ago. I was sent there quite against my will.'

She looked unhappily at the Doctor. 'It was a wasteland; all you could see were miles of red sand and, occasionally, these buildings, these cities that had been constructed from copper, which had turned green with the centuries.'

The Doctor nodded sharply. 'Go on.'

'Well,' she said, 'you have to understand that my wits were somewhat scrambled. This was just after that terrible affair with Morbius and I was still under the influence of the magicks and arcane trickery of the Sisterhood of Karn.'

The Doctor raised his eyebrow.

'The only life on Makorna,' she said, 'came in the form of the archaeologists, who claimed to have found the principal city and who swore blind that it was full of treasure. Also, it was full of evil spirits...'

Verdigris chuckled, deep inside his hollow, cavernous body. Instinctively Jo drew back from that terrible sound. 'And tell us,

Iris,' he rumbled. 'Tell us the rest.'

Iris hung her head. 'It was on the planet Makorna that I at last heard what the Time Lords had done to you, Doctor. Your own people! They had sentenced you to a lifetime on the Earth, to wander like an Ancient Mariner... Well, this news was more than I could bear.'

The Doctor made a noise in his throat. 'I wasn't too delighted, myself.'

'You were the kindest, most generous, most self-sacrificing person I had ever met. I couldn't bear the idea that, just for the crime of helping people out in their troubles, you had been exiled. So, I'm afraid I got rather drunk that night... and stole out of the tavern where I'd been drinking with the archaeologists. I stole their maps, one of their pack animals and all of their equipment...'

'Iris!' gasped Tom. 'What did you do?'

Verdigris took up the tale.

'She found my city. She descended into the ruptured bowels of my ruined home. She clambered down, drunkenly, through level after level and, when she reached the very bottom, in a chamber all of verdigrised copper, she enacted a ritual to call up the spirits of the place.'

'Black magic!' cried Jo.

Verdigris chuckled. 'Green magic!'

'And from the flames that I had summoned,' said Iris dolefully, 'out stepped the creature you see before you now. The city's spirits fashioned him from the very fabric of their remains. He was invincible and would last until the end of time. This I was promised.' She sobbed then, and turned beseechingly to the Doctor. 'But I was addled! I didn't know what I was doing! If I'd been in my right mind, I'd never have... But I was upset...'

'And drunk,' Tom pointed out.

Verdigris said, 'She made me her champion. She instructed me to free the Doctor from his vile exile. I was to do whatever was necessary to set him, her beloved, free once more.'

Everyone stared at Verdigris.

'I set off immediately. I flew off into the sky; streaking away from my native Makorna. I was bound to do whatever my mistress bade me.'

He looked angry for a moment. 'For hundreds of years I floated through space, alone. An unnatural creature, without a home. It took me millennia to reach Earth's solar system. I had to reach the right century, in which you, Doctor, were held prisoner. That was when I found the Meercocks in their ship, looking for a new world of their own.'

'You hitched a ride!' said Kevin.

'Exactly,' said Verdigris. 'They have been a very useful race.'

'This is all very well,' said the Doctor, 'but I honestly didn't ask anyone for any help! I've been managing quite well on my own, thank you very much.' He fixed Iris with a beady glare.

She shook her head. 'That's what I did, anyway.'

'Well, I wish you hadn't, Iris. Just look at the fuss you've caused everyone.'

'Never mind him, Iris,' urged Tom. 'Go on with the story.'

'In the morning,' she said, 'I woke up, lying on the floor, beside the dying embers of the fire I'd lit. And I could only vaguely remember what I'd been up to.' She shrugged. 'I had a nightmare of a hangover.'

'You couldn't remember?' cried the Doctor.

'It was as if I'd blocked it all out,' she said. 'Until now. One thing I do remember now, though... is that when I woke up I had a new handbag with me. One I wasn't sure how I'd come by.'

'Ah!' Saldis cried, pleased to be back in the picture. 'That will have been me, then!'

The Doctor couldn't believe the fantastic tale he had been told. 'You unleashed a creature of sorcery upon the universe?

Really! Iris!'

Jo was shaking her head. 'I still don't understand what he thought he was doing. I mean, if he was sent by Iris to help you, Doctor, then he's been doing the very opposite, hasn't he?'

'That's right,' said Marsha. 'He's been trying to discredit him! He used us to make the Doctor look like an evil fake!'

'And he's been trying to kill us all, over the past few days,' added Kevin gloomily.

'Well, Verdigris?' asked the Doctor, his mouth twitching. 'Explain that bit to us.'

'It's quite simple,' the green man said. 'The Doctor's work for UNIT is what has kept him trapped on the Earth.'

The Doctor frowned.

'How do you work that out?' asked Jo.

'If he wasn't spending all of his time fending off the invaders from space, he'd have more time to find a way to end his exile and mend his TARDIS.'

'Of all the preposterous claptrap!' cried the Doctor. 'I've never heard such nonsense! What would I do, carry on tinkering with my TARDIS while the invaders came?'

Verdigris had it all thought out. He nodded. 'More and more invaders would come and one day, eventually, would arrive aliens with the requisite time-travel technology that would enable you to free yourself from your prison.'

The Doctor stopped in his tracks. He looked at the others. 'Do you know? He's right!'

'Doctor' said Jo. 'You can't be serious!'

He put his arm around her. 'Well, obviously not, my dear. But his logic is right, even if a little callous. With alien technology to hand on the Earth, I could have repaired the TARDIS and reminded myself of the correct codes and procedures ages ago.'

Verdigris bowed gracefully, as if he was being congratulated on his plan.

'But,' said Jo, 'where did you take UNIT? What did you do to the Brigadier and everyone?' Her voice faltered. 'Are they all dead?'

Verdigris shook his head. 'Oh no, Miss Grant. At the moment, the Brigadier and his men are running a small supermarket in the next village but one to their usual headquarters. It was rather easy to infiltrate their minds and convince them that this was the life they had always lived. Likewise the Ministry and Geneva; no one there really wanted to believe, at any rate, that UNIT was doing a very credible job.'

They all stared at him, letting all of this information sink in.

Iris turned to the Doctor. 'Do you forgive me?'

'That rather depends on what happens next,' he said curtly.

The Doctor squared his shoulders and faced up to his green champion. 'Verdigris, this has all got to stop. On my command.'

'You cannot command me to stop my mission, Doctor. It is my only reason for living.'

'Can I command you?' asked Iris. 'I was the one who brought you to life, after all.'

Verdigris shook his head. 'I shall continue to work to free the Doctor and only then will I cease my efforts.'

'But you can't go on hurting people and changing their lives for them!' the Doctor said.

Verdigris was impassive.

'This,' said the Doctor, 'is what I want you to do. I want you to send each of the ambassadors in this faked council back to their rightful place in the galaxy.'

The ambassadors, on the whole, didn't look very pleased at the sound of this. They had rather enjoyed being thought of as intergalactic VIPs.

'Continue,' said Verdigris.

'I want you to free the UNIT people of their mind control and return them to their headquarters.'

The green man nodded.

'I want you to stop dabbling with the teenagers known as the Children of Destiny and to allow them to discover their latent talents for themselves, and then to make their own contacts with extraterrestrial species.'

Kevin and Marsha looked quite pleased at this.

'Anything else?' asked Verdigris.

'Destroy this mountain facility. Make it look like it was never here. Then send us back home. And don't send any more killer sheep or living trees or monstrous globular creatures after us. In short, stop interfering in my life!'

Verdigris considered and everyone held their breath.

'I agree,' he said slowly, 'to undo the damage I have done thus far. Perhaps it all got a little out of hand.'

'A little!' exclaimed Iris.

'But I cannot consent to stop interfering in your life, Doctor. I am your servant until you find yourself free again and only then will I give up my efforts on your behalf.'

'Some servant!' hissed Jo to Tom.

The Doctor nodded grimly. 'Very well. Then do as much as you can and do as I have bade.'

Verdigris bowed low and it struck Tom then that he was behaving exactly like a genie from the lamp in one of the very oldest stories of the world.

With startled squawks and cries of dismay, the various ambassadors shimmered out of existence.

The hand on which they stood began to close up into a fist, pitching the small gang together, where they stumbled and toppled, one into another.

'The whole mountain!' cried Iris. 'The whole thing is falling down, like a pack of cards!'

In the centre, as the vast room about them fell to pieces, Verdigris folded his arms impassively, and carried on with his work.

Chapter Twenty-four
Back to Work

Verdigris tried to disguise himself once more, but his heart wasn't in it.

He was ashamed of himself, causing all this fuss. He was trying to convince himself he'd only been trying to help.

He wore a long coat to conceal his oddity and his coarse green flesh, and tried to keep out of the Doctor's hair.

He went to see his Master.

They met, in South London, in a Chinese takeaway. It turned out the Master was similarly attired. They sat together watching the pallid, bored fish swirl around an illuminated tank as they waited for their orders.

'I honestly thought, when the truth came out, that he would be pleased.'

'The poor Doctor,' purred the Master. 'Can't ever see further than his nose. He's far too attached to those wretched human beings he gets involved with.'

'But even when it means he might get away from this world!' gasped Verdigris. 'He still prevented me...' The creature shook his head dolefully. 'I can't give up. What can I do now, Master?'

The Master stroked his beard and stared at the menu again, wishing he'd asked for some prawn crackers with his order. 'Why don't you just hang around and generally make his life a misery?'

Verdigris looked uncomfortable.

'Go on,' said the Master eagerly. 'I'm not going to be around to do it.'

'You're leaving?'

'I've had quite enough of this absurd world. I'm going to see what I can get up to elsewhere. I've planned a few meetings here and there... Skaro, for example.'

Verdigris looked shocked. 'You never give up, do you?'

The Master was smug. 'I'm ruthless, obviously. That's what you never understood when I allowed you to use my persona for that little while. You were far too lenient towards them. And as for kissing Miss Grant...' He shuddered.

Verdigris found himself becoming utterly miserable.

'Never mind,' the Master slapped his back. 'You just hang around and do your worst.'

'The Doctor scares me.'

'Oh, come now,' chuckled the Master. 'You've got to interfere with his life. That's what you were created to do!'

Verdigris nodded. 'But I can do it without meeting him again, can't I? I can work from the wings...'

'How so?' asked the Master, to whom such subtlety was, at present, quite novel.

'I've been thinking about anti-matter,' said Verdigris. 'There's a whole universe of it out there and one I've thought about visiting. The Doctor has no idea it exists yet. But in that odd, antithetical dimension, there exists a being, by all accounts, quite livid and set upon the idea of visiting revenge upon this universe.'

'Really?' the Master's interest was piqued.

'Someone whispered about in the legends of Makorna. Someone called Omega. If we could somehow arrange it that Omega learns of the Doctor's presence on Earth, we might just...'

Firmly, the Master shook his head. 'Not "we", Verdigris. Just you. I'm not popping off into any universe of anti-matter. It sounds ghastly. You can do what you want.' He started to stand up. 'As I say, I'm leaving this world and I'm leaving you to your own devices.'

At this point a Chinese woman appeared at the counter with carrier bags steaming with a whole fragrant banquet. 'Menu D?' she asked hopefully. The Master nodded, bowed at her and took the bags from her. He turned to the doleful-looking Verdigris. 'You'll just have to go it alone. I'm off.'

Verdigris watched him stride out into the dark, rainy street with his dinner, and climb into a battered Hillman Imp. He watched the girl at the counter blink in surprise as the vehicle vanished with a peculiar wheezing, groaning noise.

'I ordered menu D, as well,' he reminded her.

'But your friend,' she stammered, as Verdigris drew himself up to his full, impressive height. 'He took both.'

Verdigris turned on his heel and left. Typical. He should never have let himself get involved with the Master. As he walked out into the night, contemplating his trip into the antithetical universe, he consoled himself with the thought that, surely, this Omega person would be a much more balanced individual, and one whom he could persuade to help him.

Verdigris almost had a spring in his step as he prepared to make the necessary jump, sideways, into the other world.

The next week or so was rather difficult.

There was a period of resettling at UNIT HQ as the Brigadier and his men readjusted to a military life. There was one, further, curious episode, as a taxi pulled up outside the building and a troll-like being personally delivered Mike Yates into the Brigadier's hands. The missing captain was brought in a bag that Jo Grant recognised as her own, lost since that terrifying night when UNIT HQ had been turned into a peculiar and maddening parody of itself.

All the troll would say was that he had been looking after Mike Yates, along with his wife, and after the Brigadier slipped him a fiver in gratitude he was off, never to be seen again.

The Brigadier shrugged and then watched in amazement as the two-dimensional Mike Yates shook himself, stood up and seemed to return to a semblance of three-dimensional life.

The Brigadier found himself heartily glad that he himself had been susceptible to mind control for once, if this was what had happened to those who could see through the supermarket illusion. Actually, thought the Brigadier, as he consigned the shaky captain to sick bay, his short spell in retail had done his nerves a power of good. Not that he'd ever tell anyone that...

The Doctor and Jo had given up any pretence of a holiday, returning only once to the Doctor's ruined house to have the TARDIS transported to headquarters. The Doctor intended to work on it night and day until it was fixed and he would be bothered by Verdigris no longer.

On Monday morning Jo brought him a cup of tea and said, 'Is there still no sign of him?'

He sighed and tossed aside the lumpy component on which he had been working. 'Not a thing.'

Jo shuddered. 'I dread to think what mischief he might be causing right now.'

'Don't rub it in, Jo.' The Doctor stood up and started pacing up and down.

'I'm just glad everyone's safe and well again,' she said. 'Mike Yates back to normal, the Brig back at the helm...'

She frowned then, because the Brigadier still wasn't quite right. He was still talking about some kind of shoplifter everyone had to be on the lookout for. And he kept telling her what was on special offer this week.

'And,' she added brightly, hoping to cheer the Doctor up, 'the Meercocks have found their new home on the planet Makorna!' Though she found it hard to imagine a world populated by creatures from English literature; ruled over by Red Riding Hood and her husband, the wolf.

'That's if Iris has done as she promised and shown them the way,' said the Doctor gloomily. 'She's just a bit unreliable, that one.'

'Oh, I'm sure she has,' said Jo. 'After all, she was very upset and contrite over the trouble she's caused everyone. Dabbling in black – I mean, green – magic and all.'

The Doctor sighed deeply. 'Well. Maybe Verdigris will stay out of my hair long enough for me to fix the TARDIS.'

'Maybe!' said Jo, with more enthusiasm than she felt.

'And maybe Iris will come back from space and help me. She knows a thing or two about TARDIS technology. She's virtually remodelled that bus of hers all on her own...'

'Mm!' agreed Jo, but she thought that they'd seen the last of Iris Wildthyme for some time. When the old woman had boarded her bus in order to help the Meercocks find a new planet, she had been accompanied by Tom, of course, but also the Children of Destiny. Kevin, Marsha and Mary were very keen on seeing a little more of the universe. The real universe.

Jo didn't think they'd be back for a while.

They were off on the trip round the galaxy that the Doctor had always promised for her.

At this point the Brigadier marched in.

'Life goes on,' muttered the Doctor.

The Brigadier was clutching a sheaf of reports. 'Any sign of that green chap?'

'I sent him out looking for the Master. I suggested that he might be able to take his TARDIS off him and bring it here, for me.'

'Splendid,' said the Brigadier. 'I would be happier with both that Verdigris fella and the Master out of my way, once and for all.'

'So would I, Brigadier,' said the Doctor.

'Well, come on, old man! Buck up! We've got work to do!'

Jo smiled. 'What's on file this week, Brigadier?'

Lethbridge-Stewart leafed through the sheets of paper he had brought with him. 'Lots to interest us! Apparently, up on the west coast of Scotland, there have been sightings of the entire cast of characters from the whole of Wagner's Ring Cycle!'

The Doctor coughed, took the sheet and crumpled it up. 'We've already dealt with that one.'

The Brigadier frowned and tried again. 'What about this? Robot sheep with red laser eyes? Murdering people in...'

'And that one's sorted out too, Lethbridge-Stewart. You were managing a supermarket, rather badly, at the time.'

The Brigadier flushed red. 'Now, here's one I'm sure we haven't had a crack at yet. Look, apparently junior cabinet ministers have disappeared from their London homes and there's a report in to say that we have reason to believe they are being held captive on the moon!'

'Let me see that,' said the Doctor thoughtfully. He read the report and rubbed his neck. 'It could be the Cybermen, I suppose. They used to have a base up there...'

Jo gave the Brigadier a look, as if to say: See? He's cheering up already!

'Oh, and there's this,' said the Brigadier, glancing down at the final report. 'More disappearances. Someone at a bird sanctuary. Apparently these horrific globs of something or other are appearing out of nowhere and attacking people!'

The Doctor beamed. 'Now, that's more like it, Brigadier!'

Chapter Twenty-five
Space

It was some time later, after the thrilling, extraordinary affair of the Three Doctors (in which Doctors One, Two and Three were reunited somewhere over the rainbow in a nightmarish universe of antimatter to defeat a common and lunatic foe called Omega), that the Doctor eventually regained his freedom.

As a reward for saving their bacon (and not mentioning a word of it to anyone), the august -not to say hypocritical- Time Lords of Gallifrey granted the Doctor back the use of his TARDIS.

He was free to roam once more.

He hopped gleefully back into his police box and plugged the brand-spanking-new dematerialisation circuit into the console and it went in like a dream.

The various, rather complicated codes he needed in order to pilot the ship slipped back into his head with exactly the same sensation as a dream coming back to you, the morning after you've dreamed it.

He took Jo Grant by the hand and offered her, at last, that quick whiz around the galaxy he'd been promising her for so long.

The Brigadier didn't fancy it. His feet were staying firmly on the floor.

Jo clambered aboard the police box, dressed up especially for the occasion, though she fully expected to be flung straight into another terrifying adventure.

But to her surprise, however, the TARDIS materialised with blissful ease, inside a bar.

It was a swanky cocktail joint on a far-flung outpost, and it was full of the most extraordinary creatures she had ever seen.

Some of them even waved acknowledgement at the Doctor. The barman winked and welcomed him back.

The Doctor grinned at her. 'I'm a citizen of the universe, all over again!'

At the end of the bar, though, where they stood to order cocktails of the like, the Doctor promised, she had never tasted in her life, they found themselves confronting two rather familiar faces.

Tom and Iris were sitting at the bar with drinks of their own. Iris was in a low-cut black dress and perched high up on a bar stool. She lit a cigarette and looked the Doctor up and down.

'You took your time getting here,' she said.

And that night, celebrating, becoming friends again, they all got rather drunk.

They last saw Tom dragging Iris out to the car park, where the bus was waiting. Iris was singing Shirley Bassey songs again.

Jo had forgotten to ask what had become of the Meercocks and the Children of Destiny. But she supposed there would be time enough in the future. She was sure she would see them again.

Likewise, Iris, in her cups, had neglected to ask what had become of Verdigris.

And, as the Doctor and Jo tottered happily back into the now fully functional, gleaming white space of the TARDIS console room, he was waiting for them.

'You!' cried the Doctor as the doors slid closed. He sobered immediately.

Verdigris lifted his head slowly and gave them both a ghastly smile.

'I hope you're not here to cause more trouble,' said Jo.

The green man shook his head. 'I came to congratulate you, Doctor. Iris was right. You deserve to be out here. Out in the galaxy. Your time isn't over yet.'

Then the green drained out of him like dirty water from a bath and his bulky silhouette hovered for a moment in the bright white air.

'Farewell, Doctor. Farewell, Jo. *Bon voyage!*'

Then he was gone.

Jo and the Doctor both stared at the green, desolate dust he had left behind on the shining floor.

Then, without a word, the Doctor turned to the control console and expertly flipped the switch that would send them both spinning off into another exciting adventure.

About the Author

Paul Magrs was born on Tyneside in 1969. He has written two previous novels for the BBC *Doctor Who* series: *The Scarlet Empress* and *The Blue Angel*, which he co-wrote with Jeremy Hoad. In addition to his work on *Doctor Who*, Paul has written three novels: *Marked for Life*, *Does it Show?* and *Could it be Magic?* as well as a short story collection, *Playing Out*. All are published by Vintage. He lives in Norwich where he lectures in English Literature and Creative Writing at the University of East Anglia.

PRESENTING

DOCTOR WHO

ALL-NEW AUDIO DRAMAS

Big Finish Productions is proud to present all-new *Doctor Who* adventures on audio!

Featuring original music and sound-effects, these full-cast plays are available on double cassette in high street stores, and on limited-edition double CD from all good specialist stores, or via mail order.

Available from April 2000
RED DAWN

A four-part story by Justin Richards.
Starring **Peter Davison** as the Doctor
and **Nicola Bryant** as Peri.

Ares One: NASA's first manned mission to the dead planet Mars. But is Mars as dead as it seems?

While the NASA team investigate an "anomaly" on the planet's surface, the Doctor and Peri find themselves inside a strange alien building. What is its purpose? And what is frozen inside the blocks of ice that guard the doorways? If the Doctor has a sense of deja-vu, it's because he's about to meet some old adversaries, as well as some new ones...

If you wish to order the CD version, please photocopy this form or provide all the details on paper. Delivery within 28 days of release. Send to: PO Box 1127, Maidenhead, Berkshire. SL6 3LN.
Big Finish Hotline 01628 828283.

Still available:
THE SIRENS OF TIME (Doctors 5,6,7)   THE LAND OF THE DEAD (Doctor 5, Nyssa)
PHANTASMAGORIA (Doctor 5, Turlough)   THE FEARMONGER (Doctor 7, Ace)
WHISPERS OF TERROR (Doctor 6, Peri)   THE MARIAN CONSPIRACY (Doctor 6, Evelyn)

Please send me   [ ] copies of *Red Dawn*
                [ ] copies of *The Marian Conspiracy*   [ ] copies of *Whispers of Terror*
                [ ] copies of *The Fearmonger*   [ ] copies of *Phantasmagoria*
                [ ] copies of *The Land of the Dead*   [ ] copies of *The Sirens of Time*

each @ £13.99 (£15.50 non-UK orders) – prices inclusive of postage and packing. Payment can be accepted by credit card or by personal cheques, payable to Big Finish Productions Ltd.

Name...

Address..

Postcode..

VISA/Mastercard number..

Expiry date.................................Signature..

For more details visit our website at **http://www.doctorwho.co.uk**

THE DEVIL GOBLINS FROM NEPTUNE *by Keith Topping and Martin Day*
ISBN 0 563 40564 3
THE MURDER GAME *by Steve Lyons* ISBN 0 563 40565 1
THE ULTIMATE TREASURE *by Christopher Bulis*
ISBN 0 563 40571 6
BUSINESS UNUSUAL *by Gary Russell* ISBN 0 563 40575 9
ILLEGAL ALIEN *by Mike Tucker and Robert Perry*
ISBN 0 563 40570 8
THE ROUNDHEADS *by Mark Gatiss* ISBN 0 563 40576 7
THE FACE OF THE ENEMY *by David A. McIntee*
ISBN 0 563 40580 5
EYE OF HEAVEN *by Jim Mortimore* ISBN 0 563 40567 8
THE WITCH HUNTERS *by Steve Lyons* ISBN 0 563 40579 1
THE HOLLOW MEN *by Keith Topping and Martin Day*
ISBN 0 563 40582 1
CATASTROPHEA *by Terrance Dicks* ISBN 0 563 40584 8
MISSION: IMPRACTICAL *by David A. McIntee*
ISBN 0 563 40592 9
ZETA MAJOR *by Simon Messingham* ISBN 0 563 40597 X
DREAMS OF EMPIRE *by Justin Richards* ISBN 0 563 40598 8
LAST MAN RUNNING *by Chris Boucher* ISBN 0 563 40594 5
MATRIX *by Robert Perry and Mike Tucker* ISBN 0 563 40596 1
THE INFINITY DOCTORS *by Lance Parkin* ISBN 0 563 40591 0
SALVATION *by Steve Lyons* ISBN 0 563 55566 1
THE WAGES OF SIN *by David A. McIntee* ISBN 0 563 55567 X
DEEP BLUE *by Mark Morris* ISBN 0 563 55571 8
PLAYERS *by Terrance Dicks* ISBN 0 563 55573 4
MILLENNIUM SHOCK *by Justin Richards* ISBN 0 563 55586 6
STORM HARVEST *by Robert Perry and Mike Tucker*
ISBN 0 563 55577 7
THE FINAL SANCTION *by Steve Lyons* ISBN 0 563 55584 X
CITY AT WORLD'S END *by Christopher Bulis*
ISBN 0 563 55579 3
DIVIDED LOYALTIES *by Gary Russell* ISBN 0 563 55578 5
CORPSE MARKER *by Chris Boucher* ISBN 0 563 55575 0
LAST OF THE GADERENE *by Mark Gatiss* ISBN 0 563 55587 4
TOMB OF VALDEMAR *by Simon Messingham*
ISBN 0 563 55591 2

SHORT TRIPS *ed. Stephen Cole* ISBN 0 563 40560 0
MORE SHORT TRIPS *ed. Stephen Cole* ISBN 0 563 55565 3
THE BOOK OF LISTS *by Justin Richards and Andrew Martin*
ISBN 0 563 40569 4
A BOOK OF MONSTERS *by David J. Howe* ISBN 0 563 40562 7
THE TELEVISION COMPANION *by David J. Howe and Stephen James Walker*
ISBN 0 563 40588 0
FROM A TO Z *by Gary Gillatt* ISBN 0 563 40589 9
DEMONTAGE *by Justin Richards* ISBN 0 563 55572 6
REVOLUTION MAN *by Paul Leonard* ISBN 0 563 55570 X
DOMINION *by Nick Walters* ISBN 0 563 55574 2
UNNATURAL HISTORY *by Jonathan Blum and Kate Orman* ISBN 0 563 55576 9
AUTUMN MIST *by David A. McIntee* ISBN 0 563 55583 1
INTERFERENCE: BOOK ONE *by Lawrence Miles*
ISBN 0 563 55580 7
INTERFERENCE: BOOK TWO *by Lawrence Miles*
ISBN 0 563 55582 3
THE BLUE ANGEL *by Paul Magrs and Jeremy Hoad*
ISBN 0 563 55581 5
THE TAKING OF PLANET 5 *by Simon Bucher-Jones and Mark Clapham*
ISBN 0 563 55585 8
FRONTIER WORLDS *by Peter Anghelides* ISBN 0 563 55589 0
PARALLEL 59 *by Natalie Dallaire and Stephen Cole*
ISBN 0 563 555904
THE SHADOWS OF AVALON *by Paul Cornell* ISBN 0 563 555882
THE FALL OF YQUATINE *by Nick Walters* ISBN 0 563 55594 7

DOCTOR WHO: THE NOVEL OF THE FILM *by Gary Russell*
ISBN 0 563 38000 4
THE EIGHT DOCTORS *by Terrance Dicks*
ISBN 0 563 40563 5
VAMPIRE SCIENCE *by Jonathan Blum and Kate Orman*
ISBN 0 563 40566 X
THE BODYSNATCHERS *by Mark Morris* ISBN 0 563 40568 6
GENOCIDE *by Paul Leonard* ISBN 0 563 40572 4
WAR OF THE DALEKS *by John Peel* ISBN 0 563 40573 2
ALIEN BODIES *by Lawrence Miles* ISBN 0 563 40577 5
KURSAAL *by Peter Anghelides* ISBN 0 563 40578 3
OPTION LOCK *by Justin Richards* ISBN 0 563 40583 X
LONGEST DAY *by Michael Collier* ISBN 0 563 40581 3
LEGACY OF THE DALEKS *by John Peel* ISBN 0 563 40574 0
DREAMSTONE MOON *by Paul Leonard* ISBN 0 563 40585 6
SEEING I *by Jonathan Blum and Kate Orman*
ISBN 0 563 40586 4
PLACEBO EFFECT *by Gary Russell* ISBN 0 563 40587 2

VANDERDEKEN'S CHILDREN *by Christopher Bulis*
ISBN 0 563 40590 2
THE SCARLET EMPRESS *by Paul Magrs* ISBN 0 563 40595 3
THE JANUS CONJUNCTION *by Trevor Baxendale*
ISBN 0 563 40599 6
BELTEMPEST *by Jim Mortimore* ISBN 0 563 40593 7
THE FACE EATER *by Simon Messingham* ISBN 0 563 55569 6
THE TAINT *by Michael Collier* ISBN 0 563 55568 8